# IN HIS SILKS

PATRICIA D. EDDY

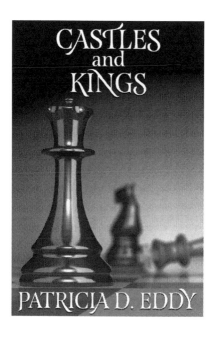

If you love sexy romantic suspense, I'd love to send you a short story set in Dublin, Ireland. Castles & Kings isn't available anywhere except for readers who sign up for my mailing list! Sign up for my newsletter on my website and tell me where to send your free book!
http://patriciadeddy.com.

# CHAPTER ONE

The skies opened and let loose a frigid downpour the second Elizabeth stepped out from under the awning. Within seconds, her cardboard box was soaked through. A gust of wind ripped open her coat, exposing her to the worst of November's dismal weather. She hurried, the large box clutched in her arms, but before she reached the stairs of the T station, the bottom fell out, and her entire professional life spilled onto the sidewalk.

"No, no, no," she moaned and dropped to her knees. Her stockings ripped as she crawled along the ground, gathering her papers and precious mementos. A throng of commuters exited the T station and swamped her. When a booted foot kicked her purse and sent her wallet tumbling towards the sewer drain, Elizabeth yelped and dove forward, landing with a bone-jarring impact across a pair of very expensive dress shoes.

A firm gloved hand grasped her arm and pulled her to her feet. Her wallet forgotten, she looked up into a pair of eyes so green she thought they might be emeralds. Trim black brows matched a shock of black hair peeking out from under a gray wool cap. An umbrella bobbed above the man's head, held by a uniformed driver in an oilskin raincoat. Everything about the man who held her screamed money from those expensive shoes to his soft leather gloves. With his free hand, he took the wallet his driver offered. "I believe this is yours, *chérie*." A posh British accent dominated his smooth words.

"Th-thank you," Elizabeth stammered. She couldn't tear her gaze away from his face. Alexander Fairhaven. The richest man on the East Coast. The entire Fairhaven family—Alexander, Nicholas, and the matriarch, Margaret, had more money than God and at least as many connections. They were famous around the world, but particularly in Boston, as the American headquarters for their multibillion-dollar conglomerate, Fairhaven Business Group, made its home here.

"Thomas? Her things." Alexander raised a brow at the man in uniform and released Elizabeth's arm to accept the umbrella. Thomas ducked his head into the trunk of a limo idling beside them and returned with a large plastic garbage bag. He gathered Elizabeth's belongings and deposited the entire bag back into the trunk.

"Wait, that's my stuff!" Elizabeth protested. "I need—"

Alexander cut her off with a finger to her lips. "I know what you need, *chérie*. A ride. Get in." He gestured towards the limo and fastened his hand around her elbow.

"I don't get into cars with strange men." Elizabeth tried to pull her arm from his firm grasp. "Not even rich and famous ones who save my wallet."

"I am getting wet. As are you. I won't ask you again. Nor will I harm you in any way," Alexander said. "Get in, and Thomas will drive you home."

"I could live in Leominster for all you know."

"Yes. And if that is where you live, then that is where Thomas will take you." He guided her towards the limo, and Elizabeth found herself sinking into a buttery leather bench seat that hugged and warmed her ass. My God. The man had heated seats in his limo. Alexander turned and withdrew a towel from behind his seat across from her. "Dry yourself off, Elizabeth."

"How did you know my name?" She took the towel and dried her face and hands as the limo pulled away from the curb.

He grinned, the flash of white teeth almost predatory as he glanced at the open wallet in his palm. "The same way I know your address. I cheated. Hollander Street, Thomas. Number forty." A privacy screen rose to seal the two of them in the passenger compartment.

Elizabeth snatched the wallet and shoved it into her purse. "That's not fair."

"Oh, I think it's very fair. After all, you know *my* name, don't you? I was only trying to level the playing field."

Elizabeth glared at him. Alexander was the playboy of the Fairhaven family with a string of conquests as long as Elizabeth's arm and a reputation for tiring of women after no more than two dates. "Why am I here?"

"Because you were wet and injured." He gestured towards her scraped knees. "And I dislike seeing a beautiful woman in distress." He removed his gloves. "Now, we have a few moments to get to know each other. Tell me who sacked you and why."

Elizabeth flushed and shrank back against the leather. "H-how—"

"Really, *chérie*. Why else would you be carrying a cardboard box of your personal items through the rain at four in the afternoon?"

When she didn't immediately reply, Alexander tapped his palm against a wood panel across from her, and a small door whispered open. He poured two glasses of an amber liquid and then pressed one into her hand.

"Drink."

"I can't," she protested.

"You can, and you will. You are pale and shivering, and I will not have that when it is in my power to fix it." Alexander set his glass down on the sideboard before sliding across the limo to sit next to her. He lifted the glass to her lips. "Sip slowly."

His tone brooked no argument, so she parted her lips and a scotch so smooth it was practically caramel slid over her tongue. Since her parents had disowned her and she'd moved to Boston five years ago, Elizabeth could scarcely afford anything above bottom shelf. She barely stifled the moan at the rich taste of the expensive liquor.

"Good girl." Alexander tipped the glass up again. Three more sips and a pleasant warmth settled in Elizabeth's belly. "Now tell me who sacked you."

"Carter, Pastack, and Hayes."

Flecks of rich cognac danced around the midnight pools of his pupils. "Why?"

"I can't."

"Didn't we already establish that you can and will?" When she tipped her head up to meet his eyes, he tucked a lock of wet hair behind her ear. "Tell me."

She lowered her gaze to her hands clasped in her lap. The cheap gray skirt molded to her thighs, directly above the blood that oozed from her scraped knees. Under her thin coat, the dark blue silk blouse clung to her breasts, and she shuddered. "I, um, apparently I made a mistake," she whispered. "One of Hayes's clients had an independent audit done. We didn't know anything about it. Hayes was out of the office, and Carter pulled the file. Their tax due—what their independent auditor found—was off for each of the last four years. Carter didn't want me to see the file, but I caught a glimpse. I *know* I did those returns correctly. But the bill they paid—the one that Carter had—it wasn't the bill I prepared. I tried to tell Carter that we had to go back over the numbers, figure out what happened. But he insisted they had, and it was my mistake. 'One of many,' he said. Last year alone, the discrepancy was almost three hundred thousand dollars. The client was livid. Carter fired me on the spot."

"You don't strike me as a woman who makes mistakes."

"I'm not. My track record is impeccable. Numbers...they stick in my head. Always have. I can tell you every phone number I've ever had. What I paid in taxes down to the penny. But last year was so busy. I worked my ass off to try to get ahead. Carter's a misogynist. I handled two hundred clients last year. More than any other accountant in the firm. Carter wouldn't let me see the whole file. Only one return. But it wasn't right. I *know* it wasn't right."

Tears gathered in Elizabeth's eyes. She didn't know why she'd confessed all of this to Alexander Fairhaven. Or why he'd care. Her gaze shifted out the window, the gray skyline of the city she loved streaming by. The silence in the car grew until it developed a physical presence all its own.

A quick rap on the glass alerted her that the car had stopped. How long had it been? Alexander tapped once in return, and the door opened. Thomas held Elizabeth's bag in his hand, her apartment looming behind him. Even the torrential downpour couldn't quash the stench of garbage that wafted up from the bins next to the building. Alexander unfolded his six-foot-three frame and extended his hand to help her out.

She climbed awkwardly to her feet, trying not to flash him as her skirt hiked up her thighs.

"Give me your key."

Elizabeth took a step back, shocked, but Alexander caught her wrist and drew her against him. God, he was hot. Under the gray business suit and crisp blue shirt, he was a mass of sculpted muscle. His arm banded tightly around her back, pressing her breasts against his firm chest.

"Your key, Elizabeth. Now."

She dug into the inner pocket of her purse and fished out her sopping wet keys. Alexander slid them from her chilled fingers and walked her to the building's door where she punched in her code.

"I'll be a bit, Thomas. I intend to see Miss Bennett upstairs. Get out of the rain," Alexander said to his driver as he took the plastic bag filled with Elizabeth's belongings.

"You're double parked," Elizabeth murmured as Alexander led her into the foyer and punched the elevator button.

"It doesn't matter," he bit out, distracted, as they stepped into the lift. "This elevator is a death trap."

"I usually take the stairs. Fourth floor." The scotch had loosened her tongue. Or perhaps it was Alexander's scent, the sandalwood, cedar, and cloves that invaded her nose. And he was warm. So very warm. Her clothes were still soaked through, and she shivered in the crook of his arm.

When the elevator sputtered to a halt on her floor, Alexander leaned down so his lips brushed her ear. "Which unit?"

"Four-oh-six."

Alexander led her down the hall and then slid her key into the lock. He kept her tight against his body as he surveyed the apartment with a critical eye. All of Elizabeth's furniture was second hand, well used, and worn. But there wasn't a speck of dirt anywhere. Her orange tabby cat, River Song, padded out of the bedroom, and when she saw Alexander, she meowed once and wound around his legs.

Stepping over the cat, Alexander urged Elizabeth into her bedroom. "Change clothes. Do you drink coffee or tea this late in the day?"

"Tea. Left-hand cabinet, second—"

"I will find it." The door shut and River meowed. Elizabeth gave the cat an absent-minded scratch behind the ears. "I don't know, sweetie. But I think he's trouble."

---

ALEXANDER COULD BARELY CONTAIN his anger. He knew of Carter, Pastack, and Hayes. His family even used them for some of their holdings. Not his division, but his brother's. Carter was an ass, but he'd thought they were a reasonable company on the whole. Still, there was no reason for him to harbor such anger towards them over a woman he'd only met half an hour ago. Why was he even here? Elizabeth Bennett was nothing. A low-level accountant. But there was a spark in her eyes that hinted at a dizzying intellect. She spoke with the refinement of one who'd had a top-notch education, but she lived in a ramshackle building with second-hand furniture. There was obvious pride, both in her demeanor and her flat's cleanliness. She carried herself as if she belonged in his social circle, but no one he'd ever associated with lived in such conditions. One of his suits probably cost more than her monthly rent. Even in Boston.

Withdrawing his phone, Alexander dashed off an email to his brother. As part of the business agreement between Fairhaven Exports and Carter, Pastack, and Hayes, Nicholas had easy access to their basic employee information.

While he waited for a response, Alexander set a kettle on the tiny two-burner stove, then casually inspected the contents of Elizabeth's cabinets and her fridge. She had good taste in tea, he'd give her that. And she liked grilled cheese sandwiches and red wine.

Withdrawing two mismatched mugs from the cabinet, he took his time preparing the Fortnum & Mason Queen Anne tea.

As the floral aroma wafted up, his phone buzzed with Nicholas's reply. Apparently, Elizabeth had worked for Carter, Pastack, and Hayes for five years. She was Harvard educated, but her salary was a mere sixty thousand a year, barely enough to live in Boston.

"You're still here," Elizabeth said as she emerged from the bedroom. She probably thought the oversized green sweatshirt and ill-fitting gray fleece pants hid her figure, but in fact, they enhanced it. Her breasts would be heavy in his hands, and she had a small waist, which gave way to the generous curve of her hips. He'd caught a glimpse of her long legs in the limo. Perhaps she was a runner. Her hair, the color of spun gold, was now dry and secure in a knot at the back of her head, and her makeup was gone.

"Sit down," Alexander said.

Her blue eyes narrowed, but she did as he asked, watching him warily as he carried the mugs of tea to where she sat on a threadbare sofa.

"I hope you do not mind. I took the liberty. I am sorry to say that you're now out of tea." He lifted his mug in a small toast, and she nodded.

Alexander could read her body language easily—the defensive set of her shoulders, the furrow between her brows, and the tiny lines around her lips. So expressive, though he'd bet she thought she gave away nothing.

"Why did you stay?" she asked, eyeing him over the top of her cup as she took a sip.

"You are quite direct, Elizabeth."

"People call me Lizzie."

Something about the way she said the nickname made him think she didn't like it much. "Elizabeth suits you better." He lifted a brow, challenging her. "Does it bother you?

The tiny quirk of her lip gave everything away. "No."

An honest answer. In fact, she liked the use of her full name. He filed that information away for later. He'd already decided he was going to need it.

"What will you do now? Your position?" He sipped the light, fragrant tea as he crossed his legs, watching Elizabeth. She fascinated him. The insipid women who moved in his usual circles held no sway. They'd fuck him if he did nothing more than nod in their direction, but it had been years since he'd found a woman who aroused his more unconventional desires or held his interest for more than a single date. Elizabeth Bennett was born to fill that role. Spirited, with a strong vein of submission running through her. He wondered if she even realized it.

"I don't know. No one's going to hire me a week before Thanksgiving. The busy season doesn't start for another two months. I'll hold out until then. Find somewhere to volunteer through the holidays while I look for work." She slumped, losing the fight she'd displayed ever since she'd fallen over his feet outside that pitiful company.

Alexander drained the last of his tea and then returned the cup to her kitchen. Elizabeth didn't move from the couch when he returned and stood over her, pinning her with his eyes. Would she look away? No. A smile tugged at his lips, but he schooled his features into a stern mask. Withdrawing a gold case from his jacket, he removed a single business card, setting it on the small table in front of her.

"It was a pleasure to meet you, Elizabeth. If there is anything I can do for you while you look for work, please do not hesitate to ring me."

"Thank you for your help, Mr. Fairhaven. I'm afraid you did not see me at my best." She unfolded herself from the couch and held out her hand.

Alexander brushed a kiss over her knuckles. "You will call me Alexander or if you must, *sir*. Nothing else."

Her lower lip caught between her teeth and her breathing stuttered. What would she do? In truth, Alexander did not enjoy being called *sir*, but if she used the word, he'd know his suspicions were correct.

"Elizabeth, did you hear me?"

"Yes, sir."

Alexander smiled, intrigued. "I hope to see you again soon, Elizabeth. Lock the door after me."

He waited in the hall until he heard the *rasp* of the tumblers. The lock was a joke. He could kick the door in with no effort or pick the lock in under five minutes. Like most boarding school brats, he'd learned how to nick a bit of the headmaster's scotch from his locked office.

Alexander eschewed the rickety elevator and jogged down the four flights of stairs. Thomas waited on the stoop with the umbrella at the ready.

"Where to, sir?" the driver asked.

"Home." Alexander smiled. He had some serious thinking to do.

# CHAPTER TWO

*A*lexander tossed and turned half the night. He'd thought of Elizabeth all through dinner, and had scarcely been able to concentrate on the movie he'd thrown on while he perused his schedule for the rest of the week. The way she'd submitted to him had made his heart quicken, and his cock harden uncomfortably. This woman recognized the Dom within him, but unlike some of the women he'd played with in the past, there was a quiet strength to her. Her backbone had shone through her submission. Elizabeth could and would stand up for herself—at least outside the bedroom. She'd tried when they'd sacked her—or so she'd said. He'd bet a chunk of his sizable fortune that she was not responsible for that cock up.

Alexander was used to reading people. As CEO of Fairhaven Charities, he was responsible for appropriating vast amounts of money to deserving recipients. Applicants came out of the woodwork every day, and many were not worth the paper the applications were printed on. Along with his charitable foundation, he also oversaw the British arm of the conglomerate, traveling back and forth across the Atlantic every month. He had another trip in three days that would extend through Thanksgiving.

*Bloody inconvenient timing.*

The thick black satin sheets whispered over his naked body and his hardening cock. He stretched out an arm and snagged his Piaget watch from the nightstand. Four-thirty in the morning. Good enough. Another few minutes fantasizing about Elizabeth's voice or her body and he'd have to take a cold shower.

He tugged on a pair of running shorts, and ten minutes later, he was downstairs in his personal gym. He programed a high energy music mix for a long set of free weights, some Pilates, and a six-mile run. By the time he checked the clock, it was close to seven, and though he was dripping with sweat and spent, his mind was still on Elizabeth.

He might need that cold shower after all.

AT PRECISELY 9:00 A.M., Alexander reclined in his chair inside his top floor office overlooking the Charles River. He glanced down at his watch. "Three. Two. One."

He smiled as his brother Nicholas burst into the room. "Alex, what the fuck were you thinking?"

Alexander chuckled. "You saw the morning papers?"

"Eight million dollars in one donation? Are you a fucking dolt? Do you care nothing about the future of this company?"

"Eight million won't even give the board heartburn. You lost half that much gambling last year alone. And it will pay for the cancer treatments for at least fifteen children. The Jimmy Fund is the best charity in the city. Before Father died, he told me to make sure this company never sold its soul. I'm trying to keep his spirit alive."

"More like trying to buy its soul back at a fifty percent markup with how much you've given away this year." Nicholas paused, narrowing his blue eyes. "Are you ill? You look terrible."

Alexander rubbed his hands over his face, annoyed. "Bugger off, Nicholas."

Yet again, Alexander wondered how he and Nicholas could be from the same family.

Nicholas had moved to the States at twelve with their father, while Alexander chose to remain in England with Mother until he'd completed his requisite two-year stint in the Royal Army. A business degree from Yale followed, and Alexander had been happy running Fairhaven Limited in London until their father's cancer diagnosis. There were days he regretted agreeing to run Fairhaven Charities and taking a position as co-chairman of the board at Fairhaven Exports.

Still, Nicholas and Alexander were the two youngest members of the Forbes 400 Top Ten List, despite his brother's penchant for betting on horses and his poor luck at the tables.

Nicholas dropped into a chair across from Alexander. "Then what is it? Have a hot date last night? Please tell me you finally fucked someone."

Alexander's gaze returned to the window, seeking out a cluster of buildings across the river he knew surrounded Elizabeth's tiny flat. Strange that he couldn't get her out of his head.

"Your vulgar Americanized English offends me. As does your insistence on prying into my affairs."

Undeterred, Nicholas leaned forward. "Does your poor mood have anything to do with the name you asked me to look up last night? Elizabeth Something-Or-Other?"

"Bennett," Alexander answered without thinking.

"Oh, so it *does!*" Nicholas slapped his knee. "Who is she? And how did you meet her?"

"It's none of your bloody business. Don't you have a meeting to attend? I'm off to the Jimmy Fund in an hour." Alexander tapped a few keys on his laptop and then raised a brow at his brother. "That is your cue to clear off, Nicholas. But answer me this. Will you be returning to England for Mother's holiday extravaganza on Sunday?"

"Adequate deflection, Alex." He grinned. "But believe me. I *will* find out what you're hiding. Perhaps I'll go chat up Elizabeth Bennett myself. See what all the fuss is about."

Alexander saw red as he bolted around his desk. In a single breath, he hauled his brother to his feet. "If you so much as run her social security number, I will tell Mother that I had to bail you out of jail last year after you got piss drunk at the Celtics game and fell onto the court." Alexander couldn't keep the dominant edge from his voice. But Nicholas, though smaller, was a Dom as well and could hold his own.

Nicholas threw up his hands. "Calm down. *You* had me look her up last night, remember? If she's hands off, I respect that."

"She's hands off."

"Okay. You got it. You won't tell Mother, yeah? It will ruin her ball."

Alexander inclined his head. "No. I won't. Go back to your tower, Nicholas. I'll see you soon."

When he was alone again, Alexander turned to his computer. Anyone who ran a multi-billion-dollar company had access to data the average American couldn't possibly envision. If he'd wanted to, he could have ruined many a career. Only his moral code and a firm belief in his father's core values kept him from abusing this power. Alexander entered Elizabeth Bennett's name and address and waited impatiently for the background check to arrive in his inbox. It was unethical, but he couldn't help himself. He took three phone calls and two dozen emails before he got the information he'd been looking for.

*Elizabeth Bennett*
*Thirty-two years old*
*Born in Seattle, Washington to Avery and Mark Bennett, owners of Bennett Pharmaceuticals*

*Moved to Boston in 2009 and took a job with Carter, Pastack, and Hayes as a mid-level accountant*

*Promoted to senior accountant in 2011*

Bennett Pharmaceuticals was worth fifty million dollars and employed three thousand people. They held the patent on an anti-nausea drug for cancer patients, and they'd been in the news a few years ago for hiking the price of the drug more than 500%.

Alexander scowled as he skimmed the news stories surrounding the company, including one scathing expose from an unnamed internal source.

Why had Elizabeth left their employ? She'd started working there right out of Harvard and had stayed for six years, moving to Boston only a month after leaving her parents' company. But she hadn't taken her next job for two months after that.

Alexander could request a detailed report on Elizabeth, but he paused. Did he really want to learn about her through a file? *No.* He wanted to acquire his knowledge the old-fashioned way. From the woman herself.

---

PUNCHING in the code for her building's outer door, Elizabeth pushed inside, then practically collapsed into the hallway. She'd managed a four-mile run and a light weight workout at the Y today. Not bad for someone with an extra twenty pounds on her five-foot-six frame. But now the rain had soaked her to the bone, and her fingers were blue. She retrieved her mail and climbed the stairs to her apartment. At the front door, a small box wrapped in gold paper sat on the thin, beige welcome mat. She looked up and down the hall. No one was around. Retrieving the gift, she flipped over a small tag sticking up from the emerald green ribbon.

*Fondly, Alexander Fairhaven*

When had he come by? Or had he sent someone? A man as

busy as he was wouldn't have come himself. His driver maybe? Too cold to deal with whatever was in the box, she unlocked her door and tossed the package on the coffee table. She showered, changed into sweats, and curled up on her couch with River to watch *Love Actually*. Whenever she was in a rotten mood, that movie always seemed to do the trick.

Absently, she toyed with the tag on the box from Alexander. Might as well see what Mr. Powerful-and-Handsome had sent her. She ripped through the paper, opened the box, and gaped. Inside rested a handwritten card and a metal tin of her favorite tea. She inhaled deeply, and the strong, floral scent calmed her nerves.

*Elizabeth, my apologies for finishing the last of your tea and for not delivering this in person. Obligations will keep me in meetings all day. I would very much enjoy your company for coffee tomorrow morning. Perhaps 8 a.m. at Thinking Cup in the North End? If you decide to accept my invitation, kindly text me. My mobile number is on the card I left you. -Alexander*

Elizabeth tossed the note on the couch, and River started playing with it.

What did Alexander think he was doing by inviting her for coffee? Men like him didn't date women like her. That only happened in books, and she'd never been one to believe in fairy tales. She snorted. Whatever. She'd let him buy her coffee. But for now, she wanted a cup of tea.

———

THE NEXT MORNING, at precisely eight, Elizabeth ran into Thinking Cup. The rain was incessant today, and she couldn't find her umbrella. Tossing the soaked newspaper she'd used as a substitute into the trash, she scanned the room. Handwritten menu boards lined the back of the shop. Conversation hung thick in the air, though all awareness of the din faded when she saw him. Alexander sat at a secluded corner table, a French Press pot on the table in front of him. The patrons around him stared and tittered, snapping surreptitious photos and whispering. He looked casual, unaffected, his phone in his hand and an untouched croissant on a plate. A smile broke out over his face when she approached. As he stood, he offered her his hand. "I wasn't certain you'd come."

Elizabeth allowed his warmth to envelop her palm.

"I didn't have anything else to do this morning. My work schedule is a bit...light these days."

Alexander frowned and pulled out a chair for her. "I'll get you a coffee. A croissant as well? Or perhaps a breakfast sandwich?"

"All right." She smiled shyly. "Bacon, egg, and cheese breakfast sandwich. Thank you."

"How do you take your coffee?"

"Black."

"A woman after my own heart. How refreshing."

Elizabeth watched him walk away. Everything about his gray suit whispered understated elegance, although his confidence was anything but subtle. His ass filled out the trousers nicely. Smiling at the barista, he asked about her morning, paid cash, and dropped a twenty in the tip jar. Elizabeth respected that. So few people took the time to be courteous to baristas, waiters, and shop clerks, but it was something Elizabeth's father had instilled in her at an early age.

When Alexander returned to the table with another press pot and mug, she tried to return his smile, but couldn't quite muster the emotion. This was a waste of time.

"I have been thinking about you," Alexander said.

"Why?"

His green eyes flashed with a dangerous glint. "Why not? I'm not allowed to think of an intelligent and beautiful woman?"

"Mist...Alexander. I'm unemployed, and your shoes probably cost more than my rent this month. There is nothing we could possibly have in common." The barista rushed over with her breakfast sandwich and gave Elizabeth a wink. This was a mistake. Nothing good could come of it. "I'm sorry. I should go."

"Stay." With a single word, Alexander sent a shock of warmth to her core. "I cannot drink all this coffee alone, and even if we have nothing in common but our good taste in tea, I believe the next hour will be more interesting than the rest of my day. Board meetings are my least favorite task. Steel me for the day with your smile, will you?"

He depressed the plunger on her press pot, and even in a busy coffee shop, the fresh scent of the brew invigorated her. She inhaled deeply and couldn't help but smile.

"Now that is better. You have a lovely smile, Elizabeth. We will eat first, and then perhaps you will tell me how you came to discover Fortnum & Mason."

Alexander poured her coffee, then his own, and unfolded a paper napkin across his lap. Elizabeth did the same and then bit into her sandwich. She watched him eat, deft fingers tearing into the flaky pastry. His lips twitched into a half smile after every sip of coffee, and she found that hers did as well. By the time she polished off the last bite of her sandwich, she was nearly grinning. Alexander's energy was magnetic. He had long finished his croissant, but said nothing, waiting for her to answer his question.

Elizabeth sat back and wiped the cornmeal from her fingers. "I used to travel to London and Paris every year with my family. I fell in love with Queen Anne ten years ago. There's a tea shop on Newbury Street that carries it. It reminds me of all those trips. Well, the good parts of them anyway. The lights of the Eiffel Tower, riding the London Eye overlooking the Thames. I used to love to travel." She dropped her gaze to her cup.

"Used to?" he prompted.

She cleared her throat and took another long sip of coffee. "I don't see my family any more. We had a falling out."

"Is that when you left the family business?"

"Yes."

"Family is important, Elizabeth. They do not wish to see you? The holidays are fast approaching. You do not even visit at Christmas?"

"No. This...I'm sorry. Will you excuse me for a moment?" Elizabeth shoved back from the table, nearly toppling over her chair. The air in the shop was too thick. Too hot. It pressed in on her like a blanket. Where was the damn bathroom in this place?

Alexander shot up and took her arm, steadying her. "Elizabeth." Her name rolled off his tongue with such a commanding and calm tone that she looked up into his sharp green eyes. "Take a deep breath. I'm sorry that I pried. Forgive me."

She inhaled his spicy scent. Coffee, cloves, pine, and freshly cut wood. "I don't like talking about my family," she said after she managed to catch her breath.

"Clearly. Will you answer one more question about them?"

"You can ask. I may or may not answer." She allowed Alexander to pull out her chair again and she sat. Her hands shook, so she shoved them under her thighs. She hadn't had a panic attack in years, but between losing her job and Alexander's prying questions, she was close.

"Why did they shut you out?"

Anger rolled over her, drowning the panic. "Do you have any idea how much it costs to manufacture Zocazim?"

"I do not know what Zocazim is, so no." Alexander leaned forward, his gaze fixed on her.

"It's an anti-nausea drug for chemo patients. It costs six cents a pill to manufacture. For years, you could get a month's worth for under twenty dollars. Until my parents' divorce. Then they raised the price to more than seventy dollars a pill. Insurance companies won't cover more than ten percent of that cost. We—" Elizabeth shook her head. "Bennett Pharmaceuticals used to donate pills to low-cost cancer treatment centers for women without insurance. But then my father had an affair, and everything went to hell. My parents still run the business together, but since they have to share the profits now, all they care about is making as much money as they can."

"And you do not."

"Money's great. Don't get me wrong. Speaking as someone who doesn't have a bank account the size of a small country, it's a necessity. But my parents have enough to last three lifetimes. I tried to get them to listen to reason, but they told me I was acting like a child. That I didn't understand the finances."

Alexander's brows rose. "You're an accountant."

Elizabeth rolled her eyes. "I couldn't, in good conscience, keep working for them. But..." Her cheeks flamed, and her heart thumped painfully in her chest.

*Just stop, Lizzie. He doesn't need to know the rest.*

Alexander's warm fingers feathered over hers around her coffee mug. With that one move, he tore through her defenses, and she crumbled. "I gave the *Seattle Times* an anonymous interview," she began reluctantly. "Explaining how much the drugs cost to make. The stock price collapsed. And then my ex-fiancé told my parents that I was the source. They fired me, disowned me, and told me they never wanted to see me again. That's how I ended up in Boston."

Elizabeth tried to extricate her hands, but Alexander's fingers tightened on hers, and a muscle in his jaw ticked. "I admit that I did a bit of research on you, Elizabeth. And I am sorry that you lost your family, but knowing why, I find myself even more interested in getting to know you."

He *researched* me? Normal people didn't *research* their dates. Sure, maybe they looked up their Facebook profile, checked out their Twitter account, but they didn't *research* them. Anger flared again. "Am I a project to you?"

"A project?" He chuckled dryly. "No. Why do you ask that?"

"I don't appreciate being researched. Do you know my bank

account balance now? My dress size? My credit rating? What about my Internet search history?"

"Calm down, Elizabeth. I know none of those things. I was curious about the firm that fired you. We use them for some of our accounting. I asked my Human Resources department to pull a basic report on your employment with Carter, Pastack, and Hayes. I know you are thirty-two and that you were born in Seattle and moved here five years ago. I know when you started at Carter, Pastack, and Hayes. And that is it. I do not wish to learn about you from a report."

Elizabeth yanked her hands free. "You're a pompous ass, Alexander. Thank you for the coffee and the breakfast. Enjoy your board meeting." With that, she turned and marched out into the storm.

---

"Welcome home, sir." Samuel, Alexander's majordomo, held the front door open for him.

Wearily, Alexander climbed the Brownstone's stairs, giving only a passing glance to the holiday lights that hadn't been there this morning.

He needed a drink. All day, his thoughts had continually strayed to Elizabeth and her dismissal of him. "I'm knackered, Samuel. Once you've set out my luggage, take the rest of the evening off."

"It's already done, sir."

Once in his suite, Alexander stripped on the way to the bath. Four shower heads massaged his body, the hot water sluicing down his well-muscled back. He braced his head on his forearms pressed against the wall. After Elizabeth's indignant departure at the Thinking Cup, he'd tried to focus on his work, but had failed miserably. She wanted nothing to do with him.

His cock sprang to life under the heat of his thoughts. He

hadn't had more than a passing fling in recent memory. Every woman he'd dominated or tried to dominate had left him unfulfilled. Since he'd moved to Boston, he'd had no trouble enticing a playmate, but they were all interested in one thing. Bedding a billionaire. Few were adventurous enough to put themselves in his silks and those that were always seemed to treat their play like a game, not the true submission he craved.

He spilled soap into his hand and wrapped his fist around the hardening flesh of his cock. His hips took on a mind of their own as thoughts of Elizabeth consumed him. The brilliance of her smile, the light in her eyes, and even the indignation when he'd told her he'd researched her. Everything about the woman fascinated him. He imagined her moaning his name, blindfolded, her slender wrists confined in his silk restraints. *"Alexander, please, fuck me."*

He wanted her begging for release, screaming his name. His balls tightened, and he groaned as his load hit the shower's polished rock wall.

He'd not fantasized about a woman in years. Not a specific woman anyway. A woman's body, perhaps. Breasts, pink from his silk and suede flogger, buttocks reddened from his hand, nipples held in his clamps with the black silk tassels.

Alexander favored hemp and silk, as the sensual textures enhanced a woman's pleasure. He cared little for his own release. He took his enjoyment from a woman's submission. He always came, of course, but long after his subs had given up multiple orgasms.

A bit of his tension gone, Alexander toweled off and then flopped down naked on his bed. He had Elizabeth's number and resolved to try one last time. Just a text; what harm could it do?

*Elizabeth, my apologies for this morning. I was curious about you. I suppose I could have stalked your Facebook page—assuming you have one. But that's too personal.*

He ran out of characters and swore, then reworded.

*I merely wanted to know a bit about you. A starting point for more. I was wrong. Please forgive the cock-up.*

After the message disappeared, he set the phone down but kept checking the device as he went about his evening. It wasn't until nearly eleven that his phone buzzed.

*Thank you. It was rude of me to storm out. You were wrong, but I was too. I'm sorry.*

He grinned. An opening.

*What is your favorite color?*

*Purple. What an odd question. But fine. I'll play your game for a moment. Yours?*

*Blue. I said I wanted to get to know you. How else do you propose I do so? Night owl or early bird?*

*Early bi taew ho;aier wafsd vho;x*

He frowned at her response.

*Elizabeth? What's wrong?*

*Sorry. My kettle went off, and while I was in the kitchen, River played with my phone.*

Alexander sat up. Who the hell was River? A child? The text had been gibberish. His fingers fumbled with his next message.

*River?*

*My cat. River Song.*

He laughed with relief. *Doctor Who?* Everything Alexander learned about her left him hungry for more, but his eyes were gritty and tired, and the clock tormented him.

*I must sleep now. I'm up at five. May I text you tomorrow night? I will be in England for a few days, but I would like to continue to get to know you.*

*Why?*

*Because you have a spark about you. And I wish to see how bright it burns. Sleep well, chérie.*

*Good night, Alexander.*

He fell asleep with a smile on his face.

# CHAPTER THREE

*L*ying in bed with River pressed against her, Elizabeth tried, and failed, to concentrate on her book. She'd applied for three jobs today, gone for a run, cleaned her small apartment, and put in two hours down at the food bank. She was exhausted. As the clock ticked past eleven, she yawned. After staying up past midnight exchanging text messages with Alexander Fairhaven the previous night, she needed sleep, but he'd asked her if he could text her again tonight. So far, though, her phone had remained silent.

She had, however, received three unwanted calls from her former employer. They wanted her to come in for an exit interview. She'd politely declined the first time, and they'd called twice more, leaving terse messages that chilled her. Harry Carter wanted nothing to do with her—he'd made that abundantly clear when he'd fired her—but apparently, Hayes felt differently.

After yet another check of her screen, she let the phone slip from her fingers and turned to River. "I don't know why I'm still up, sweetie. There's no point in starting anything with that man. He'll only drop me like a hot potato when someone more interesting comes around." The cat rolled over and exposed her belly, begging for more. "At least *you* love me."

Elizabeth sighed as she rolled over and yanked open her nightstand drawer. Her vibrator sat in the neatly ordered space, next to a box of old condoms, a silk blindfold she'd bought on a whim and never used, and a small tube of lube. Desperate to prove herself at her job, she hadn't dated anyone in over a year. Friendships, romance, and even her passion for cooking had suffered. At least she'd discovered her love of running. It was the only way to reliably beat the stress.

Her fingers had just brushed the vibrator when her phone buzzed.

*What are you doing tonight, Elizabeth?*

Her heart skipped a beat, and she slammed the drawer shut, the vibrator forgotten.

*Reading. It's late. I was about to turn out the light.*

*I'm sorry. It was a terrible flight. I've made this trip for years and never encountered such turbulence. I went to bed ill last night. What are you reading?*

*Principles of Forensic Accounting.*

*For the love of God, why?*

She kicked herself for her honesty. This afternoon, she'd sat down at her computer and reconstructed most of the data from the Museum of Contemporary Art's tax return, one of the accounts she'd been accused of screwing up. She'd kept backup copies of a few files on her laptop, and her uncanny ability to remember numbers had helped her piece together the truth. Someone *else* at CPH had altered those returns. Not her. Now she had to decide what to do with this knowledge.

*Elizabeth?*

Shaking her head, she responded: *I'm trying to keep my skills current.*

*It has been less than a week since you were sacked. I do not believe you need a refresher course already. You were well educated, yes?*

*Harvard.*

*Yale here. You did not make a mistake, did you?*

Biting her lip, she stared at the screen, then sighed as she tapped out her reply: *I don't want to talk about this.*

Only a few seconds later, he returned: *Is there anything I can do? My brother's division uses CPH. I could speak with him. He might know one of the partners.*

*No. I'm tired now, Alexander. I have to be up early. I'm spending the day at the soup kitchen in the North End tomorrow.*

Several long moments passed before his reply popped into the box. *Happy Thanksgiving, Elizabeth. I am sorry we did not have more time to chat tonight. I find myself missing your company.*

She frowned. *You haven't had the pleasure of my company enough to miss it. Good night.*

Elizabeth tossed the phone on her nightstand and then turned off the light. Despite Alexander's forward and presumptive nature, she shouldn't have been so rude. She sent one last message.

*Happy Thanksgiving, Alexander.*

And then after tossing and turning for half an hour, she sent another one.

*I'll chat with you tomorrow?*

His reply came immediately.

*Yes. Without a doubt. Sleep well, chérie.*

---

ON FRIDAY MORNING, Benny Hedgeman, a representative from the Red Sox, Elizabeth's biggest client, called her to discuss the work she'd done for them the previous year.

"I'm sorry, Mr. Hedgeman. I'm no longer employed by CPH." She unclenched her jaw, trying to ease the near-constant headache she'd carried around for the past three days.

"I'm well aware of that. Our general manager tasked me with

figuring out just how these mistakes happened. We were always quite pleased with your work. The GM in particular. He spoke highly of you and mentioned that you had a phenomenal memory for numbers."

"Um, yes. I do. But that doesn't mean I know what happened. I suggest you contact CPH."

"We did that. They blamed you," he said matter-of-factly.

"So why are you calling? To get ammunition for a lawsuit against me? I'm not interested."

His desperate voice stopped her from disconnecting the call. "Wait! No. We have a fax you sent last year with preliminary numbers. Do you remember?"

Tucking the phone between her shoulder and her ear, she said, "Hang on, Mr. Hedgeman. Give me two minutes." She grabbed a pad of paper and a pen and then closed her eyes. Numbers floated in her head. Thousands. Millions. Salaries, deductions, charitable contributions, depreciation, and insurance. "What's the bottom line of that fax? The estimated tax owed?"

"Twenty-three million, four hundred and sixty-two thousand."

"And how much did you pay CPH? Not counting their fees?"

Elizabeth's stomach twisted into a knot. She'd seen the file on Carter's desk just a few days ago. She knew exactly how much they'd supposedly paid.

"Twenty-six million and change. What I need to know, Miss Bennett, is where the mistake happened. The IRS has a six-week turnaround time for information requests—if we're lucky. Our independent audit suggests we owed a sum much closer to your fax than the final return. All the owners want to know is whether another set of hands touched our return besides yours."

She chewed her lip. "I can't answer that, Mr. Hedgeman. I'm under a strict confidentiality clause. It binds me for five years after my employment ends. Believe me, I wish I could. Please tell Larry that I'm sorry."

Her hands shook as she set down the phone. Every return at CPH went to one of the three partners before it was delivered to the client. When she'd sent the Red Sox files to the partners last year, their tax owed was within five thousand dollars of the preliminary fax she'd sent to their offices. Most clients didn't ask for interim numbers, but the GM was a little OCD and had demanded them.

Something happened to those returns. But who was responsible? And what the heck could she do about it now?

Elizabeth wasn't any closer to answering those questions when Alexander texted her that night. Still, she found herself laughing more with him than she felt she had right to given her situation

They'd texted half of Thanksgiving night, and now, she was up past her bedtime again. She slipped into bed with her phone and grinned as she typed out a reply.

*Why are you up so early on a Saturday morning?*

*There is no rest for me here, Elizabeth. My employees get weekends off. I often do not. Though if I am successful this week, I might have more free time soon.*

Alexander was bored out of his mind with meetings. He was trying to hire someone to handle the day-to-day operations of the London office and had found no one suitable.

*Who would you hire? The woman with the string of successful companies under her belt who claims to want a new challenge? Or the man who retired as the COO of British Airways and decided he was too bored to stop working?*

Elizabeth pondered before returning: *I haven't met them or seen their resumes. But the woman would be my gut. If the man changed his mind once, he could do it again.*

*That was my assessment as well. Thank you. How was your day?*

She didn't know what to say to him. Awful? Frightening? Stressful?

*I've had better.*

*What's wrong? Can I help?*

*No. I'm sorry. I shouldn't have said anything. Don't you have your mother's party tonight?*

*I do. Nicholas arrived late last night. Mother is thrilled. The two of us haven't been home together in three years. He's staying at the house.*

*You're not?*

*Bloody hell, no. I love Mother dearly, but she'd drive me mad if I had to spend every moment with her. Nicholas might not survive the weekend.*

A sudden pang of jealousy hit her. She never thought to ask. Did Alexader have a date for the party? She wasn't sure she wanted to know. It was well after one in the morning before he bid her goodnight. She didn't think she'd sleep a wink wondering about his social life, but then he texted her one last time.

*I will miss you tonight, Elizabeth.*

She smiled, and to her surprise, drifted right off.

———

SATURDAY MORNING, Elizabeth went out for her customary five-mile loop along the Esplanade. A thin layer of ice covered the grass at the edges of the path. This early, only a few other joggers exhaled matching white clouds from their chapped lips as they hurried over the Boston University Bridge. Running typically freed her from the chains of stress that wound around her life, but today, not even the adrenaline helped.

A block from her apartment, a man called out to her. "Miss Bennett, a moment of your time."

She skidded to a halt. Cold black eyes peered at her, deep set in a non-descript face. With her finger on her watch's panic button, she asked, "Who are you?"

"Salvador Perez. I work for Carter, Pastack, and Hayes. Leonard Hayes would like you to come in for an exit interview. The legal department has copies of the non-disclosure you signed when you started that you are to review in front of them. There are also several post-employment agreements they'd like you to sign. If you do so, you'll be given a small severance package."

"Are you following me?" she demanded.

"Your address was in your employment records, Miss Bennett. I was waiting for you to emerge, yes."

"I'd like you to leave. I'm well aware of my non-disclosure agreement. I haven't—and won't—violate it."

"You spoke to the Red Sox." Perez took a step closer to her.

"Get the hell away from me before I call the police. The Red Sox called *me*. I told them if they had any questions, they should contact the office because I couldn't tell them anything—exactly what my non-disclosure agreement requires me to do. I have nothing else to say to Carter, Pastack, *or* Hayes. I'm trying to move on with my life, and no severance package is worth going back to that place."

Sprinting towards the building, Elizabeth was relieved when she tossed a quick glance behind her and saw that Perez made no move to follow her.

After a shower and a quick snack, she returned to her work. Numbers swam in her head. Some clients, like the Red Sox, she could remember with almost perfect clarity, and she wanted to recreate their returns as best she could. The snow started to fall around mid-afternoon, but she barely noticed. Her back ached. The tension behind her eyes spurred her on.

After dinner, she brought her laptop to bed. Surrounding herself with tax forms that she'd printed out from the Internet, she checked, rechecked, and verified. The baseball team had paid more than three million extra in taxes. Why? She was so distracted by the numbers that she didn't see the caller ID when she answered the phone.

"Hello?"

"Elizabeth. I have missed hearing your voice." Alexander's deep tones sounded odd, echoing over the line, but the joy in his voice was hard to mistake.

"Oh, hi. Are you still in London? You sound so far away."

"As do you, *chérie*. But not physically. You're distracted. Another book?"

"No, I'm—" If Alexander knew, he'd interfere. Rich and powerful men were like that. Her father could never leave well enough alone either. "It's nothing. It was a long day."

"What did you do? And, if you would indulge me, are you in bed?"

"Excuse me?"

Alexander cleared his throat. "It's 7:00 a.m. here, Elizabeth. I'm sitting here in my hotel room after another sleepless night aching to know what you're doing. What you're wearing. Anything about you. I cannot stop thinking about you."

"Alexander, we can't do this. I'm...what I mean to say is that...shit. Men like you don't date women like me."

"Women like what? Intelligent? Witty? Am I some sort of cretin? An ogre with such poor manners that I would embarrass you at dinner?"

"No, but I've been in your type of social circle before. You need someone who'll stand up to scrutiny in the press. Someone who doesn't live on Hollander Street and shop at Goodwill. Regardless of my former station in life, right now I don't have a job, and my bank account is hemorrhaging."

*And I'm involved in a sticky situation with your accounting firm.*

"I do not care what your financial situation is," he snapped. Then he sighed, and his voice softened. "That came out wrong. I care very deeply that you are struggling, Elizabeth. But not for the reasons you believe. Do you know how long it has been since

I found a woman I could converse intelligently with? A woman who did not want me only for my bank account? My position in life?"

"I don't know. The society pages aren't my home. They're yours. Didn't you date Pippa for a time? How am I supposed to follow that?"

"You don't have to. Pippa is a lovely woman, but she and I have nothing in common. I *did* accompany her to the theater once at my mother's urging, but we didn't hit it off. Nary a peck passed between us."

"You don't have to justify yourself to me, Alexander. I've no claim on you." She didn't want to hear about his dates.

"Bugger it. Can we simply chat? I have several social obligations this morning, none of which promise to offer me anything stimulating in the way of conversation. Being needled by my mother's friends is not my idea of a rousing good time. You are a bit of sunlight amid all of this dreary rain we are having in London. And I'd hoped that you would agree to have lunch with me on Monday when I return."

"That's not a good idea," she said quietly.

"Lunch is almost always a good idea."

Elizabeth couldn't stop herself from laughing at the matter-of-fact tone he'd used. "Touché. Skipping meals isn't usually a good idea. Still, what are you expecting from me?"

"I enjoy hearing you laugh. Will you stay up for a bit? I realize it's late there."

"I don't have a job. There isn't exactly a reason for me to get up early in the morning. Why will your mother's friends needle you?"

"Because I am thirty-five and have not had a relationship that lasted more than three dates in almost a decade. My mother feels as if she is entitled to a grandchild. Neither my brother nor I are inclined to give her one."

Elizabeth set aside her laptop. "Your brother is older?"

She slid down so she was curled on her side with River tucked against her, purring.

"Yes. Nicholas just turned forty. We both have certain...unconventional requirements in a partner. Nicholas needs a woman with an extreme submissive nature. He currently lives his life as a Master. You know what that is, yes?"

"You're talking about BDSM." Something in Elizabeth's core warmed at the thought. She'd always preferred her sex vanilla and quick. Orgasms were nice, but they were messy and usually left her wanting.

"Yes. But while Nicholas has a complete power exchange with his current slave, I don't want that. I prefer a true partner. One who enjoys my silks, the tools I use as a Dom, but who does not wish me in control of her life outside of the bedroom."

His voice oozed heat, and Elizabeth squirmed under her cheap cotton sheets.

"Oh."

"Does this frighten you, Elizabeth?"

"No. But I'm not a submissive, Alexander. Once or twice, I've thought it might be fun to be blindfolded, but that's as far as I'd ever take it."

"You are indeed a submissive, *chérie*. I knew it the very first time I spoke to you. When I return, I will show you the truth of your nature if you will allow it. I admit that the vision of you in my silks has haunted my dreams each night since we met. Perhaps this is why I have not slept." He sounded amused. A knock echoed through the phone. "I'll be a moment, Elizabeth. I believe my breakfast has arrived."

Elizabeth hung up on him. How dare he? She was no one's plaything or wet dream. Especially not his. She fired off a quick text.

*If you'd like to "chat" as friends, that's one thing, but nothing will ever come of it. No more talk of sex, or submissives, or whatever the hell*

*your silks are. And stop fantasizing about me when you jerk off. I'm
going to bed now.*

The phone rang, but Elizabeth sent it to voice mail. A text
flashed on the screen a moment later.

*Please do not deny me the only light I have had in my days, Eliza-
beth. Your voice, your wit, your sense of humor.*

And then another.

*I am sorry that I have offended you. You unsettle me. A feeling I am
quite unused to.*

Foregoing an answer, she turned the phone off completely.

# CHAPTER FOUR

*A*lexander spent the whole day cursing his honesty. He wanted Elizabeth like he had wanted no other woman. But despite his desire to see her lovingly restrained, he wanted her mind even more.

She was smart, funny, and unassuming. She said what she meant, not what he wanted to hear and he couldn't wait to return to Boston, if for no other reason than he would be in the same city as this delightful, infuriating, and beautiful woman he'd found himself fascinated with.

"You are distracted, Alexander," his mother chided after the third time he'd asked her to repeat herself.

Heat crept up his neck and flushed his cheeks. Suddenly he was ten years old again. Only his mother could bring about that reaction. "Apologies. Please forgive me. What did you ask me?"

"This woman you're so taken with," Margaret mused. "She must be quite something to put you in such a state." His mother's blue eyes danced under her wrinkled brows. She might've been getting up there in years, but her mind was as sharp as a tack.

"She's brilliant. Harvard-educated, beautiful. And completely maddening. She refuses to believe I could be interested in her. I intend to prove it to her when I get back." Alexander ran a hand through his wavy black hair. "Her name is Elizabeth."

"Does she know what you need in a lover?"

"Mother!" The last thing he wanted to do was discuss his bedroom proclivities with his mum.

"Your lifestyle hasn't been a secret for some time. Nor has your brother's. I do not care what either of you does in the bedroom as long as it doesn't besmirch my name or our company. But you did not answer my question."

"She knows a bit. But this discussion is premature. We've not been on a single successful date."

"Well, get on it then."

He smiled. "I intend to."

---

THOMAS DROVE Alexander to Elizabeth's neighborhood late the next morning. The harsh tone of her buzzer set him further on edge.

"Yes?" she answered, her tone weary.

"Elizabeth, may I take you to breakfast?"

"Oh God. Alexander, what the hell are you doing here? I told you, I'm not interested in a relationship."

"A meal does not make a relationship. I have a favor to ask of you, and I'm peckish. I thought we might revisit the Thinking Cup with better results. Or if you'd like something more substantial, I have a diner in mind."

"I'm not even dressed yet."

"It is nearly ten. Are you ill?"

A long pause. "No. I...haven't been sleeping much lately."

"Elizabeth, I'm worried about you now. This is hardly the way to get me to leave." Alexander entered the code he'd memorized the day they'd first met, and the door clicked open. "I'm coming up."

"Oh, for fuck's sake," she said and severed the connection.

By the time he'd climbed the stairs to her floor, she was dressed in a pair of worn jeans and a green sweater. The dark smudges under her eyes alarmed him, as did her pallor.

Even so, she took his breath away. The subtle swells of her breasts filled out the sweater nicely, and her feet were bare and slim, with deliciously red toenails. He dragged his gaze away from her with some difficulty and stared past her.

From what little he could see, her flat was a mess. Papers were strewn about her coffee table, her laptop was on the floor, and a blanket lay crumpled next to the couch. A clutter of mugs spoke of hours or even days spent without a break.

"Working?" he finally asked.

Following his gaze to the mess in her living room, she blushed. "I'm trying to get organized. You've been out of town less than a week. I haven't found a job if that's what you're asking."

"Relax, Elizabeth. I was only trying to make conversation." Alexander stepped forward and touched her cheek. Her eyes fluttered closed for a single breath, and she leaned into his palm. Too soon, she stepped back. He tried not to let his disappointment show. "You look knackered. When was the last time you had a decent meal?"

"I had a grilled cheese last night," she said defensively. "And you're not my mother."

"No. Definitely not. Come to breakfast with me. I've missed you these past few days." He smiled and withdrew a tin of her favorite tea from his coat pocket. "A peace offering."

She made no move to take the green tin. "I feel like this is made of strings."

"As in strings attached to my offer? No. No strings, *chérie*. Silk or otherwise. As I told you, I'm peckish. Both for food and for your wit. Indulge a jet-lagged and desperate man?" He held the tin of tea out in front of him.

Elizabeth huffed and plucked the canister from his hand. "Fine. Let me get my shoes and put on a better shirt."

"You look fine the way you are," Alexander insisted as she left him in the hallway. He was dressed casually himself: jeans, brown leather loafers, and a burnt orange sweater. Still, her terse acceptance rang like melodious bells in his ears.

A few minutes later, Elizabeth emerged with her thin rain coat and a knit hat that hid her hair. He'd been right about that luxurious mane. It did shine, and he ached to run his fingers through it, to grab the thick locks, and gently, but firmly, angle her head back so he could nibble her throat.

He offered his elbow to accept Elizabeth's hand. She kept looking up at him, her eyes uncertain.

"Are you hungry?" he asked her once they'd descended the four flights of stairs.

She slid across the supple leather seat in the back of his limo. "Yes."

"Mike's Diner, Thomas," Alexander said as he took the seat across from Elizabeth. He wanted to touch her, but he didn't think it would be welcome.

The ride passed largely in silence, Elizabeth fiddling with the belt on her coat and Alexander unable to look away.

At the diner, they found two seats at the counter, and soon they had cups of coffee and plates of eggs Benedict in front of them.

"I cannot get you out of my mind, Elizabeth."

Her eyes widened, and he caught the hitch in her breath and the flush on her cheeks.

Alexander reached over and brushed a knuckle along her jaw. "I think about you every morning when I wake up and every night when I fall asleep. But I do not only want you in my bed. I want you in my life. You say you won't fit in my social circles, but I say you will. You're a Harvard-educated woman. Summa cum laude? And before you say anything, I did not research you."

Her lips twitched into a small smile. "Magna cum laude. I got pneumonia in my third year. One of my professors was a dick and refused to let me make up an exam." She forked up a bite of eggs and washed it down with a sip of coffee. Her eyes fluttered, and a satisfied moan escaped her lips. "I haven't had eggs Benedict this good in years."

"I'm pleased. Elizabeth, you are brilliant. And you are lovely. You carry yourself with such grace. You know who you are. Well, mostly. I still believe there is a true submissive inside those walls you've erected around your heart." Alexander leaned closer. "Give me a chance. Please. Do you find me a pleasant companion? Enjoy talking to me?"

"I changed my mobile plan so I had unlimited text messages," she admitted. "I had to drop my cable to do it."

Alexander chuckled. "And I was late to the office every day while I was in London. My mother interrogated me that last day after you hung up on me. She could see the effect you had on me. Let us see where this goes, shall we? I have a fundraiser to attend on Friday night. A black-tie ball for the Jimmy Fund. Come with me. If you don't, I'll be stuck with my brother and his insufferable date for the evening."

Elizabeth set down her fork and folded her napkin. The dark cloud that settled over her features dimmed Alexander's smile immediately. "The nicest dress I own cost less than your socks, Alexander. I would *not* fit in. I can't go with you."

"Nonsense. I can easily have a dress sent over for you."

Elizabeth slid off her stool. "I'm not one of your *causes*. You can't throw money at me and expect that it'll fix everything or make me come to heel and be your pet. I don't need you to swoop in and save the day."

"I am well aware of that, Elizabeth. You are a strong and beautiful woman who has found herself in circumstances unbefitting of her intelligence, kind heart, and moral code. I can help. Why won't you allow me to do so? I'm not asking you to let me pay your rent, move you into one of my properties, or find you a job, though I would be happy to do any of those things. But right now, I am offering a dress. Nothing more."

He barely suppressed his ire. Any other woman would have jumped at the chance to join him. But every other woman he'd dated paled in comparison to Elizabeth.

"No." She shook her head. "No dresses. No meals. They all come with strings. And right now, I have enough on my mind without figuring out how to escape your knots." She shoved her hand into her pocket and withdrew a crumpled twenty-dollar bill. Tossing the cash in the middle of his plate of eggs, she said, "Good bye. Enjoy the party. Don't call me again."

Before Alexander could rise, Elizabeth stalked out of the diner and disappeared down the street.

---

How dare Alexander try to buy her with an expensive dress and celebrity shoulder-rubbing.

"I am not submissive," she muttered over a dinner of stale popcorn and half a bottle of wine. River butted her head against Elizabeth's ankle. "You don't think I'm submissive, do you, sweetie?" The cat meowed and rolled over. *River* was submissive. Not her.

Merlot sloshed into her glass, more than was prudent. She didn't want to stay sober tonight. Loneliness pressed in on her like an unforgiving prison from which she had no escape. Not even wine could unlock the cell. When Alexander had buzzed her this morning, she'd allowed herself a brief moment of hope. He desired her. No one had desired her for a very long time.

By the time she climbed into bed, the effects of her over indulgence had largely worn off, and only the headache remained. She looked longingly at her phone. Dammit, she missed him.

*Enough,* she chided herself.

Alexander was a rich man, and he was used to getting what he wanted. Darren, her last serious boyfriend back in Seattle, had been the same way.

They'd dated for five years. She'd found him rude and dismissive at first, but at her parents' urging, she'd tried to adapt to his strong personality. She'd adapted too well. Within a year, they'd been living in an apartment he chose, eating at restaurants he liked, and associating with his friends—not hers.

He'd told her what to wear and how to act. Gradually at first. Snide comments about her preference for loose sweaters. Glares when she laughed too loudly for his tastes. A raised brow when she took a second helping of dessert. Every time they had a social engagement, he'd bring home a dress or pick something out of her closet that *he* liked. She hated it, but she'd never said a word. He signed her up for a gym because she'd gained five pounds and even went so far as to have meals delivered to their apartment to try to help her stick to the diet *he'd* prescribed.

Darren's true colors came out when her parents disowned her. By then he was one of Seattle's best cardiologists and flush with cash.

A few tears escaped her eyes, and she dashed them away. The controlling, arrogant asshole wasn't worth her tears. Nor was Alexander.

# CHAPTER FIVE

On Tuesday morning, there was a potted African Violet outside her door.

*Elizabeth, the only string here is the one attached to this card. I keep offending you. For that, I am sorry.*

"Nice try, but I'm not buying it." She left the plant on the mail table on the first floor on her way out of the building.

The snow swirled in violent eddies along the street and blew up her deep blue pencil skirt as she trudged to the T station. Pants would have been smarter.

Huddled against the train's window, she held onto the strap above her head to stay upright. She wrinkled her nose at the odd smells—eggs, stale sweat, and a hint of urine.

Her phone found its way to her hand without conscious thought. No messages. *Dammit.*

She scrolled back through some of the older texts she and Alexander had exchanged, unable to hide her smile.

He'd told her several times that she was lovely or beautiful, but mostly he'd complimented her personality and the stories she'd told about her life. He never failed to ask about her day and seemed genuinely interested in the little things she had to say.

She'd learned much about him through those messages. His preference for running over cycling. His love of red wine, scotch, and a thick steak. And he was kind to his employees. That she'd discovered when he'd asked her opinion on the best holiday bonus for them.

Chocolate gelato and the Beatles. *Doctor Who, Firefly,* and *NCIS.* The beach rather than the mountains. Winter over summer. Would they have found more common ground if she hadn't broken it off?

Elizabeth emerged from the T station into a biting wind. Damn the expense, she *had* to get a warmer coat this winter.

By the time she arrived at Fenway, she was numb. A pretty, young secretary showed her in to a richly paneled office in a building adjacent to Fenway Park, then offered her coffee.

Elizabeth practically dove for her phone when it buzzed, but Benny Hedgeman strode into the room before she retrieved the device. Wire-framed glasses rested low on his nose, and he smiled, his thin face heavily lined.

"Miss Bennett. It's a pleasure." He extended a bony hand and shook hers firmly. "I'm glad you came in today."

She swallowed hard. "I don't know how I can help you, Mr. Hedgeman. I can't divulge company policies and procedures. Not for five years. My confidentiality agreement prohibits it. I can't tell you what I...know."

He set an open Manilla folder on his desk in front of her, a knowing smile curving his lips. "And I cannot give you copies of the last tax returns we received from your former employer. If you'll excuse me for a moment, I need to speak with my secretary."

Proof. Inches away. She watched the door snick closed and then quickly tucked the copies into her bag and shut the folder. Unfortunately, she had no idea what to do with the documents. Call the cops, confront CPH, do nothing...every option frightened her.

Benny came back in a moment later and nodded when he saw the closed folder. "I appreciate your time, Miss Bennett. As does the club's GM. I'll walk you out."

Elizabeth didn't think about checking her phone until she walked in the door of her apartment. She couldn't help her disappointment when the only new message was from her best friend, Kelsey.

---

ON WEDNESDAY, a fresh tin of tea waited at her door, wrapped in a pink silk ribbon.

Elizabeth thought about dumping the tea out the window, but there hadn't been any response to the jobs she'd applied to, and she couldn't afford much more tea on her own.

Those damn copies of the Red Sox's tax returns mocked her, daring her to make a decision. Should she go back to the Red Sox and show them *her* numbers? Take her suspicions to the police? Or let Carter, Pastack, and Hayes get away with what looked more and more like embezzlement?

She called ten Boston lawyers over the course of the morning, but as soon as she mentioned CPH, every one of them refused to speak with her. More than once she picked up her phone and contemplated calling Alexander. He ran a multi-billion-dollar business. He had lawyers at his beck and call. Though if CPH *was* guilty of embezzlement, his company was likely affected. If she admitted her suspicions to him, he could and would force her hand, and she'd never be able to think of him fondly again. Though she'd abandoned all hope of a relationship with him, the memory of his smile, his eyes, and his scent brought warmth welling up inside of her.

She cleaned up her files, made copies of everything, and sent an overnight package with a USB drive and a one-hundred-dollar check to her former lawyer in Seattle.

THURSDAY DAWNED with a freak ice storm. Still, Alexander managed to send a gift. Thomas arrived at her door with a black silk dress in a large box.

The man was obsessed with silk.

Elizabeth sent him away, the box still tucked under his arm.

An hour later, the bell rang again. Elizabeth ran down the stairs, determined to tell Alexander to bugger off in no uncertain terms, but when she opened the door, a young man bundled up in a down jacket was waiting for her.

"Elizabeth Bennett?" he asked hopefully.

"Yes. How can I—?"

He shoved a manila envelope into her hands. "You've been served."

Elizabeth's hands shook as she opened the packet. The legal documents contained within accused her of breaking her non-disclosure agreement. Among the papers was a summons instructing her to appear in court right after the first of the year. There was also an ominously worded note that advised her to cease all contact with her former clients immediately, or she'd be subject to arrest.

"What the hell? How did they know?"

Were they following her?

A shiver raced up her spine, and she thanked her lucky stars that she hadn't been responsible for any of the Fairhaven Exports accounts. Hayes and the senior pool accountant had handled those personally. On her way to the stairs, she paused at the table underneath the row of mailboxes. The African Violet was still there. She carried it up to her apartment. Today, she needed something good in her life.

"So what's going on with you, Lizzie? You're a million miles away."

Kelsey's mop of curly red hair bobbed as she reached for a set of chopsticks. A thick scar perpendicular to Kelsey's wrist sent a pang of sadness through Elizabeth. Three years ago, Kelsey had lost her husband to a mugging gone wrong. David had tried to protect his wife, taking the knife meant for her.

A month later, Elizabeth had found Kelsey on her bathroom floor, her wrists covered in blood, and had gotten her friend to the hospital just in time.

"Stress. Nothing serious, Kels. I need to find a job, and it's not going well. I'll pick up one easily in January, but I hate feeling...useless." She shoved a bite of chicken curry into her mouth.

"You okay for cash, babe?"

"Yeah. I've got enough in my savings for rent and food for a few months. If I have to, I'll sell my stock or liquidate some of my retirement. Not ideal, but you do what you gotta do." She hated owning the stock anyway. "I really appreciate dinner tonight, but I'll be fine. No presents this year. Okay? For Christmas, let's you, Toni, and me go to a movie and gorge ourselves on popcorn."

"Whatever you want, Lizzie. I mean it."

Elizabeth smiled. She didn't care that Alexander was at some stuffy charity ball and she was wearing sweats, eating greasy Thai, and hadn't bothered to put on makeup in more than two weeks. This was what she needed. Time with her friends. This would clear her head, and on Monday, she'd call her lawyer and figure out what to do. She'd make it.

A tear burned in the corner of her eye, but she forced it away and hugged Kelsey so hard, the redhead dropped her chopsticks in surprise.

"What was that for?" Kelsey asked.

"It's been too long since we did this and I want you to know that I love you."

"I love you too. Now eat. You're too skinny."

Elizabeth laughed. "Hardly, but you don't have to tell me twice. It's been *ages* since I had Golden Tiger for dinner."

---

SHE WOKE early on Saturday with a headache. That second beer at Kelsey's hadn't been a good idea.

After pulling on sweats, she opened her laptop, determined to apply for at least five jobs today.

Heading to the *Boston Globe*'s website to browse their job ads, she choked on her tea. Plastered across their home page, in full living color, was a photo of Alexander.

He stood in a trim black tuxedo amid a hoard of people. Next to him, with a hand on his arm, was a woman dressed in a blood red gown that dipped low to expose what had to be expensive but obviously fake breasts. Diamonds glittered at her ears and throat, and her lips and long fingernails matched her dress. She gazed up at Alexander, her mouth slightly open and her tiny body completely out of proportion with her massive chest.

Elizabeth huffed. So *that* was his type then. Well, it was a damn good thing she'd shut him down. She threw the latest tin of tea across the room, sending River yowling under the sofa. She'd almost managed to get over her case of sour grapes when her phone buzzed.

*I need to see you. Last night was bloody awful, and I've missed you terribly. Come to dinner. I'll even cook.*

"Oh, hell no," Elizabeth swore. She jabbed her finger at the screen and called him back.

"Elizabe—" he said joyfully, but she didn't let him get a word in.

"Are you calling me with her still naked in your bed? Or did you kick her out right after you tied her up and did God knows what with her?" Anger mounting, she paced the room.

"I have no bloody idea what you are talking about. There is no one in my bed but me and I have not tied up *anyone* recently. I thought I had made myself clear. *You* are the one I want, Elizabeth. Who am I purported to have slept with and when?"

"Last night. Blond. A chest that looks like it costs more than my net worth. Red dress."

She nearly dropped the phone when he started laughing.

"What's so funny? I'm asking you a serious question. Answer me, dammit."

He gasped a couple of times, trying to catch his breath. "Candy? You think I shagged Candy? Oh, that is brilliant, *chérie*. Candy does not even possess the intelligence of a log. But she's my brother's conquest of the month. As long as he continues to support her expensive shopping habit, she will enjoy being his slave. I take it there was a photo?"

She paused. "Yes."

"And is she wearing a diamond collar around her neck?"

"Yes."

"That is my brother's. The collar symbolizes their relationship. If you meet him some day, he can explain. It isn't a dynamic I enjoy, but it works for him. He left her with me while he got her a drink. It was the longest ten minutes of the entire night. She asked me why none of the players attending were wearing red socks and where Jimmy Fund was. When I tried to explain that the Jimmy Fund was a charity that the Red Sox support, she was quite indignant that Mr. Fund warranted an entire ball when he couldn't be bothered to show up."

Elizabeth laughed in spite of herself. "Really?"

"Yes. Admittedly, Candy was knackered when she arrived, and alcohol does nothing for her intelligence level. My brother is usually more responsible than that. He was distracted last night."

Alexander sounded worried, and she regretted jumping to conclusions. "Is Nicholas all right?" Elizabeth curled up on her couch.

A long pause hung in the air. "I don't know. My brother has a gambling problem, Elizabeth. I fear he lost a significant amount at the tables last weekend. I worry about him, but I'll talk to him on Monday."

Alexander's admission touched something in her. He trusted her with information that could be detrimental to their company's reputation after she'd jumped down his throat.

She swallowed hard. "And you didn't..."

"I spent the entire evening with my brother and Ryan Lavarnway. He's a fellow Yale grad, but he's all of twenty-six. We have very little in common other than our alma mater. After a disappointing meal and more small talk than anyone should tolerate, I went to bed at midnight. Alone. Wishing desperately that I'd sent my regrets to the party's organizers and shown up at your flat with a pizza and a bottle of wine instead."

"I'm sorry. I shouldn't have jumped on you like that."

"You were jealous, yes? Don't lie to me."

"I was...something. Angry with myself maybe. And yes, a little jealous. And sad. I wish I fit into your world."

"You are the one who seems to think you do not. *I* think you'll fit in perfectly. I want no one but you, Elizabeth. Come to dinner tonight. Wear anything you want. Jeans. Flannel pajamas. Nothing at all. Third time's a charm for a meal?"

God, she'd missed his voice and that slightly arrogant swagger his words seemed to convey. She needed something to focus on besides the abysmal state of her life.

*One meal doesn't make a relationship.*

She could have dinner with him, enjoy his company, and maybe even see what it would be like to kiss him without any strings attached. "Okay."

"Really? And you won't run out on me halfway through dinner? I require your promise, Elizabeth." There was a hint of amusement in his words, but also a hard edge. He did want her promise, and God help her, she was going to give it to him.

"I won't run away. I promise."

"Thomas will pick you up at six. Thank you, Elizabeth."

"You're welcome." She hung up and stared at the photo of him on her laptop. She hoped she wouldn't regret this.

# CHAPTER SIX

*A*ll through her run, Elizabeth tried to ignore her worries, with little success. She was being sued, she didn't have a job, and she was having dinner with a man who both intrigued and baffled her.

After four miles, she stopped for a sip of water. Peering across the Charles River, she spotted a photographer, his camera pointed right at her. After staring at her for a moment, he turned and fled, and despite the bright sun illuminating the city, a shiver ran down Elizabeth's spine.

She raced back to her apartment, every inch of her exposed skin tingling with pinpricks of almost-pain. Her eyelashes were frozen.

As she rounded the corner and caught sight of her building, she skidded to a halt. A police cruiser idled out front with its lights flashing. Her neighbor, Mrs. McGillis, waved to her from the front steps. Approaching eighty, the woman still lived on her own and played bingo every Friday and Saturday night. Next to her, a young uniformed policeman with a round face and bright hazel eyes scribbled on a notepad.

"Elizabeth! Oh dearie, I was worried about you," Mrs. McGillis said.

"Why? What's wrong?" Elizabeth rubbed her hands up and down her arms. "And whatever it is, can we discuss it inside? I'm freezing."

"Miss Bennett, I'm Officer O'Hara." The policeman followed her inside. "Have you had any trouble the past few days? Anyone approach you, claiming to forget their key and asking you to let them in?"

After seeing the photographer, all she wanted was a cup of tea and a hot shower. Was this all a coincidence? Or had CPH come after her again? "N-no. Why?"

"A man followed your neighbor here into the building. She hit him with her purse, and he pushed her, but then ran off," the young officer said.

"Oh God. That's awful. Did you get a good look at him?" Elizabeth leaned against the mail table, unsure her legs would hold her much longer.

*Please let it just be a random would-be thief.*

Officer O'Hara glanced down at his notebook. "White. Mid-forties. Blond hair."

Elizabeth pressed her hand to her chest. At least this hadn't been Perez, the man CPH had sent to intimidate her days ago.

"I'll...keep an eye out in case he comes back," she stammered. "Come on, Mrs. McGillis. I'll walk you back upstairs."

By the time Elizabeth locked her apartment door, her tears had spilled over.

---

ELIZABETH PACED in front of her closet. Alexander was too wealthy, and she owned nothing suitable for a date with a billionaire. Clothes littered the bed, dozens of options tried on and discarded.

As the clock ticked ever closer to 6:00 p.m., Elizabeth gave up and tugged on a shapeless black dress several sizes too big. Belting her coat tightly, she stepped out into the night's chill to find Alexander's driver waiting.

She bit her lip before ducking into the back of the car. Warm air surrounded her, spiced with Alexander's distinctive scent. When the door shut with a soft *click*, she sat back and dug her fingers into her bare thighs.

What the hell was she thinking?

A divider rolled down with only a whisper, and the door that hid the scotch popped open. "It's a twenty-minute ride, Miss Bennett. Help yourself to a drink."

"I don't think that's a good idea," she said more to herself than the driver.

The man met her gaze in the rearview mirror and offered her a small smile. "Mr. Fairhaven hasn't been himself since he met you. Nor has he ever, to my knowledge, cooked dinner for a woman."

"Thank you for that." She almost smiled as the divider rolled up and the limo pulled away from the curb.

The city flew by as they crossed the Charles River, and Elizabeth couldn't help but stare out the window like a kid at Christmas. Snow dusted the streets, and her love for the city swelled, a welcome distraction.

Once the limo stopped, her door opened. Alexander's lips curved into a grin as he held out his hand to help her up.

*God, he's handsome.*

The tight jeans and black button-down shirt suited him, though she felt increasingly out of place in her old dress and scuffed heels. Hell, she'd had to color in the abrasions with a Sharpie before leaving the apartment.

"Elizabeth. I confess until Thomas called me from the car, I wasn't certain you'd come," Alexander said as he drew her closer and then kissed her cheek.

"Well, my social calendar hasn't exactly been overflowing recently."

He frowned as he led her inside the gate. "A woman of your beauty and intelligence should be fighting off the suitors, not sitting home alone on a Saturday night."

"Well, I'm not alone now." Despite her nerves, she couldn't deny the connection she felt to this man.

Resting a hand on the small of her back, Alexander guided her up the steps. White columns framed the dormer with large windows radiating light through thinly veiled curtains. Real pine needles pricked at her palms as she ran her hand over the Christmas garland lining the door.

Stepping over the threshold into such elegance tugged a sigh from her lips. A massive Christmas tree in a sitting room greeted her as Alexander led her to a dark gray leather sofa. "May I take your coat?"

Fumbling for the knot on her belt, Elizabeth tried to keep the heat from blooming on her cheeks. Alexander slid his hands under hers, deftly undoing the belt, then flicked the buttons open one-by-one before easing the wrap from her shoulders.

Alexander looked her up and down with her coat draped over his arm, then shook his head. "You hide so much, Elizabeth. Your body, your heart. I hope soon you'll stop hiding from me."

The dress was a mistake.

Shrinking back, she hugged herself tightly. "I'm sorry if my fashion choices disappoint you."

A closet door snapped shut as Alexander turned back to her. "You are *not* a disappointment. Don't ever think that." Two steps later, he pulled he against him, eyes smoldering. "I want you, Elizabeth. In my silks, in my bed, in my life. I can't explain it to you. Hell, I can't even explain it to myself. You are the single most intriguing, beautiful, and infuriating woman I have ever met and by God, you smell amazing."

When his teeth nipped along her collarbone, Elizabeth's

knees threatened to buckle. "I don't know that I can resist you much longer," she whispered.

"So don't. Surrender." More kisses to the sensitive flesh behind her ear, and she ached to do just that.

*God, he knows how to kiss a woman.*

Elizabeth shuddered. "I can't. You scare me. Your life. You have...staff." She managed to extricate herself from his embrace and backed towards the sofa.

"I do. Samuel is my household manager. He and Thomas, my driver, have small flats on the lower level. My chef, Donatella, lives in the South End."

She nodded, dazed.

"I won't apologize for my wealth, Elizabeth. I was fortunate to be born into a family of means, but I've worked hard to keep Fairhaven Limited and Fairhaven Charities solvent for years. I'm more than my bank account. As are you."

They stared at one another until the silence grew uncomfortable. Alexander sighed, then schooled his features back into an unreadable mask. Wine?"

"Yes, thank you."

*Anything to change the subject. Please.*

The delicate crystal goblet rested heavy in her hand as she sank down onto the couch. Alexander raised his glass. "To a fulfilling evening, I hope."

He had good taste in Bordeaux, she'd credit him with that. Unable to stare into his eyes a moment longer, she trailed her gaze over the rest of him. What she wouldn't give to unbutton that shirt.

By the time she realized she'd been staring, Alexander had draped his arm across the back of the sofa only inches from her shoulders.

Resisting the urge to scoot away—or climb into his lap, she stammered, "I-I like you. I've missed you this week. But I still don't know why you want a relationship with me. I'm not fishing for compliments here. I really want to know. How can you think I'll possibly fit into your world?"

Alexander raised a brow. "Despite the abysmal cut and fit of that dress, you are stunning, Elizabeth. But that isn't why I wanted the pleasure of your company tonight. I enjoy talking to you. You're smart, witty, and you laugh at my poor jokes. You care. You were livid with me this morning, once you knew I was concerned about my brother, you worried about him too. In today's society, we've all grown less and less compassionate. We go about our lives without forming deep, personal connections. But I think I could have one with you. And I think that feeling is mutual. Ever since that day in the rain, I've been unable to stop thinking of you.

"Do you know what drew me to you in the first place? What compelled me to do more than help you up and offer you a ride home?"

Elizabeth tried to still her nervous fingers so she wouldn't spill her wine. "No."

"You were soaked to the skin, clearly a bit frightened of me, of being in a limo with a man you knew by reputation only, and determined to give nothing of yourself away. But the moment I held the glass of scotch to your lips, you told me everything I needed to know."

"I don't understand," she said.

The energy that passed between them calmed her pounding heart as he slid the wine glass from her hand and set it aside. Alexander looked at her like she was the only woman in the world.

*No one's eyes should be that green. No man's touch should be that reassuring.*

Alexander moved even closer on the leather sofa until the heat from his body warmed her, and she breathed in his scent. If he kissed her, the bit of stubble darkening his cheeks would tickle. What would he taste like?

"Close your eyes and don't move until I say." His voice took on a commanding tone she couldn't—or didn't want to—ignore.

For several breaths, she waited.

Then, a gentle kiss took her breath away. No other part of their bodies touched, but his demanding lips sent heat flooding through her until she fought to stifle her moan.

He tasted of wine and the promise of passion. A quiet sound, almost animalistic, rumbled in his throat. A lingering tug on her lower lip punctuated the kiss, and she tried to follow him, but then remembered his order. Squirming, she dug her hands into the leather.

Alexander chuckled. "Look at me, *chérie.*"

Her eyes flew open. He sat a few inches from her with light sparkling in his gaze.

"Why are you laughing?" Frustration sharpened her tone.

"Because, Elizabeth, you gave yourself to me. You trust me, even if you don't want to. I saw such amazing strength in you that first day. A woman strong enough to know what she wants and go after it, yet self-aware enough to consciously trust me with her body and maybe even her heart. You fascinate me. I want to know everything about you. Down to the smallest detail."

Alexander's words were too smooth, too perfect. Yet they drew her in, so when he offered her his hand, she took it.

He kissed her knuckles. "Relax. Make yourself at home. I have to finish up the meal. I'll be a few minutes."

"Can I come with you?" She gripped his hand firmly, not letting him pull away from her. When he cocked his head, she tried a tentative smile. "You want to get to know me. Leaving me alone in this imposing house isn't the way to do that. Aren't you afraid I'll run away again?"

"*Touché,*" he said with a smile. "I wanted to cook for you. Unfortunately, I'm not the best in the kitchen. Donatella is going to be very upset with me tomorrow. I'm a tad bit embarrassed to show you the mess I made."

Now *this* was a side of Alexander she could deal with. "You want me to share my secrets? Then you'll share yours. I want to see the great Alexander Fairhaven fumble around in the kitchen. Maybe it'll knock a bit of that swagger out of his step."

He led her through the cavernous dining room and into the kitchen. A bubble of laughter fought to escape as she took in the mess. A tossed salad rested in a large wooden bowl on the counter, small bits of greenery scattered all around. On a cutting board, a lopsided loaf of bread rested. Flour covered every prep surface, splatters of marinara sauce dotted the six-burner Viking stove, and various bits of vegetable detritus littered the floor around the sink.

"When was the last time you cooked?" Elizabeth asked, biting the inside of her cheek to keep from embarrassing him further.

In this room, the confident, self-assured billionaire disappeared. Rolling up his sleeves, the corded muscles of his forearms flexed as he reached for a set of potholders.

"Something more complicated than scrambled eggs? Three years ago," he said, cursing under his breath as he pulled a bubbling dish out of the oven. Lasagna. "Shite. It isn't supposed to look this...runny."

Elizabeth stifled a snort. "It'll set. Give it a few minutes. It smells delicious." The smile she earned warmed her down to her toes. "You're not planning on us eating in that big formal dining room, are you?"

He paused halfway to the door with the salad bowl in his hands. "I was. Why?"

"Because that's not the way to get to know me. That's a party. *This* is an intimate dinner for two." She slid off her stool and withdrew a bread knife from the knife block on the counter. Arching her brows, she drew the knife across the loaf of sourdough. "Pull up a stool."

Alexander stammered for a moment, but whatever he saw in her eyes convinced him. "I'll get the wine."

*This is more like it.*

Despite the grandeur of the kitchen, the mess and the familiar smells calmed her. They both wanted the same thing—to find out if they had anything in common besides the basic chemistry that burned between them. If she was going to be off balance, she wanted him just as unsteady. Sharing a meal tucked close enough for their knees to touch at a messy counter leveled the playing field.

"This is amazing," she said, savoring a generous bite of the slice of lasagna he'd served her. "Nonno Giuseppe would be proud."

"Nonno Giuseppe?" Alexander sipped at his wine.

"Toni's grandfather. Antonia," she clarified when he frowned at her. "A friend of mine. Her family owns a pizza restaurant in the North End. I'll take you one of these days." As soon as the words left her mouth, she regretted them. She'd just committed to another date. Oh, who was she kidding? She *wanted* another date. She worried she wanted a lot more than that.

"I look forward to it, *chérie*. To Nonno Giuseppe." They toasted Toni's grandfather and exchanged smiles—hers shy, his triumphant.

*Change the subject.*

"Tell me something about you I can't learn from the press," Elizabeth asked, eager for a change of subject.

"I'm not sure what that would be," Alexander grumbled. "My mother claims my first word was 'shite.' Though Nicholas insists I ran around the house shouting 'binky.'"

"Were you always this...imposing?" Elizabeth scooped up another bite of lasagna as Alexander sat back and took a sip of his wine.

"I fought with the other children. Once I joined the Royal Army, I met other men like me who helped me realize why I couldn't leave well enough alone. I embraced being a Dom, and my life suddenly made sense."

Elizabeth soaked up the knowledge about the man next to her. He was so open, much different than she'd expected him to be.

Still, she couldn't find her bearings. Alexander often paused to caress her cheek or arm, and at the end of the meal, scooped up a bite of lasagna for her from his own plate and held the fork to her lips. Despite the absurdity of the action, Elizabeth squirmed, and heat flooded her.

"Dessert," Alexander said as he withdrew a plate of chocolate-covered strawberries from the fridge. "These, I did not make. A tragedy for which you should be supremely thankful."

Something inside her melted at his self-deprecating statement. "You did quite well with everything else. There's always next time."

"We're up to two future dates now." He grinned. "This is progress." He fed her a strawberry, following it up with a firm kiss and a swipe of his tongue over the corner of her mouth. "Delicious. The strawberry and the woman."

"I enjoy your company," Elizabeth said, throwing his words back at him. "I still think you're making a mistake pursuing me, but it seems that I can't stop you. And the more time we spend together, the less I think I want to."

"And *I* still do not understand why you insist on referring to yourself as a mistake," he said, his words clipped. "I've made mistakes before. Miss Massachusetts was a mistake. She thought James Bond was a real British agent. The newscaster, Paola Larkinson was a mistake. She had us followed by a cameraman on our one and only date. You are *not* a mistake." He took her hands, and his strong grip almost convinced her of the truth of his words. "I've never felt as much myself as I do when I am with you. With everyone else in my life, even my brother, I've always been guarded. But with you, I think all of those walls can come down."

"You're different than I thought you would be," Elizabeth said. "Less...arrogant."

Alexander chuckled, earning him a punch in the arm. "Oh, you're still arrogant. Your whole tea-gifting, dress-sending penchants, and insistence that I'm going to end up in your silks? Arrogant. But there's another side to you that comes out when you're relaxed like this. Playful."

"I'm not sure anyone's called me playful before." Alexander fed her another strawberry.

Elizabeth savored the sweet fruit as she watched the man in front of her. "You're a mystery, Alexander Fairhaven. One I want to solve."

# CHAPTER SEVEN

"*K*iss me."

Elizabeth tried to look away, but Alexander slipped his arm around her waist, and her body won the battle with her mind. As their lips met, her eyes fluttered closed. This time, he let her set the pace. Hesitant at first, she slid closer. Teasing her tongue over his teeth, she took in the taste of him. Arousal prickled her nose as her body responded to the feel of his tongue against hers, the tug of his teeth against her lip, and the firm grasp he had on her. She couldn't move if she wanted to, but at that moment, she couldn't fathom a single reason why she'd ever move again.

"Oh God," she whimpered when she broke the kiss. "What are you doing to me?"

"Showing you who you are. Why I want you. I have very specific needs in the bedroom. Needs that I believe you can fill. And in turn, I will take care of *your* needs—even the ones you refuse to acknowledge."

"You want to tie me up." The words shot a thrill through her, raising gooseflesh on the backs of her arms. Her core practically

ached with a need she hadn't felt in years. But giving up control...
she couldn't.

"That is part of it. I require your surrender. Total and
complete trust. And in exchange, I promise that you will always
be safe and protected. No harm will ever come to you in my care.
That is the role of a Dom, *chérie*."

"You want to make me—"

"No." The single word practically exploded from his lips,
though he'd never raised his voice. "I will *never* force you. Is that
what you think submission is?"

While she'd read the occasional romance novel that teased
BDSM in a relationship, she'd never experienced it firsthand.

"I'm not a...a sub. I'm sorry, Alexander. You have the wrong
woman."

Alexander slid his arms around her. His breath whispered
against her ear as he nibbled on her neck. Instinctively, she
angled her head to afford him the access he demanded with his
very presence. "Only the strongest of women make true submissives. A weak-minded woman can never trust someone enough to
surrender. I want you in my silks, Elizabeth. I've made no secret
of that."

He cupped the back of her head. His stare sliced through her,
right into the depths of her soul. She looked away, unwilling to
give more of herself to this man who kept speaking as if she were
already his.

"Your silks. You keep saying that." Nothing about this situation made sense, especially not the throbbing ache between her
legs.

"All of my...implements involve silk in some manner. May I
show you?"

When she didn't respond, his lips crushed down on hers.

*Oh God.*

She wanted him.

"Come upstairs. I promise that nothing will happen you're not ready for."

He rose and offered Elizabeth his hand. She considered, and after a moment, let him help her up. Arms linked, he led her through the parlor and up a sweeping set of stairs to a dark wood door.

Elizabeth's heart pounded in her ears. Perhaps this wasn't a smart idea.

Alexander turned to her and took both of her hands in his. "You know what a safeword is?"

"Yes."

"I'd like to show you my silks. I do not intend to touch you. Not unless you ask. But for someone with no experience, even the sight of a crop in this context can be too much. If you say 'red' to me at any time, everything stops. If I am touching you, I stop. If I am demonstrating something, even if I am nowhere near you, I stop. If I am explaining something, and it frightens you, say red, and I stop. Do you understand?"

Elizabeth nodded, but Alexander shook his head. "I require verbal communication, Elizabeth. Inside this room, gestures mean nothing. I will ask you often if you understand me. Probably more than you think necessary, but trust me in this. Yes?"

"O-okay."

Alexander opened the door and let Elizabeth step into his private sanctuary. A reflection of the man at her side, it whispered understated elegance and power. Floors the color of dark chocolate gleamed like new. Under the glow of recessed lights, a king-size, four-poster bed sat as an island of luxury on a raised platform. In the corner, a large wooden cross made from the same rich, shining, cherry wood as the bed frame dominated the space. Black silk restraints at each point of the X drew her eyes.

While Elizabeth was taking in the room, Alexander opened the cabinet next to the cross. Inside, a pegboard held numerous pieces of braided silk and rope, what looked to be several leather crops with silk covered handles, various implements with tassels at one end and silk at the other, a collection of blindfolds, padded silk cuffs, and on the top shelf, folded blankets and bottles of water. "Come here, Elizabeth."

His voice was completely different in this room. Where downstairs he'd been playful, now he was deadly serious. His words took on a deeper timbre. They were slower and crisper—not harsh, but firm. Elizabeth chewed on the inside of her lip and stepped forward. Alexander lifted a blindfold in one hand and a piece of thick braided silk and hemp rope with suede tassels on the end in the other. "If you were ever to trust me with your pleasure, Elizabeth, this is how we would begin. This is my favorite flogger."

*Flogger?*

Her mouth went dry, and she took a half step back.

"Touch it, Elizabeth." The gentleness in his tone calmed her. He wouldn't force her. She held out her hand, and he laid the implement carefully in her palm. "Touch it. Slap it against your hand a time or two. Learn its feel."

She obeyed. The suede tickled her skin. Something about the flogger intrigued her. Alexander took it from her and held it close to her cheek. "May I?"

She nodded.

"Verbal responses, Elizabeth. Remember?"

"I'm sorry. Yes."

"Yes what? I may touch you?"

"Yes. You can touch me. With that." Her voice trembled, but she wasn't frightened. Nervous perhaps, but not frightened.

"You know what it is. Say it." Alexander stepped close enough for his heat to seep into her.

She swallowed hard over the lump in her throat. "You can touch me with your...flogger." The last word was barely a whisper.

He smiled. The suede feathered gently over her cheek. The

tassels followed the curve of her neck, across her throat, and back up towards her ear. She shivered, and the sensitive bundle of nerves between her legs throbbed uncomfortably.

"Very good, Elizabeth. Would you trust me with more of you?"

"Explain," she managed.

"I would like to show you what it is to submit to me. If you trust me, I would like to use this on you. You would remain fully clothed, as would I. There would be no marks. You would not be harmed in any way. Will you allow it?"

Elizabeth chewed on the inside of her cheek again. The spot was raw, and the hint of pain wasn't entirely unwelcome. Alexander cupped her cheek and smoothed his thumb over her lips. She sucked in a breath and closed the small distance between them. Her nipples ached for his touch. If she didn't kiss him again in the next few moments, she wasn't sure she could survive. Her tongue darted out, and she nipped his thumb.

"Not yet, *chérie*," he chided. "You must decide. Right now. Will you submit to me? Or do we end the evening?"

"I want you. It has to be...your way?" She reached for the buttons of his shirt and had loosened two of them before he captured one of her wrists and pinned her arm behind her back. His grip was firm, but not painful. Every tiny hair on the nape of her neck stood on end, and she feared the thin scrap of lace between her thighs wouldn't contain her desire much longer.

"Yes."

"We can't just have sex." She ground her hips against him.

Alexander stifled a groan. "Not in the traditional manner, no. Not tonight. Although I believe you would derive pleasure from our play, as would I."

She wasn't sure her legs could sustain her weight. She needed him to kiss her again. The bulge of his cock pressed against her. "Trust me, Elizabeth. Let me show you what pleasure is."

"God. Yes. Please. I can't stay in this room with you another minute otherwise."

Alexander's eyes lit up. He tossed the flogger onto the bed and released her. The loss of his controlling touch left her unsteady.

"You remember your safeword?"

"Red."

# CHAPTER EIGHT

*A*lexander led her up onto the platform. "Stand against the poster."

Trying not to squirm, Elizabeth tracked Alexander's every movement as he returned to his cabinet.

"It is extremely important for you to listen to me carefully, Elizabeth. You must do exactly as I say. If you cannot obey a command, either tell me immediately or use your safeword. Otherwise, you could end up hurt. Do you understand?"

She nodded, but a raised brow reminded her of his instructions. "Yes."

"Very good." He held up a black silk blindfold. "May I?"

"Um. Yes."

As the light in the room faded into nothingness, Elizabeth's heartbeat skyrocketed. "Oh God."

"Shhh. I'm right here." As he smoothed his hands down her arms, she relaxed somewhat, but once his teeth nipped her lower lip, she shivered with need. "You are doing well, Elizabeth. Is the blindfold comfortable?"

"I...yes."

Curling his fingers around her wrists, he pinned them behind her back. "Grasp the poster. Now, you must not move. Do you think you can keep your hands here or would you like me to bind you?"

Elizabeth sputtered, "N-no, don't, I don't want...I can keep still."

Alexander cupped her cheek and kissed her tenderly. "Take a deep breath, Elizabeth. Remember. One word and all of this stops. One single word. Say it for me now. Tell me you understand."

*I'm really doing this.*

"Red. I understand. I'm okay. I think."

He chuckled. "You are doing very well, *chérie*. But now we begin. Everything that happens from now until we end our play, I control. You may, however, ask me for anything you want. I may or may not grant your request. Do you understand?"

"But, m-my s-safeword?"

"Will always stop everything. I speak only of any specific desires you have as we proceed. Relax, Elizabeth. Let yourself experience the sensations of my flogger against your skin." Alexander trailed the suede from her neck, down her shoulder, all the way down to her breast. The faint touch of the tassels over her dress sent a shudder of pleasure through her.

Would it hurt if he snapped the flogger against her skin? She imagined the falls tumbling over her nipple and her clit throbbed.

A flood of dampness between her thighs had her shifting her feet. "Do not move, Elizabeth," Alexander said, his tone commanding, but not harsh. "Two strikes. Very gentle. Relax your breathing for me."

Elizabeth took a deep breath. His free hand rubbed her right thigh, below the hem of her dress. Up and down, warming, relaxing. Down again, over her knee, cupping the curve of her calf.

"One," he said sharply.

The suede bit her thigh. She yelped and jerked her hips, but she kept her hands clasped around the poster.

"All right, Elizabeth?"

"I-yes." In truth, she wasn't sure. The ache between her legs had taken on a more demanding beat and her thigh stung with a delicious warmth she couldn't call pain.

"Two." The second strike landed on her left thigh, a twin to the first. Another jerk and the ache intensified. She couldn't help the tiny moan that escaped her lips. Alexander slid his hand from her hip, over her belly, up to cup her breast. With the faintest of touches, he skimmed her nipple.

"You were wonderful, Elizabeth. Will you indulge me for more?" He punctuated his question with his lips to her ear.

She couldn't think. Hell, she could barely breathe as he kissed his way down her neck. "Answer me, Elizabeth. Four more strikes or red?"

"C-can I have a m-minute?" she asked. She didn't think her legs would hold her much longer, but heaven help her, she didn't want this to end.

"Yes, of course."

Elizabeth reached up to remove the blindfold, but Alexander grabbed her hand and returned it firmly to the poster. "No moving, Elizabeth. I was very clear about this. You may have your minute, but you will remain still."

"Alexander."

"When we are playing, I will be obeyed. Always. Or there will be consequences."

"I don't like this," she said, shaking her head. But her insides clenched and heat gathered in the lace she wore under her dress. Blind, she tried to track to his voice.

"Then use your safeword. I will not think less of you, *chérie*. This life is not for everyone. Have you made your choice?"

*God help me.*

"Four more," she whispered.

"Very good, Elizabeth. These next four will be in more intimate areas. Over your clothes. No marks. But they may be shocking. Breathe deeply. Do not tense and do not move. Two and two."

The first strike landed across her left breast. Elizabeth yelped and threw her hands up as the second strike landed across her bare forearm covering her right breast. That one hurt, so much more than any of the others.

"Elizabeth, you said you could keep still," Alexander growled as he dropped the flogger, captured her wrists, and held them tightly.

"It hurt," she whimpered. A few tears escaped her blindfold.

Long strokes of his hand against her throbbing arm soothed. "It hurt because you moved. I swung with the amount of pressure you could take through fabric. If you move again, you'll get hurt again. And as you still have two more strikes, I suggest you ask me to bind you or use your safeword."

His words were harsh, but he blew gently on the burning skin, then kissed up to her elbow, and the pain faded to a distant memory.

"Okay," she whispered.

"That's not enough, Elizabeth. I offered to bind you, and you refused. So now you must ask me."

For several tense breaths, neither of them spoke. Alexander returned her hand to the poster. Her skin cooled as his body heat faded away. "Alexander?"

She couldn't see and didn't want to disobey him by moving. A bead of her essence threatened to escape the lace of her panties.

His voice shocked her, so close he couldn't have been more than two steps away. "I'm right here, Elizabeth. During our play, I'll never be more than an arm's length from you." A reassuring hand splayed over her hip.

"Please, um, tie me up."

"Are you certain you wish to be bound?" Something soft tickled the backs of her hands and up her arms.

"Yes. I want...I *need* this. Please, Alexander."

His mouth was on hers then, his lips, teeth, and tongue assaulting her with sensations she'd never associated with sex before.

So intense was his kiss that she barely noticed the silk ropes winding around her wrists until he tightened the knot. Panic threatened, and she tested the bindings. No pain, but she couldn't move her wrists at all.

"You are truly a vision, Elizabeth. Now relax. Deep breaths. You will always be safe with me."

A thrill jolted through her, along with a desperate need. She wanted Alexander's hands on her, pinching her aching nipples. His cock filling her. She'd never felt as empty as she did at that moment.

"How are you, Elizabeth? Calm?"

*God he smelled good.*

Her breath quickened. "No. I need you to touch me."

"Oh, I plan on it." The quick pinch of her nipple had her crying out and jerking her hips, but she couldn't get close enough to press her body to his.

"Please do that again."

"Not yet. My rules. Remember?"

"Y-yes."

Alexander purred appreciatively. "Good. Now, because you disobeyed me, I am going to add an extra three strikes. Five total. This is the lightest punishment you will ever receive for failing to obey me. Do you understand?" He kissed her neck, up to her ear, and a few strands of her hair tickled her cheek.

"Five? I can't."

"Yes. You can. Punishment should not be easy. But perhaps a little indulgence for your first time is called for." Alexander cupped her breast again. A burning lance of pleasure shot to her pussy as he rolled her nipple between his fingers. "Tell me you understand."

"I under—God. Do that again."

"Another request?" He nibbled her earlobe, then tugged gently. Her entire lower body throbbed. Need coated her thighs.

"Please!"

"What do you deserve, Elizabeth?"

Tears escaped under her blindfold. "I don't understand."

"You disobeyed. What does that mean?" Alexander wiped the tears away.

"Five strikes," she gasped as he pinched the other nipple.

"You are learning well, Elizabeth. There is one additional rule that you will obey at all times. For as long as we play together—days, months, or even years—unless I say otherwise, you will not come without my permission. Do you understand?"

*How many times can he ask that question?*

"Uhh..." The way she felt, she wasn't certain she could hold back an orgasm if he touched anywhere near her clit. With only his lips on her neck and his fingers toying with her nipples, Elizabeth's body was on fire. How much longer could she hold on?

"Focus. Listen to my voice do what I say. Raise your head. Spread your legs wider. Do it now."

*Oh my God.* Her legs inched apart, and her head snapped up. She couldn't do this. It was too much.

"Five strikes now, Elizabeth. Count them for me."

The first hit her left breast, right across the nipple. The pain bloomed out over her flesh, pulling a taut thread up from her center. A trail of moisture tickled down her inner thigh. "One," she gasped. Another hit across her right nipple had her moaning in pleasure. "Two." The walls of her sheath trembled.

*Thwap.* A strike landed across her mound. This time she wailed. "Alexander," she cried. "Please."

"Please what, Elizabeth? You aren't counting," he said.

"Three. God. I can't."

"You can. Two more. Spread your legs. Wider."

Though her knees threatened to buckle, Elizabeth tried to obey. But when Alexander trailed the flogger between her breasts, she whimpered.

"Apart, *chérie*."

She inched her thighs away from each other. A swift strike landed just below the last, and she lost her mind with the sensation. "Four, ah!"

Suede bit into the lace that covered her sex, and her entire body bucked. "Please," she cried out. "Please, I need to come."

The flogger landed with a thump on the bed. Alexander grabbed her hips and held them steady. "Say that again for me, Elizabeth."

"I need to come."

"Oh, really?"

"Yes, please," she gasped. His cheek pressed against her belly. He slid his hands behind her, down her thighs, and under her dress. His strong fingers dug into the globes of her ass, massaging the firm flesh.

"You smell delicious. I wonder how you taste?" He lifted her dress, twisting the loose fabric behind her and tucking it in her fingers. "Hold onto this for me. I promised not to remove your clothing. I said nothing about moving it around a bit."

Elizabeth heard the chuckle in his voice. His jeans rustled. His teeth nipped along her inner thigh, his breath ragged and hot. He nudged her legs further apart with his strong hands. Bites and licks moved higher until he very nearly had his nose pressed to the damp lace of her panties. Elizabeth couldn't catch her breath. Every touch sent her closer to the edge.

Alexander slipped a single finger under the lace edge on her thigh, and she feared she'd come apart right there. "My God, Elizabeth, you are bare." He pressed his lips to her mound, inhaling deeply. "Are you terribly attached to these?" he asked roughly, tugging on the lace.

"No."

The rip barely registered, but his lips on her bare flesh tore a moan from her throat. Incoherent sobs escaped as his tongue darted over her skin, slipped between her feminine folds, and brushed delicately against her clit.

"Mine," he said. "This beautiful pussy is all mine."

His fingers explored, parting her dewy lips, and danced over her clit and the soft, wet heat.

"I can't," she gasped. "I need to come, please." She writhed against him, panting, desperate.

"Not. Without. Permission," Alexander growled and closed his teeth over her clit. She screamed and bucked her hips against his face. The insatiable need to come faded enough for her to draw in a breath, but built right back up again when he nibbled her inner thigh. "You taste like summer," he said, his voice hoarse. "Like rain and roses and almonds."

Alexander's fingers danced against her channel again, pulling, stroking, maddening.

"Have to," she managed. "Can't hold on."

One finger dipped inside her. Then two. Two more pinched her clit, rolling the nub of tortured flesh around in a circle.

"Alexander, please." She'd do anything he asked if only he'd stop this delicious torture.

"I have ravaged you enough for your first time? I want to see you when you come, Elizabeth. I want you to scream my name. Come now."

Three fingers inside her twisted and pressed against her G-spot. His teeth scraped against her clit, dragging her over the edge in a storm of sensation. Elizabeth came undone. A ragged, primal scream escaped her throat. "Alexander!"

He lapped at the juncture of her thighs as a fresh set of tears escaped her blindfold. She couldn't breathe, couldn't see, couldn't do anything but feel.

# CHAPTER NINE

His sweet sub made tiny, desperate noises as she came down from her orgasm. Tremors wracked her body, and Alexander wrapped his arms around her.

"Shhh. Very good, Elizabeth. You honor me." Feathering a kiss against her cheek, he savored the scent of aroused woman hovering in the air.

Her head dropped onto his shoulder as she whispered, "I don't understand."

Holding her up, afraid she'd collapse if he stepped away, Alexander nuzzled her neck. "Your trust. A woman's submission is a gift. One I never take lightly. Now, I have only one more request."

"I can't. Please, I can't take any more." Her entire body shook, and Alexander pressed closer.

"A request, not a command. Kiss me, Elizabeth."

A weak sound that might have been a giggle escaped her lips as she raised her head.

Her wanton need still coating his tongue, he claimed her mouth. Hints of wine, berries, and chocolate, the sweet honey of her release, and the unique taste of Elizabeth could sate him for days. Months. Perhaps years. Sucking her lower lip between his teeth, he groaned as his cock throbbed inside his jeans. If he didn't end the scene soon, he'd take her—or shoot his load inside his boxers.

With much difficulty, he pulled away, but Elizabeth tried to follow, leaning forward, her breath coming in shallow pants.

"Alexander, I need you. Please."

*Bloody hell, she's going to undo me.*

With a quick tug, the silk and hemp rope fell away, and her arms dropped to her sides. Sliding the blindfold from her eyes, he smiled as she blinked up at him.

"And I, quite obviously," he said as he pressed his hips against her, "want you. But not tonight, *chérie*. Tonight, I hope you'll think back to what I can do to you fully clothed. The next time we meet, you can decide if you want to know what I can do to you naked." Alexander trailed a knuckle against her cheek. "I won't have regrets between us. The next time I have you in my silks, you'll be mine completely. Tonight...will seem like child's play."

Her breath hitched, and her knees buckled, but Alexander scooped her up and carried her into the lavish bath. Depositing her on the marble counter with a gentle kiss, he started warm water running in the sink.

"Wh-what are you doing?" she asked.

As he ran a soft cloth under the water, he met her gaze. "Tending to you. Aftercare is a part of every scene, Elizabeth, and I take it very seriously."

Not to mention, trailing the cloth over her damp thighs, up to her bare pussy, and then back again gave him a delicious view he'd not soon forget. Turning the water cold, he dunked the cloth again and then took her arm.

Five welts marred the tender skin not far from her wrist.

"Shit," she whispered. Her eyelids fluttered.

Alarm quickened his pulse. "Stay with me, Elizabeth," he

ordered as he pressed the cold cloth to her reddened flesh. "A few more minutes and I'll have you warm."

"Uh huh." Though her words weren't as crisp and clear as he'd like, she blinked hard and then focused on him.

Sighing in relief, he snagged a tube of aloe from one of the drawers. "This should be gone by morning. I should have bound you from the start, even if that meant you safeworded before we even began. I'm very sorry, Elizabeth."

One didn't pass years as a Dom without mistakes, though thankfully, Alexander's had been few and far between. Still, old memories threatened as he massaged the tender skin. He wouldn't blame her for never trusting him again, but she rested her free hand at his waist, and the touch soothed him.

As he finished with her arm, he took stock of the woman before him. A little disoriented, flustered, and perhaps a bit ashamed. She glanced over at the mirror, then grimaced.

"What's wrong, *chérie*?"

"I'm a mess." Dropping her gaze, she sucked her lip under her teeth.

Alexander nudged her chin up gently. "You're beautiful. A well-loved woman is *always* beautiful."

Before she could protest, he slid his arm under her knees and picked her up, carrying her to the bed. "Lie back for just a moment. I won't be far."

Before he'd stepped off the platform, she'd closed her eyes. He needed her in his bed, in his life, and he'd only just met her.

Returning to her side with a blanket, a bottle of water, and a bar of chocolate, he helped her sit up, then wrapped her in the soft fleece. "Better now?"

She nodded. "Thank you."

Cracking the seal on the bottle, he held it to her lips. As if she'd suddenly realized where she was, Elizabeth pulled back, her eyes widening. "I can do that myself, you know."

The Dom inside him asserted control. "Elizabeth, this is part of aftercare. Let me do this for you."

She slid the bottle from his hand, then downed half of it. "Some things, yes. The blanket, the aloe. This? No."

Alexander had a hard time mustering any anger, though he tried. Frustration, perhaps. Ire, but no anger. Her spirit drew him in deeper every moment he spent with her. "I see you're going to test my limits. Not something that usually pleases me. Yet still..." A smile tugged at his lips. "Eat this, and I'll help you downstairs."

At least she allowed him to feed her a few squares of chocolate.

By the time they made their way downstairs, Elizabeth tucked firmly to his side, she'd started to shiver. "Why am I so cold?"

"Adrenaline. Or rather, the loss of it. A common side effect." Cupping her cheeks, he searched her gaze for any regret, any shame, and found none. "You could stay the night."

He cursed the hope—or was that desperation--tinging his words.

"Not a good idea," she said, straightening slightly.

Fighting against the disappointment, he led her into the kitchen. "A spot of tea then, and I'll take you home."

Silence swelled between them, and as Alexander started the kettle, he risked a glance at her. "Would you like to talk about what we just did?"

Gentle waves of her golden hair curled over her shoulders as she shook her head. "I don't know what to say. That was...so much."

"That's often the reaction a submissive's first time. Truthfully, I felt the same way the first time I restrained a partner. The orgasm I had after that was...to be crude and blunt, fucking brilliant."

Alexander followed Elizabeth's gaze to the pattern on the hardwood floor.

Her cheeks flushed. "And tonight? After I leave?"

Adjusting his jeans, Alexander grimaced. "I'll take my release remembering the sights, sounds, and—" he brought his fingers to his lips and inhaled deeply, catching a faint whiff of her arousal lingering, "—scents of you. Does that displease you?"

"N-no. I just wish—" With a sigh, Elizabeth shifted on the stool. "I feel empty."

Crossing the kitchen in four steps, he took her in his arms. "And you want me to fill you?" At her nod, he brushed a tender kiss to her lips. "Next time, Elizabeth. I want you to dream of what it will be like when I have you naked, bound, and begging."

As the kettle whistled, Alexander eased her back onto the stool. They didn't speak again until he pressed a teacup into her hand. "I can see how hard you're thinking. Don't. Let yourself feel. But...may I call on you tomorrow? Are you free?"

Her nod brought a smile to his lips. "Drink, *chérie.* I have a squash game with my brother tomorrow at seven. But, perhaps lunch? A matinee? Ice skating at Boston Common?"

Elizabeth's eyes lit up at the last option. "I've never been skating."

"Then that's what we'll do." An emotion he so rarely felt these days, the pure, unadulterated joy of his youth, warmed him until he thought of her abysmally thin coat. "You have something warm to wear? Good gloves?"

Her demeanor shifted, ire dimming the sparkle in her eyes. "I can certainly clothe myself for a day outside in the cold," she snapped. After a sip of tea, she shook her head. "Sorry. I have... issues with men not trusting me to take care of myself."

After a steadying breath, Alexander pressed himself lightly against Elizabeth, caressing her arms. "I didn't mean to offend you; I simply enjoy taking care of you. I'm sorry if I came across as condescending. That wasn't my intention."

Slumping into his embrace, she sighed. "And I don't mean to be difficult. My last serious relationship..." Her voice cracked, and Alexander tightened his embrace. "Darren was very controlling.

Told me what to wear, tried to tell me who to socialize with. By the end, he'd practically destroyed me. I can't let a man—or anyone—do that to me again. I won't survive it."

The intense desire to find this *Darren* and pummel him within an inch of his life had Alexander clenching his fists, and he stalked away so he wouldn't frighten her. "Bugger it. I'm sorry."

Though she waved her hand casually, he caught the tremble in her fingers. "It was a long time ago. I try not to think about it much, but the repercussions of that relationship... I'm kind of damaged goods. I overreact to things."

A feral growl rumbled in Alexander's chest. "You're not damaged. You're an adult. We all have baggage, Elizabeth. A good relationship helps you unpack it."

"Yeah, well, I think I want that bag to stay packed. He's a jerk who isn't worth my time. At all. I found out later that he had another girlfriend on the side."

Blowing out a breath, Alexander forced himself to calm so he could return to Elizabeth's side. If he did nothing else tonight, he had to reassure her. "I don't pursue more than one woman at a time, *chérie*. But I very much want to pursue you. Look at me."

He searched her gaze. "I believe in being faithful. Always."

"You want to be exclusive?" she asked with a hitch in her voice.

Unable to curb his grin, he replied, "Yes. For as long as this lasts. But that will mean one very important thing."

"What's that?" she asked.

"Parties, Elizabeth. It's Christmas. I have a holiday ball to attend on Friday night. Will you accompany me?" With his arm around her waist, he felt her stiffen.

"What you're really asking me is if I'll accept a dress from you."

Alexander inclined his head. "I'm asking you to let me take care of you, just a little. A dress, shoes, jewelry. Not to control you. To make things easier on you. Will you come? Meet my brother, some of my business associates? Dance with me? Maybe stay the night here, engage in some more play?"

He ran his fingers through her tousled hair, relishing the way she relaxed into his embrace.

"No jewelry. You're *not* buying me jewelry. And I get to pick the dress. You don't get to tell me what to wear."

Would he ever get enough of her scent? Of the little sounds she made when he touched her? Elizabeth arched her brows, and he pulled himself out of his musings. "I wouldn't dream of picking a dress for you. As for the jewelry... What about a loan? Something simple. Understated. This is a fire and ice ball, Elizabeth. You'll be expected to wear diamonds."

A scowl twisted her lips. "Fine."

"To all of it? Most importantly, will you date me exclusively?" Alexander held his breath, more nervous about this one question than anything he could remember. Pressing his lips together, he tried to stop the muscle twitching along his jaw.

Elizabeth studied him, and he feared she saw right through his self-assured demeanor. "Yes."

With that single word, she righted his entire world. Crushing his lips to hers, he took, tongue and teeth ravishing her until they had to come up for air. For this moment, she was completely his, and God help him, he'd handed himself over to her just as thoroughly.

"Are you sure I can't convince you to stay?" he asked as he drew back.

"I'm sure." Though her voice wobbled, her eyes held a fiery determination he wouldn't—and couldn't—argue with. "Then let's get you home."

.

THE LIMO RIDE passed in a blur. Tucked against Alexander's warm body, cosseted in the blanket and his arm, Elizabeth listened intently as he sipped a glass of scotch and told her about his meetings in London and the woman he'd hired to run the company for him. Mundane, everyday conversation, the type of easy words that passed between lovers who'd grown comfortable with one another.

Despite her interest, as they approached her apartment, exhaustion draped over her like the soft blanket she still wore around her shoulders.

"I'm sorry, she murmured, tipping her head back to gaze at him when he rubbed her thigh. "I don't know why I'm so tired. It's not even eleven."

Alexander smiled softly. "Sub drop, *chérie*. The emotions, the exhaustion, and the chills are common. Do you have more chocolate at home?"

"I think so."

"Have some. A bath, another cup of tea, a warm blanket..." He tucked a lock of hair behind her ear as Thomas rapped softly on the window, then opened the door.

He kissed her so thoroughly when they reached her apartment door that she nearly forgot how to turn the knob. Her body tingled all the way down to her toes. The man was like a drug, one she could become addicted to very quickly. It wasn't until the door was securely locked and his footsteps echoed on the stairs that she managed to break the spell of his kiss. River padded over and meowed plaintively.

Elizabeth scooped the cat up and brought her into the bedroom. She peered between the drapes and out the window to the sidewalk below. Alexander strode towards the limo that was double-parked on her narrow street, and before he ducked inside, he looked up. Four stories of distance did nothing to dim the dazzling smile that lit up his face when he saw her watching. With the cat in her arms, and his blanket still around her shoulders, she could only manage a tiny wave in return before the limo pulled away.

River protested in her arms. "Okay, sweetie. I know. Bedtime."

A flash of movement on the street caught her eye before she turned away. A lone man stood on the opposite corner, talking on his phone and staring up at her window.

With a gasp, Elizabeth stumbled back, then yanked the drapes closed. When she peered out again a few seconds later, the man was gone.

# CHAPTER TEN

*A* little after six-thirty, Alexander's phone buzzed. Setting down his coffee mug, he smiled.

*Did you sleep well? Pretty sure I passed out, but I kept dreaming about what you did to me.*

He anguished over his reply, finally settling for the simple: *Do you regret our play?*

Twenty of the longest minutes of his life passed as he headed for the athletic club. Elizabeth had captivated him, body, mind, and heart, so much that if she couldn't fulfill his needs in the bedroom, he'd probably give serious consideration to becoming a monk. By the time her message came in, he was nervous as hell and almost ready to call off the squash game.

*No. What does that say about me?*

Thank God. He sank back against the leather seat and tried to force his shoulders to relax as his fingers flew over the screen. *That you trust me. That you enjoyed a submissive role, at least once, and might again.*

Her quick reply didn't reassure him. *The last time I gave up control, I ended up Darren's pet. One he tired of once it no longer came with a pedigree.*

Once again, Alexander wondered how mad Elizabeth would be if Darren ended up with a black eye and a broken nose. How could anyone make this beautiful, strong woman feel anything but cherished and loved. He stared out the limo's window for several miles before he decided on a reply. *Darren was an idiot. Being a Dom is who I am. But that doesn't mean I will ever disrespect you or impose control over other aspects of your life.*

Her response drew a chuckle: *I want to trust you. To trust that. But you don't take no for an answer.*

Tapping the screen, he called her, hoping his voice would convey all the emotions he was bungling over text. "You walked out on me several times, Elizabeth. I'm not used to that."

"That just proves my point." She sighed. "I can't let a man control my life again."

Alexander wished he could see her face, but as she'd just accused him of being an arse, he feared she wouldn't be receptive to a video call. "I don't want to control you. Only your pleasure in the bedroom. I'd never ask you to sacrifice your spirit, your spark, or your strength. Keep those qualities in business, in life... even with me in the rest of our relationship. But in the bedroom, put yourself in my hands and let me care for you. Can you do that?"

"Will you always be so...so...?"

"Dominant? This is who I am, Elizabeth." The uncertainty in her voice put her solidly on the edge, and he didn't know how to comfort her. If he wasn't careful, he'd lose her. "When we play, I will *never* ask you give up your power. Only your control. In every way that counts, the submissive has the true power."

A hint of bewilderment crept into her tone. "I don't understand."

The limo rolled to a stop, and Alexander glanced out the window to see Nicholas tapping his watch. "I wish I'd canceled my squash game and taken you to breakfast instead. My brother is glaring at me, and I think this discussion might be easier in person. I'd like you to be able to look into my eyes when I explain. May I pick you up at two?"

"Are you going to win the game?"

Though the humor in her voice sounded a bit forced, he'd take it. "I always win."

"Then yes, I'll be ready at two."

After a quick goodbye, Alexander tossed his phone in his bag and leveled a stern gaze at his brother. "I have a lot riding on this game, Nicholas. Are you ready to lose?"

His brother raised a brow. "Bring it, Alex."

---

ELIZABETH PACED BACK and forth across the well-worn floors. Running clothes, her best business suit, three changes of underwear... As she ticked items off on her fingers, she rushed back into her bedroom for a couple of pairs of fleece pants and a sweatshirt.

River meowed and jumped in the suitcase. "I know, sweetie. But I don't have a choice." Elizabeth's lawyer had called her only minutes after she'd hung up with Alexander, and after a frantic few minutes online, she'd booked a last-minute ticket to Seattle to meet with him.

Already, dozens of variations of the conversation she'd have to have with Alexander played on an endless loop in her head.

*Not today. Not now. Give me one last good day before he dumps me.*

If she accused CPH of tax fraud, which probably wasn't an if but a when, Alexander would find out, and he'd never forgive her for not mentioning it to him earlier.

His brisk knock set loose a storm inside her: elation, fear, and arousal churned in her stomach. But the sight of him took her breath away. A green V-neck sweater the same color as his eyes, a crisp white collar open just enough to expose his Adam's apple, and black jeans screamed casual *and* wealthy. Elizabeth's cheeks flushed as she glanced down at the hole in the knee of her thermal pants.

"Every time I see you, Elizabeth, I want you all the more." Alexander cupped her ass, and when he squeezed gently, she laughed and twisted away.

"We're skating, remember. Not tearing each other's clothes off."

"We can't do both?" As he stepped inside, he frowned at the open suitcase sitting on the couch. "Are you going somewhere?"

All the joy she'd felt at seeing him fled in a single breath. "Yes. I have to fly to Seattle tomorrow. It's...complicated, but my lawyer's there. I won't be back until Thursday morning."

"You're in trouble." Drawing her into his embrace, he stared down at her. How could she possibly lie when all she could think of was his warmth and how she'd never feel it again after today?

"Don't make me answer you," she said. Alexander tightened his arms. "Please. Can't we just have fun? You asked me to give you a chance—to give us a chance. That's what I want to do today."

A single quirk of Alexander's lips spoke to his disapproval, but then he leaned in and rested his forehead against hers. A long pause and a hard stare had her holding her breath. "On two conditions."

"Anything." Too late, she realized she'd opened a door she couldn't close.

"One. When you return from your trip, you *will* tell me what is going on. And two. If I can help, you *will* ask. I care for you, Elizabeth. It pains me to see you in obvious distress. A state you've been in too often since we met."

Forcing an answer from her tight throat proved challenging, but she managed a single word. "Okay."

They stayed pressed together for another moment, and she relished in his warmth. When he drew back, concern tightened his lips, but he didn't press her further. "May I help you with your coat?"

The air in the apartment lightened with that single question. Her deep breath of relief came out almost as a laugh. "Only if you let me go." She levered up on her toes to kiss him. He tasted of mint: clean and fresh and delicious. Alexander's fingers twisted firmly through her hair. The delicious tension tightened her nipples. When he released her, she staggered back against the door jamb.

"You're terrible."

"You kissed *me*. Now get your coat." He playfully slapped her ass as she turned towards her rickety coat rack.

*Please let there be some way out of this—some way I can stop CPH without losing Alexander.*

---

ONE MOMENT ELIZABETH was laughing at Alexander's poor jokes and the next she was fighting back the tears. Each time the darkness settled over her, he seemed to sense it and nibbled on her ear, tickled her waist, or cupped her cheek and kissed her.

At Boston Common, Alexander helped Elizabeth with her skates and kept an arm around her waist as they made their way out onto the ice. They held hands, following the pace of the crowds for an hour, though she'd swear they'd only skated for a few minutes. Christmas music played, children laughed around them, and from time-to-time, someone stared or pointed at Alexander. Thoughts of CPH skirted the edges of her mind, but never settled, for Alexander kept her distracted with casual banter, frequent kisses, and the occasional brush of his hand to her ass.

"Elizabeth, do not be alarmed," he murmured in her ear, "but I'm afraid we're being photographed."

A burly man with a professional camera blocking his features aimed in their direction. Her heartbeat quickened, and she tugged Alexander's hand, urging him to move a little quicker so she could get a look at the man's face.

Alexander took her hands and swung her around in an arc, giving the photographer a show. When she righted herself and looked back over at the photographer, no longer obscured by the camera, her world stopped.

She recognized him.

Every instinct told her to run. But all she managed to do was send her legs in opposite directions and slide down Alexander's body until she hit the ice with a bone-jarring impact.

"Elizabeth!" Alexander hauled her up against him. "Are you all right, *chérie*?"

"I have to get out of here," she said before rational thought took over. "Let me go." CPH *was* having her followed, and now they'd seen her with Alexander—had evidence she was consorting with one of their clients—the lawsuit made perfect sense. Had they watched her at the diner? The Thinking Cup? She tried to pull away from his grip, but he shook his head.

"No. You're not going anywhere until you tell me what has you in a panic." Alexander pulled her towards the edge of the ice in the direction of the photographer. Elizabeth tried to drag her feet, but on skates, in his strong arms, she had no choice but to follow his lead. When the man saw them approaching, he turned and ran.

"The...photographer," she wheezed, panic tightening her throat.

Alexander swept his gaze over the crowd. "He's gone. I can have my admin make some calls. We can keep your name out of the papers for a time. At least until the Fire and Ice Ball on Friday. Money buys many things. Even privacy on occasion." He reached into his coat pocket, but Elizabeth stopped him before he could pull out his phone.

"No. Don't." All the money in the world wouldn't fix this, and his admin wouldn't find the photo of them in any newspaper.

Alexander's eyes darkened, and Elizabeth struggled to calm her breathing. If she couldn't convince him she was all right, he'd press her for details she couldn't share. "I'm not used to this. Being on display. I shouldn't have freaked out. Can we get out of here? My legs are jelly."

"Don't lie to me, Elizabeth. I read people every day. You did not *freak out*. You were afraid of that man. Tell me why." He caged her against the rail with a hand on either side of her waist.

"I can't."

A single black brow arched as he leaned closer. "This has something to do with why you're going to Seattle, doesn't it?"

Her resolve crumbled, and she struggled not to tell him everything. "Yes. But I can't tell you anything right now. Please. Give me a few days."

Facing off with one of the most intimidating men in Boston wasn't in the plans today, but Elizabeth refused to look away, and eventually, Alexander closed his eyes for a long moment, then sighed. "Come. Let's get off the ice. An early dinner somewhere?"

The way her stomach felt, she wasn't sure she'd ever eat again. "I have to be at the airport at six tomorrow. I should go home and finish packing."

"You still have to eat, and I have little confidence you'll do so left to your own devices," Alexander said tersely as he unlaced her skates.

"I have some food in the fridge that'll go bad before I get back. I promise you I'll be okay." Another lie. How many more would she rack up before they spilled over and destroyed everything? Rather than trying to explain further, she tried changing the subject. "What do you have to do this week?"

After picking up their skates Alexander relented and offered her his arm. "Year-end activities are starting. Closing out the books, planning for the next twelve months. I have a week of meetings from nine to five or longer. Nicholas plans to order a dozen new warehouses and at least one container ship. While that's his business, not mine, purchases that large require two signatories and I don't sign off on anything without doing my due diligence. Not even purchases he vouches for."

"How large is large?" Needing his closeness, Elizabeth snuggled into the crook of his arm as they strolled towards the limo.

"I believe the ship in question is approximately one hundred and twenty million."

"Holy shit." Elizabeth gaped. "Other than my rent, I can't remember the last time I spent one hundred and twenty *dollars* on any one thing. And you're going to spend a million times that."

"I told you before, Elizabeth, I won't apologize for my wealth." Alexander slid into the limo after her, then shook his head. "That was the wrong thing to say," he murmured. "I only meant that... bugger it. Forget I said anything."

"You don't have to apologize," she said. "You're rich. I knew that when I got in the limo with you that first day. I can't even fathom that amount of money. My family is wealthy, and even they'd balk at that figure."

He draped his arm around her shoulders. "I suppose when you deal in such sums daily, they lose the awe they once held. Fairhaven is responsible for more than half of the world's shipping. Each ship carries anywhere from ten to fifteen thousand containers. Think about how many computers, televisions, even cars, we can carry at once."

"I used to drive by the port in Seattle all the time. Sometimes I'd pull off the road to watch the ships being loaded," she said. The memory made her smile. "I always thought it was impressive. All those containers raised and lowered like they were dominoes."

They lapsed into companionable silence as the city flew by. *If only I'd met him a year ago. Or a year from now. Then we might have had a chance.*

"Will you see friends in Seattle? Have any fun at all?" Concern laced his tone, and he brushed his fingertips along her jaw before kissing her.

"I don't have any friends in Seattle any more. I might be able to go to the Seattle Art Museum on Tuesday. Or Pike Place Market for chowder. I have to be at the airport on Wednesday by ten, but my return trip involves three flights, something like six hours of layovers, and a red-eye."

As they arrived at her apartment, Elizabeth looked down at her hands clasped in her lap. "I had a good time today. Thank you."

"May I give your email address to my personal shopper? She can help you chose a dress for the ball while you're gone." He threaded his hand through her hair, and his smile helped her believe for a moment that things just might work out.

"That's fine."

"I could—" he pressed a kiss to her neck, "—take you to the airport in the morning."

If he did, she might never get on the plane. "No. It's a short trip on the T. I'll be fine."

At the threshold of her apartment, Elizabeth reached up and brushed a lock of hair off his forehead. His smile warmed her all over, and his kiss left her breathless. Maybe things would be okay. Maybe he'd forgive her for not telling him her fears. Maybe she wouldn't lose everything.

Maybe.

# CHAPTER ELEVEN

$\mathcal{N}$o messages waited for Elizabeth when she turned her phone back on after landing in Seattle. Alexander would be in meetings, but a part of her had hoped for something...anything to break through the dark clouds that consumed her.

Despite the rain, once she'd checked into her hotel, she tugged on her running clothes. The exercise would clear her head. Three miles from her hotel, a silver Mercedes sped past, and a torrent of dirty water splattered her from head to toe. She stopped, chest heaving, hands braced on her thighs. Grit coated her lips. "Screw it," she muttered as she turned around. On her way back to the hotel, her thoughts wandered. Where were her parents today? At the office downtown? The Athletic Club? What about Darren?

*Please don't let me run into them.*

After a shower, she opened up her email to find a message from Alexander.

*Elizabeth, please meet my personal shopper, Marjorie. Feel free to tell her exactly what you do and don't like. You'll need to be measured by tomorrow, so Marjorie found a seamstress in Seattle who can see you at your convenience. Once you choose a dress, I will pick some understated jewelry for you to wear. Nothing flashy, I promise. - Alexander*

Elizabeth and Marjorie exchanged several messages, and before long, a dozen photos from Donna Karan, Yves St. Laurent, and Jason Wu splashed across her screen. Online shopping distracted her until her phone's alarm warned her she had to leave for her appointment with Clancy. Seconds before she grasped the laptop's lid, her email dinged.

*I have one meeting left for the day, and I wish that I had a photo of your lovely face. Quite honestly, I wish I had a photo of you as you were the other night. Where will you be at 10 p.m. my time? If you're free, will you ring me? I'd like to hear your voice. -A*

The memories of what he'd done to her warmed her deep inside. They'd never had that discussion about BDSM he'd promised before his squash game, and she had so many questions. If her lawyer didn't confirm her worst fears, maybe they'd finally get a chance to have that talk tonight.

---

"HELLO, Miss Bennett. It's been some time." The old, wizened lawyer greeted her warmly and shook her hand. Clancy Poon had been her family's lawyer for more than thirty years. His hair had thinned since she'd last seen him, but his smile was as kind and his handshake as strong as ever. "I have to admit I was surprised to receive your package. You've gotten yourself into a bit of a jam, haven't you?"

"Yes," she said, taking the chair he offered her. The sweet scent of old cigars reminded her of her grandfather. Elizabeth stared out his top floor window to the rain falling on Puget Sound. "I need to know what I should do."

"Well, you start by explaining the whole situation to me. That and paying my retainer. I have reciprocity in Massachusetts, so if you don't want to find a lawyer who's local to you, I can handle your case. Though you'd be on the hook for my travel costs." The old lawyer's hazel eyes sharpened. Kindness he had in spades, but deep down, he was still a lawyer.

"I called a dozen firms in Boston. None of them would take my case. Carter, Pastack, and Hayes is a major force in the city. I have...a resource that I could probably call on now to find me someone who wasn't affiliated with them, but I really don't want to go there if I don't have to."

"Oh?"

Her cheeks warmed. "I'm dating someone with connections. But it's new, and it's complicated, particularly since his company is one of CPH's clients." Elizabeth withdrew her checkbook. "Three thousand?" she said over the lump in her throat.

"Is that a problem?"

"N-no," she lied and then handed over the check.

Clancy stared at her with an astute gaze unhindered by his advanced years. "You've been accused of leaking sensitive financial data. The repercussions could be devastating if you're found guilty."

"I didn't leak anything," she said firmly, though inside, her resolve, her strength, even her will to remain upright crumbled into dust.

Clancy folded his hands on his desk and leaned forward. "Start from the beginning."

Once Clancy's secretary had brought them both mugs of tea, Elizabeth recounted her firing, her conversation with the Red Sox, and finally, her suspicions. "The firm saved face by blaming and firing me. Probably gave the clients back their money. The USB drive I sent you contains partial tax records for the Boston Red Sox I found on my laptop. The assistant to one of the owners of the Red Sox tracked me down and I...I got copies of the files they received from CPH. The numbers don't match. I think CPH is embezzling from their clients, and they fired me to keep it quiet."

"But you have no proof that's admissible in court. No official copies of what you turned in to your employers, no one else who can corroborate your information," Clancy said.

Her heart sank. "No. It's my word against theirs. And now... they can prove—at least to a judge who doesn't know the whole story—that I broke my confidentiality clause."

Clancy scribbled on his notepad, the chicken scratch barely legible. "How? What proof do they have?"

"They had me followed." Elizabeth clenched her hands on her thighs while she told Clancy about the man outside her window and the photographer at Boston Common. "They've seen me with Alexander Fairhaven. His company is one of their largest clients."

"Fairhaven?" Now Clancy's eyes narrowed. "What were you doing with him if not violating your agreement?"

Setting the tea aside, Elizabeth unbuttoned her suit jacket. The temperature in the room must have jumped ten degrees in a few seconds. Or her cheeks were on fire. "We're...dating. Though once I tell him about all of this, I don't think he'll want to continue the relationship."

With a whistle, Clancy sat back in his chair. "I see two options, Elizabeth. You can either go to the federal prosecutor and accuse your former employers of a crime, in which case you'd be protected by whistleblower laws, or you can try to settle."

"What does that mean? That I'd be protected?"

"The lawsuit against you would go away. The government takes tax fraud quite seriously, and they know that companies will often resort to extreme measures to stop employees from exposing them. What CPH is trying to do to you falls under that category. Given the enormity of the fraud, they're going to come at you hard for the non-disclosure case to try to intimidate you. But once you accuse them of a crime, they can't touch you —*legally*. Unfortunately, they can still try to ruin your reputation, and you'd be tied up with the court case for quite some time."

"But I could work. I could get a job somewhere else at that point, right?"

"You could try. You'd be safe from prosecution, and we'd do our best to keep your name out of the papers, there are no guarantees. Before you make a decision, be absolutely certain you're right about this. Because if you're wrong, it's not going to go well for you." Clancy shook his head. "If a judge rules in their favor, they could sue you for damages."

Elizabeth bit the inside of her cheek until it cut into her own blood. Clancy wasn't making it any easier. "And what if I want this to go away?"

"If you want to settle, I can likely handle this from here. You have to pay a fine, probably well north of a hundred thousand dollars, but it would be done. You could declare bankruptcy, and most of the fine would be forgiven. You'd have to liquidate all of your stock, but your 401K would remain intact."

"Shit. I don't have much choice, do I?"

"No. And Elizabeth, if you decide to go through with the tax fraud case, don't breathe a word of it to anyone until you go to the federal prosecutor. If anyone gets wind of this before your deposition, you could lose all of your protection."

"Alexander already knows something's wrong. I can't keep this from him for much longer. If I settle and he finds out, that'll be the end of any relationship. He might forgive me if I tell him everything now, but if I have to wait…"

"You don't have proof of their crimes other than your memories. That's going to be pretty darn hard to substantiate. But if you settle and admit guilt, you probably won't be able to find work as an accountant again. At least not for any firm worth its salt. I suppose you have to ask yourself how you feel about this relationship. Is it something worth fighting for?"

*Yes. It is.*

Clancy withdrew his appointment book. "I have a three-hour block of time open tomorrow afternoon. I suggest you think about this tonight. We can meet tomorrow and go over a mock deposition. Perhaps that will help you decide. How is 2:00 p.m.?"

---

Alexander checked his watch for the tenth time. He'd been unable to concentrate on the book in his hand all evening, anticipating Elizabeth's call.

Two minutes after ten, her name flashed across the screen.

"Um, hi. How was your day?" Static crackled over the line, but it didn't dim Alexander's smile.

"You have the power to turn the most abysmal day around with just a few words," he said. "Today was full of accountants and financial discussions that threatened to put me to sleep. I'm knackered, but I've had so much coffee, I may still be vibrating."

Elizabeth started to laugh, but the sound quickly strangled into a hoarse, choking rasp.

He straightened. "Elizabeth, what's wrong? You're upset."

Muffled sounds reached him, punctuated by long moments of silence. Unable to sit still, Alexander swung his legs over the side of the bed. "If you don't answer me, Elizabeth, I'm flying out to Seattle tonight."

Damn his meetings. If she needed him, nothing would keep him away.

Elizabeth cleared her throat. "Fairhaven Charities doesn't use CPH, right?"

*Where was this going?*

"No. We use independent accountants. Nicholas has used them for the past few years, but I've suggested he find a new firm. I don't like the idea of associating with a company that would fire my...girlfriend. But that doesn't answer my question. What is wrong?"

Her words tumbled out, almost too fast for him to discern over the scratchy connection. "Can we...I hate to ask. I know you're busy with meetings. But can we talk on Thursday when I get back? I have to go through San Diego and Vegas and I don't land until six in the morning, and I'll need a nap, but maybe eleven?"

"Breathe, Elizabeth," he said, adopting the tone he used in the bedroom. "I'm going to switch to video. I want to see your face."

Her splotchy cheeks swam in and out of focus as she moved from a pitiful looking hotel bed to the desk. The phone rattled, and then she sat back in a rickety chair.

"Shite. You've been crying," he said. "Why?" Alexander tightened his grip on his phone. How quickly could he get to Seattle? If the company jet was free...

"Please don't." She swiped at her cheeks. "I'm fine. There's just something we have to discuss before—well, before things are irrevocably fucked up for both of us."

*Fucked up?*

"Are you saying what I think you're saying? There's something wrong with our accounting? Something that got you fired? Explain."

"I...can't. Please don't ask me to. Not yet." Her eyes shone with unshed tears, and she sniffed loudly.

*Fuck.* Alexander couldn't stand being this far away from Elizabeth. His frustration and helplessness turned to anger as he ran through all of their encounters over the past few weeks. "Why won't you trust me?"

On screen, she started to shake. Her breath wheezed in and out, heaving her chest under the oversized sweatshirt. She swore under her breath—or tried to—as the word escaped as more of a vague "shiiii" sound, and then the phone swung around, showing him the drab wall of her hotel room.

"I need...a minute."

He could hear her struggling to inhale, and his own panic crawled up his spine.

"Elizabeth?" Alexander yelled. "Elizabeth? Bloody hell, answer me!"

"A...minute," she rasped.

"Goddammit. Turn the phone around, or I'm headed for Seattle." He stalked over to his closet, yanked open the door, and grabbed the first shirt he found.

The video shook as she righted the phone. "I'm here," she said in a small, hoarse voice.

Alexander stared at the terrified woman on screen, and his heart thudded in his chest. "Fuck me, Elizabeth. I won't just sit here while you try not to panic on the other side of the continent. Where are you? What hotel? I can be there...well, by morning."

"No!" She shoved away from the desk, but when she tried to rise, her legs buckled and she ended up falling to her knees next to the bed. The top of her head bobbed almost off camera until she pushed up and glared at him. "Before I left, you promised to let me handle this until I got back. That's all I'm asking for."

How could he make her understand she was killing him?

*Focus.*

Years of experience had honed his skills. He could cut to the root of any problem with a few pointed questions—one of the reasons he'd been so successful over the years. CPH. She'd gone to Seattle to see her lawyer.

"They're after you."

Her eyes widened. "Don't. Please. Don't say anything else. Just...give me until Thursday."

Another, darker thought chilled him. "Did you work on the

Fairhaven accounts?" Struggling to keep the phone in his field of vision, he stalked across the room to pour himself a stiff drink.

Elizabeth shook her head. "No. But...you should bring your brother when we talk on Thursday."

The scotch burned a path down his throat as he tossed back the double shot in one swallow. "I need to call Nicholas."

"Talking to him now could *ruin* me!" Her phone shook as she dropped back into the chair. "I knew I shouldn't have called. Clancy told me not to..."

Alexander's blood ran cold. "Clancy? You're harboring secrets that could affect me, Nicholas, and our company, and you talked to someone else *before* you talked to me? How is that trust?"

"Clancy is my lawyer," she cried. "Fine. CPH is suing me. Saying I violated my confidentiality agreement. I didn't. The photographer at the ice rink—he wasn't a reporter. He was following *me*. Our relationship is the evidence CPH has against me. My lawyer says I have two options. I know which one I have to choose, but before I do, we need to talk. Really talk. But I can't do this over the phone. I've...shit. I think I've fucked this whole thing up. Whatever this is...between us. All of it. Maybe my entire life."

Every word widened the chasm between them until Alexander wondered if she'd ever truly trusted him at all. "I care for you, Elizabeth," he said, emotion threatening to choke him. "Why won't you tell me everything now?"

"If I do," her sob ended as a hiccup, "and you tell *anyone*...I can't...I won't have anything left."

Alexander staggered back to the wet bar and poured himself another two fingers of scotch. Was this how they were to end?

"You don't trust me." Each word hurt more than the last, and Alexander didn't know how to stop the pain. After he'd emptied his glass again, he cleared his throat. "I believe in honesty, Elizabeth. Without that, what do we have?"

She swiped at her cheeks. "I've never lied to you."

"Maybe not." He struggled with his next words. "However, you believe I'd let you come to harm, that I'd *ruin* you over business matters. We're new, Elizabeth. But you should know me better than that by now. You said you trusted me, yet clearly, you do not."

Desperation pinched her features as she pulled the phone closer. "I let you tie me up," she whispered. "I trusted you—"

"With your body, yes. Not your mind. Your heart. I thought you were willing to take a chance on me. On us. But now, you're across the country, crying, implying that your former employer did or is doing something that could be detrimental to my company *and* to you, and you won't trust me to help. What am I supposed to think?"

Her answer, when it came, didn't reassure him—nor was he surprised. "That I thought I could handle this on my own." She squared her shoulders, and when she focused on the screen again, her eyes held a hint of the fire he'd seen that very first day. "I'm not one of your causes, Alexander. Nor am I perfect. I—" Her voice wobbled, but she swallowed hard enough for him to see the muscles of her throat clench. "I swear—on my grandmother's grave—that I never touched your accounts. When I get back, I'll explain everything. I'll even go to Nicholas myself. On one condition."

Ultimatums didn't sit well with him. Nor did seeing the woman he—Alexander stopped himself before he finished his own thought. Without trust, there couldn't be love. Elizabeth waited, three thousand miles away, her lower lip tucked under her teeth.

*I can't do this. Not when she doesn't trust me.*

"What is your condition?" Alexander wasn't proud of the cool edge to his voice, but if he didn't detach himself, he'd end up on a plane to Seattle tonight, and he wasn't sure he could handle having his heart broken in person.

"You can't say anything to anyone until then. No lawyers. No one at CPH. Not even your brother." The phone shook, and her voice dropped. "Please."

"You have my word. Good night, Elizabeth."

Alexander threw the phone across the room, and as it shattered against the wall, along with his fantasies of a future with Elizabeth.

# CHAPTER TWELVE

*A*n hour before dawn, Elizabeth's phone woke her, and she nearly fell out of bed fumbling for the device. As she read Alexander's message, her heart cracked in two.

*I arranged the meeting for Thursday. Be outside your flat at 11. A car will be waiting.*

A car. One without Alexander in it.

Elizabeth moved through the rest of the morning in a fog. Not even Seattle held enough coffee to make her feel human. After a long run, she forced down another cheap burger and fries, then visited her financial planner. When she returned to her room after the long and stressful meeting with her lawyer, she took a chance and fired off a text message to Alexander.

*I'm sorry. I thought if I handled this on my own, we'd have a chance. I was wrong. I miss you.*

She paced and tried to read, chided herself for being needy, and then chided herself again for chiding herself. On the off chance she hadn't thrown away the relationship before it had a chance to flourish, she spent the evening learning everything she could about BDSM.

*The Dominant in the scene has control at all times, but the true*

*power lies with the submissive. In a mutually respectful D/s relation-*
*ship, the submissive can always end things with an agreed upon safe-*
*word or gesture. In this way, it is the sub who has the power for the*
*Dominant can do nothing (and should do nothing) without the sub's*
*total and informed consent.*

Alexander's words came flooding back to her. *"If you say 'red'*
*to me, at any time, it means that this all stops."*

Her eyes burned. The clock ticked over to eleven, and she
shut her laptop. After glancing at her phone one last time and
fighting a losing battle with her tears over Alexander's silence,
she turned off the light and tried to sleep.

---

ALEXANDER TURNED his new phone over in his hands. The hunk
of glass and metal held no appeal without Elizabeth to talk to,
and though he'd tried, more than once, to find a suitable reply to
her text, each attempt had left him cold.

"I should have gone directly to the airport," he muttered on
the way home from the cinema, where he'd passed a horrible two
hours trying to distract himself from the complete cock-up he'd
made of their relationship.

"I'm sorry, sir?" Thomas met his gaze in the rearview mirror.
"Did you say something?"

Alexander ran a hand through his hair. "Nothing of any
importance."

"Mr. Fairhaven, perhaps this is too forward, but are you all
right?" The driver gave him a quick glance as they idled at a
stoplight.

"I'm afraid I've made a real mess of things with Elizabeth," he
replied. "I'm not sure I can fix it."

"Shall I take you to her apartment?"

If only life were that simple. "No, she went to Seattle."

"The airport, then." Thomas flicked the turn signal, his gloved hands tightening on the wheel.

Alexander shook his head, then turned to stare out the window. The city, for all its beauty, felt empty without Elizabeth in it. Despite his promise to her, he'd done a little research on Harry Carter, Phillip Pastack, Leonard Hayes. Pastack had just turned eighty and retired, but he'd been a career military man with three cases of sexual harassment and two wrongful termination suits to his name—all settled out of court long before trial. Carter was clean, other than some unpaid parking tickets, but Hayes... Something rubbed Alexander the wrong way about that man. His father had embezzled millions as a stock broker in the seventies. How far did Leonard's apple fall from the father's tree?

With a sigh, Alexander checked his phone again. Nothing.

*You should have known. Her sacking. The avoidance every time you asked her what was wrong. You're a fucking dolt, and you'll be lucky if she gives you the time of day when she comes back.*

The chasm he imagined between them had grown so wide, he wasn't sure he could ever bridge it.

"Sir?"

Alexander rubbed his temples as Thomas held open his door. "You have someone special in your life?" he asked his driver as they stood nearly eye-to-eye.

"We've been together for six months, sir. I'm going to pick her up from work in a few minutes." Thomas's eyes lit up, and he smiled. "If it's not too forward, may I make a suggestion, sir?"

At this point, Alexander would take suggestions from anyone who'd managed to make a relationship work. "Of course."

"Samuel can arrange for flowers or a gift."

"No. I'm afraid I must earn her forgiveness the hard way." He turned to head up the stairs but paused with his hand on the railing. "Thomas?"

"Yes, sir." Hat in his hand, the driver paused to meet Alexander's gaze.

"Tell your girl that you'll take her out for a nice dinner—on me—over the weekend."

Thomas stammered his gratitude, but Alexander stopped him. "Don't thank me yet. I need you to get me to the airport tomorrow by 6:00 a.m. Elizabeth's flight lands then, and I want to be there to pick her up."

With a smile, Thomas nodded. "I'll be ready at five, sir."

LATER THAT NIGHT, Alexander sat in his living room sipping an eighteen-year-old Macallan. The door shook as someone banged insistently, rang the doorbell, then banged again. He'd already dismissed the staff for the night, so he trudged down the front hall himself.

His brother stood on the doorstep, wrapped in a camel-colored wool coat. Snow fell steadily, giving the street an eerily calm facade.

Alexander stepped aside. "Nicholas, to what do I owe this unexpected pleasure?" He tried to keep his tone friendly, but he'd spent most of the past two days dancing around his brother's schedule so he wouldn't have to answer any questions about Elizabeth or CPH.

His brother entered silently, divested himself of his coat, gloves, and hat, and then arranged everything precisely on the arm of one of the sofas. "Got any more of that scotch?" Nicholas asked.

Once he had his own drink in hand, Nicholas threw himself down in the chair across from the hearth and drained half of the scotch in a single swallow. "Why did you suggest we dump our accounting firm?"

*Shite.*

"Because the woman I'm dating was let go from Carter, Pastack, and Hayes two weeks ago. They claim she didn't do her

job, but I don't believe that for a moment. I thought it unseemly to give our money to a firm that caused her such grief."
Alexander tried not to dwell on the fact that he might not be dating Elizabeth anymore.

"That's it? That's the only reason?" Nicholas leaned forward, his piercing blue eyes searching for answers.

"It *was*. But I'm afraid there is more now. I can't talk about this, Nicholas. Not tonight. I made a promise to Elizabeth."

"Did she work on our accounts?" Nicholas slammed his glass down on the coffee table, shattering Alexander's tenuous hold on his emotions along with the lead crystal. "Shite."

Welcoming the distraction of retrieving a fresh glass and pouring Nicholas another two fingers of scotch, Alexander shook his head. "Leave it. The housekeeper comes in the morning."

"Well?"

His brother could be insufferable when an idea stuck in his head, and Alexander tried not to snap at him. "No. Elizabeth had nothing to do with any accounts tied to Fairhaven Exports. That's all I'm willing to say tonight. Tomorrow's meeting is at her behest. She's frightened. I have my suspicions as to why, and she promised to explain everything tomorrow. We can't do anything tonight anyway."

"Goddammit, Alex. You're taking her side over the company our father entrusted to us. We overpaid our taxes by at least ten million last year. I had Cynthia run a quick audit of the numbers. Standard practice since I was investigating new accounting firms. She and I both nearly missed it, but our charitable contributions were listed as two-point-three million last year. Do you remember that bet we had?"

Alexander chuckled. "Of course. I beat your arse five weeks in a row on the courts, and you had to donate an amount proportional to your total score."

"I scored twenty-one points over those five weeks, so to keep it sporting, I donated two-point-one million. In one go. Cynthia totaled up the rest of the donations, and we should have been credited for three-point-nine million. I have her going over every line of our taxes for last year." Nicholas finished off his scotch and rose to pour himself another.

Alexander grabbed his arm and spun him around. "Did you share your suspicions with *anyone* other than Cynthia?"

Shaking his arm free, Nicholas glared at his brother. "Of course not! Cynthia's handling this personally. If CPH screwed us, they're going to pay. We'll sue them for everything they're worth. They're arseholes. I've seen them go after former employees who exposed their insane overtime requirements. I dismissed it. Business sometimes requires us to be cold and unfeeling. But I never liked it. Knowing that they screwed us, even if it was unintentional, I'm hitting them as hard as I can."

Alexander had two inches and fifty pounds on Nicholas, all muscle, but his brother was older, and his stare could still reduce Alexander to a ten-year-old boy. Exhaustion washed over Alexander like a tidal wave, filling his lungs, tumbling him head over heels. The boy he'd been wanted Nicholas to throw him a life preserver. The man he was now swam to the surface alone.

"Elizabeth begged me not to say anything. Even to you. She's not the type of woman who begs. At least not outside the bedroom. We had a row about it, and I'm afraid I was an arse to her. I've never asked you for much at all, brother. But I am asking now. Give her—us—twelve hours. Please. Don't tell a soul."

"Shite, Alex. You're really falling for her, aren't you?" Nicholas poured them both more scotch, then took a seat, Alexander joining him.

"That I am. She's a natural submissive, Nicholas. But there's also a tremendous amount of strength in her. She's everything I've always wanted and didn't know I needed. A woman who'll stand up to me, challenge me, but will give me her total trust in the bedroom. It's easier for you, I think. What you want. Finding a slave when you're...well, us...isn't difficult. Throw some cash around, and you've got it. At least for a time. I'm glad that dynamic works for you. It doesn't work for me."

"You think it's easy dealing with Candy? She's as dumb as a box of rocks. No. Scratch that. She doesn't even have the brains of a single rock."

Alexander's dry laugh echoed against the high ceilings. "No, she does not. Are you saying it's finally over?"

"Not yet. I need someone for all the holiday parties, and she does fill out a dress quite well." Nicholas ran a hand through his blond hair. "But after the first of the year, I'll find her a new Master and be done with her. I want someone who can hold their own in a conversation. After Lia..." Sadness swam in Nicholas's eyes and he shook his head. "I told Terrance that I'd take him to a club I joined out in Dorchester. I found Candy there shortly after they opened. Perhaps I'll find a better match there now. I was going to see if you wanted to come with us. They're quite exclusive. All members and guests are required to sign a strict confidentiality agreement. I know you were recognized a time or two at Midnight Sin."

"I saw Terrance on Monday. He mentioned the club. Chains, is it?"

"Yes. You should see their dungeon. I had Candy begging after mere minutes."

*"I need to come. Please."*

The memory of Elizabeth's voice brought a smile to his lips. "I do not believe I'll have need of it. Not if Elizabeth forgives me." Alexander drained the last of his drink. "It's late, and I need to pick her up at the airport in the morning. Or try to anyway."

"Try to?" Nicholas deposited his glass on the end table next to the broken one.

"I haven't spoken to her since we fought on Monday night. She's all alone—or was. I won't let her be alone any longer. Not when I can do something to protect her. Do I have your word that you'll wait until our meeting to speak to company counsel about the tax discrepancies?"

"Yes. You're my blood, Alex. If you trust her, I'll give you those twelve hours you asked for."

"Thank you."

Nicholas donned his coat and tugged on his gloves. Alexander stopped him just before he reached the entryway. "We have not always seen eye-to-eye, but you're a good man."

Nicholas gave Alexander a quick clap on the shoulder. "I hope she's worth it."

"She is."

# CHAPTER THIRTEEN

*A*lexander shoved his hands into the pockets of his coat as he strode towards Terminal A at Logan Airport. Only one flight was arriving from Vegas at this God-awful hour, but he'd already arranged for a back-up plan in case he'd been wrong. Samuel waited at Elizabeth's apartment with a note Alexander had poured over for several hours.

An influx of weary travelers streamed through the security gates, and Alexander scanned the crowd. His heart inched north into his throat as the throng of people started to thin. As he wrapped his fingers around his phone, he spotted her, and his entire world righted until he got a good look at her.

The bright, shining light that *was* Elizabeth had faded, leaving an empty shell: sunken, puffy eyes, slumped shoulders, pale skin. Heading for the T on auto-pilot, she didn't even look up when he approached, just whispered a quiet "sorry" and veered out of his path.

"Elizabeth." His voice cracked, and he reached out to touch her arm.

She jolted, her hand flying to her mouth to cover her gasp.

They stared at one another as tears welled in her eyes. "What are you doing here?"

"Trying to apologize for my truly abhorrent behavior on the phone. I was a sodding bastard, and I've no excuse for it." He stepped closer, too afraid to touch her, but aching to embrace her and never let her go.

"Y-you s-said..." A tear tumbled down her cheek.

Alexander pulled Elizabeth into his arms. "I know what I said." He'd thought of nothing else since he'd hung up on her. "I'm sorry. You were so far away, I could do nothing to help, and I couldn't see past my own frustration."

"I just needed two days." Her muffled words cut him even deeper, and he wasn't sure he could ever bleed enough to make this up to her. "Why couldn't you give me that?"

"Because I'm an idiot." Alexander drew back, hoping that seeing his face would help Elizabeth believe him. "Can I bring you home?"

She chewed on her lip for a moment, and he held his breath until she nodded. With his arm around her shoulders, Alexander guided her to the curb, then into the limo.

The silence ate away at his composure, as did the sight of Elizabeth shying away from him, braced for his rejection. Why hadn't he called to apologize? Or even sent a text?

Once they were on their way, Alexander cleared his throat. "Have you slept?"

Whatever she'd expected, it hadn't been that. "N-no. I can't sleep on planes."

"You've never been on the right plane." He slid closer to her. "I missed you."

Another tear fell. "If you missed me, you wouldn't have ignored me for two days."

Alexander cursed under his breath. "I deserved that. When I hung up on you on Monday night, I was hurt and frustrated. This was never about the tax fraud." Elizabeth's eyes widened, and

Alexander took her hand. "It's not a stretch to realize that's what's going on. And you should have told me about it from the start. You knew my company was involved. But that's not why I was angry. You feared I would *ruin you*. I care about you, Elizabeth. Even if we break up and never speak to one another again, I would *never* ruin you. You should have trusted me—" Alexander held up his hand when she started to protest. "But I should have trusted you as well. In the middle of a very long, sleepless night, I finally realized I hadn't given you the very thing I was demanding. By then, however, I imagined this chasm between us, and I had no idea how to atone for my mistakes. Will you forgive me?"

Her lower lip quivered, but she didn't look away. In her eyes, a storm raged, and when the turmoil broke free, her words tumbled out quickly, as if she couldn't hold them in another moment. "We didn't have a relationship when I got the summons. I couldn't find a lawyer here. No one would represent me because CPH has ties to *everyone*. That's why I called my lawyer back in Seattle. I wanted to tell you. But then I saw the photographer at the ice rink. He was outside my building after you dropped me off on Saturday night too. I was scared. I'm going to—" Elizabeth choked on a sob, but wouldn't let Alexander pull her closer. "I have to go to the federal prosecutor. Clancy is filing the paperwork now. But until I know I'm protected by federal whistle-blower laws..."

"You'll be protected by a lot more than that," Alexander murmured.

Elizabeth lost all fight and crumpled into his chest. "I'm sorry. I can't be with you. I can't drag you further into this mess."

Alexander reclined in the seat and pulled Elizabeth closer, a hand in her hair angling her face up to look at him. "Do you want to be with me? If this whole cock-up wasn't an issue, would you want to see where this goes?"

The look in her eyes calmed his raging emotions. "Yes."

"Then everything else will wait until you've had some sleep.

We've a bit of a ride in this traffic. I'm afraid you would have been home sooner if I'd let you take the T, but then I wouldn't have been able to do this." He cupped her cheek and brushed his lips to hers. "Rest a bit. I canceled my meetings this morning so I could stay with you."

"You don't have to," she said against his neck.

"I have my laptop. I'll work while you rest. I've missed you, *chérie*. And I feel terrible about how I treated you. I was upset, but that is no excuse. You don't do that to someone you care for."

"S'okay," she murmured. Her breathing evened out, and the tension in her shoulders eased.

He stroked a hand down her back. "No. It isn't. The partners are guilty, aren't they?"

"Uh-huh." She burrowed closer to him. "They can't know."

"They won't."

Thomas pulled onto the turnpike and almost immediately slowed to a standstill in the morning commute traffic.

"Shhh," Alexander soothed. "I've got you. I'm not letting you go, Elizabeth."

She settled closer to him and sighed, falling asleep in his arms.

---

ELIZABETH COULDN'T REMEMBER ARRIVING HOME, TAKING off her shoes and sweatshirt, or getting into bed, and she had a sneaking suspicion that Alexander had carried her up from the car and tended to her. Now, armed with a few hours of sleep, a shower, and the fresh memory of Alexander's arms around her, she felt almost steady as she opened her bedroom door and stepped into the living room.

Alexander sat on her couch, working on his computer with River on his lap. When he looked up at her and smiled, something in Elizabeth's belly flipped.

"You stayed."

"That I did. I do not know how much you feed this behemoth, but she seemed quite pleased with me when I filled her bowl. Coffee?" He stood, then deposited River where his ass had been moments before. The cat curled up in the well-warmed space with a single glare before she started cleaning herself.

Elizabeth stared at the travel mug he offered her, uncertain if they'd managed to resolve anything—her memories from the limo were muddy at best.

As Alexander pressed the mug into her hands, his scent enveloped her, and damn if she didn't want to lose herself in his strong arms again.

"Everything will work out, Elizabeth. I have a lawyer on retainer. He'll be joining us."

Backing away, Elizabeth clutched the mug to her chest. "My lawyer didn't want me to tell you. He warned me...this would happen. I need to call—" Her airway constricted, and she turned, ready to sprint for the bedroom, but Alexander wrapped his arms around her.

"Relax, Elizabeth. The lawyer is for you. I have no doubt Fairhaven Exports will sue them for all they're worth, but we won't do a bloody thing until you're protected."

"I can't accept that much from you. This isn't your fight—"

He silenced her with a kiss. "Do you really think I care about the amount of money the lawyer is going to cost? Nicholas started looking into the work CPH did for us last year." Elizabeth stifled a gasp. "I said nothing to him, but Nicholas found discrepancies on his own. He came to me first, and he agreed to keep his findings a secret until we sorted this."

He gestured to a garment bag hanging on the back of her front door. "If you need another sign that I'm not giving up on us, I brought your dress for tomorrow's ball."

"I...uh...don't know what to say." A few hours ago, she'd been alone, terrified, convinced she was going to lose everything.

Now...could she actually have a chance? Both to survive CPH's lawsuit and be with Alexander?

Alexander trailed a knuckle along her jaw. "Say you'll still dance with me tomorrow."

Elizabeth forced a weak smile. "I'll still dance with you tomorrow."

THE LIMO RIDE to an upscale Boston restaurant passed in silence, but Alexander kept his arm around Elizabeth's shoulders the whole time. Inside the empty restaurant, three men waited for them in a large, circular booth.

"Elizabeth, please meet Ben Hetherington, my lawyer." Alexander gestured to a man with salt-and-pepper hair and an easy smile. "Yours too, now."

Ben offered a firm handshake and a smile. "If anyone from CPH contacts you again, send them right to me. They won't touch you."

"Th-thank you."

"And my brother, Nicholas." Elizabeth turned to a blond man who shared many of Alexander's features. His eyes were blue rather than green, and he didn't match his brother for height, but he held himself with the same pride and air of dominance.

"Nick, please." He smiled and clasped her hand in both of his. "My brother is quite taken with you. I'm sorry that we're not meeting under better circumstances, but I'm afraid the seriousness of the situation precludes all the usual pleasantries."

"It's a pleasure—well, it would have been. If this hadn't happened," Elizabeth stammered.

Nick angled his head to the last man, a tall, thin, and dour man with a small laptop open on the table in front of him. "This is Paul Foyle. Lead council for Fairhaven Exports."

They sat, and Alexander twined his fingers with Elizabeth's under the table. "What would you like to tell us, Elizabeth?"

She bit her lip. "How much did Fairhaven Exports owe in taxes last year?"

"Forty-point-three million," Nicholas replied. "According to CPH. Though we all know that number is wrong."

"I didn't touch your account, but my cube-mate did. One day, she asked me to make copies for her—she'd misplaced her code for the copier." Elizabeth glanced down at Alexander's hand on her thigh, blushing. "You don't get a file in your hands of that magnitude and not take a peek. You owed thirty-seven-point-four million. I remember because my copier code is 37400. Or...was, anyway."

As she spoke, Nicholas flipped through a stack of papers in front of him. "She's right. That's the number Cynthia and her team calculated and what CPH sent to the IRS on our behalf. But that's *not* the number that CPH gave us."

"I was fired because the Red Sox discovered a discrepancy during an independent audit ordered by Major League Baseball. I had partial copies of their returns on my laptop, and I compared them to the altered returns the Red Sox got from CPH. They don't match."

Ben cleared his throat. "Elizabeth, I need you to be very clear. You're accusing Carter, Pastack, and Hayes of embezzlement and tax fraud. Correct?"

Somber faces around the table waited for her to speak.
*No turning back now.*

With a glance at Alexander, who nodded encouragingly, Elizabeth forced herself to take a deep breath. "Yes. I suppose I am."

With copies of her paperwork strewn across the table, Elizabeth summarized everything that had happened since she'd been fired. "My lawyer said if I went through with this, I might never work as an accountant again."

Ben snorted as he flipped through the papers. "If you tried to fight this alone, perhaps. Not now. These documents are designed to intimidate you. You're protected once the lawsuit is filed. You do, however, need to tread carefully until then. CPH doesn't suspect that you ever saw the original Fairhaven returns, correct?"

"They'd have no reason to. It wasn't my account. There were fifty of us. We each had our own clients. No overlap."

With a nod, Ben stacked the papers neatly. "All right. You've already been seen with Alexander, so we can't do anything about that. I'd like to arrange for some press that focuses on your personal relationship, not business. Make it clear to CPH and the public that you're not associating with the Fairhaven brothers for business purposes. It'll make it easier when the lawsuit's filed. A kiss or two or ten wouldn't be a bad idea. Can you do that?"

Elizabeth's stomach flipped, and Alexander smiled. "Elizabeth is accompanying me to the Fire and Ice Ball tomorrow. We can stop and talk to a reporter or two on the way in. Being affectionate with her won't be a problem." He slid his hand up her thigh, and she tried not to shift in her seat.

"Good. Have you contacted any of your other clients?" Ben asked.

"Just the Red Sox," she replied. "And *they* called *me*. CPH filed the lawsuit after they first saw me with Alexander. Since he wasn't my client, they probably assumed I was doing...well...what I'm doing now. They called several times when Alexander was in London, and someone came to my apartment a few days before we had breakfast together."

"I don't want them around her," Alexander said roughly. "At all."

Ben shook his head. "Neither do I, but there's nothing illegal about it. Still, if anyone comes to your door again, Elizabeth, do not answer and call me immediately." Ben slid a business card across the table, and she tucked it into her purse. "I will take care of all of your representation from here on out. If we're lucky, the federal prosecutor will be able to see us first thing Monday morning. We'll have the weekend to get all of our ducks in a row first."

Nicholas cleared his throat. "And what do we do about Fairhaven Exports? We'll need to hire a new accounting firm very soon, and Hayes is going to find out. He knows everyone in this town."

Paul, who had spent the entire meeting so far taking notes on his laptop, looked up. "You do exactly what you have been doing. I want to meet with the team that you're having re-run the numbers. They'll sign confidentiality agreements. Once Miss Bennett finishes with the prosecutor, we can file our own suit." He leveled a stern gaze at Elizabeth and Alexander. "It might be a good idea if Elizabeth was tucked away somewhere the press and CPH's lawyers can't get to her after she's given her deposition. A little vacation out of town or even a few nights in a hotel under an assumed name would force them to deal with Hetherington. Whistleblower laws protect her, ultimately, but that won't stop CPH from doing their worst."

"That won't be a problem," Alexander said. "A trip up the coast can easily be arranged. I won't let anyone get to her."

Elizabeth gaped at him. "I...I don't think—"

"Don't be ridiculous, Elizabeth. It isn't as if I'm planning a trip to London for you to meet my mother." Alexander's grin flashed, hungry and almost predatory. "Yet."

Her breath hitched, but she was saved from further embarrassment by Nicholas rising. "I have to get back to the office." Nicholas extended his hand. "It was lovely to meet you, Elizabeth, despite the circumstances. I've never seen Alex quite so unsure of himself. It's very entertaining. I'll see you tomorrow at the ball."

The next ten minutes passed in a flurry of papers to sign and a dizzying number of legal terms Elizabeth had only heard in passing—on *Law and Order*. By the time the lawyers were done, Elizabeth's head pounded, and her stomach twisted into knots.

*Why did my life have to turn so complicated?*

Before she'd been fired, other than the occasional dinner with Toni and Kelsey, Elizabeth rarely socialized and never dated. Endless stretches of solitude broken up only by her daily runs and long hours of work made up her life. Now, she was dating a billionaire, about to accuse a very powerful and influential company of tax fraud, and oddest of all, almost happy.

"Elizabeth?" She leaned in to the warm hand on her shoulder, unsure how long she'd been absorbed in her own musings. "What's wrong?"

"Everything I've worked for...five years of sitting at that desk, doing my job, is about to go down the drain. But then...there's you. I don't know why you're bothering with me. All I'm going to do is make trouble for you. I figured you'd drop me as soon as I told you what was going on. But instead you came to get me, and I don't understand why."

"Because I find you irresistible," Alexander said, sliding into the booth next to her and cupping her cheeks. "Your strength, your intelligence, the spark in your eyes, your smile, your laugh..." He leaned in and claimed her mouth until all she wanted was to lose herself in him. When he pulled away, his eyes darkened, threads of copper shining through his somber gaze. "I understand why you didn't tell me. Why you didn't feel like you could. But can we agree that for however how long this lasts, we won't keep secrets from one another?"

Elizabeth linked their fingers. "No more secrets."

# CHAPTER FOURTEEN

"Stop fidgeting, sir. You're not helping the matter."

Alexander glared at Samuel. "All the advances in science and technology over the years and no one's found a way to make this simpler?"

"It's a bowtie, sir. It's not supposed to be simple." Samuel coaxed the tie into place, then stepped back. "There. Now don't go fiddling with it. And for God's sake, snap out of this snit before you go and pick up Miss Bennett. I'm quite certain she will not appreciate the attitude."

Samuel strode out of the room after Alexander's withering glare. It didn't help that his majordomo was right. He had been in a bloody awful mood all day. Alexander shrugged into his jacket and gave his appearance a once-over in the mirror. His tense shoulders interrupted the lines of the jacket. With a deep breath, he forced himself to relax. Spending the past day and a half trapped in stuffy conference rooms with even stuffier lawyers had soured his mood. Only the prospect of seeing Elizabeth tonight kept him sane.

He usually hated parties, but with Elizabeth at his side, perhaps the drudgery of arranged seating, speeches, and making small talk with some of his business associates wouldn't be quite so awful. And later...she'd agreed to spend the night with him. He wanted her bound to his bed, blindfolded, and begging.

At Elizabeth's door, Alexander fought the urge to fiddle with his tie as he waited for her to answer his knock.

When she did, he forgot to breathe.

Her golden locks tumbled from a messy up-do over her shoulders. Only a hint of makeup enhanced her features, a touch of glitter to her eyelids, a shine of gloss on her lips. Her fingers fluttered over the string of citrine diamonds around her throat, the necklace, bracelet, and matching earrings on loan, with an option to buy.

Sparkling golden fabric swathed her body in gentle waves and curves. The shimmering gown wrapped her in sunlight, and the heels put her at least three inches taller.

"Eliz—" He cleared his throat. "Elizabeth, you are a vision. Your hair..." Alexander reached out to touch the silky locks, but she stepped back, nearly losing her balance. Gripping her elbow, he steadied her.

"No touching. Kelsey worked on me for two hours to get my hair to stay this way. If I'm photographed with my hair a mess, she'll have my ass."

"Kelsey doesn't get your arse, *cherie*. I do." Alexander slid his arm around her waist, fighting the urge to take her home and skip the ball completely. "Tonight, I intend to show you what I can do to you naked. You *have* been thinking about that, have you not?"

"Every night."

Despite her quiet tone, she held his gaze, though her cheeks flushed a delicious shade of pink.

Alexander leaned in and brushed his lips to her cheek. The faint scent of almonds and gardenias wafted over him. He'd smelled that scent before. The night she'd come to dinner. "What else did the talented Kelsey do to you, Elizabeth?"

She squirmed, and the blush spread down her neck to her chest.

"What," he kissed up to her earlobe and twirled his tongue around the drop of ice that dangled, "else."

"She...ah...oh... She works at The Waxing Spa on Newbury Street." Elizabeth's legs trembled as Alexander skimmed his hand down her hip until he found the slit in the dress just above her knee. Trailing the pads of his fingers as high as the dress would allow, he reveled in the tiny mewls and moans she made as she clutched at his shoulders.

"We should go before I lose all of my resolve and take you right here." Once Alexander was confident she could stand on her own, he stepped back enough to drink in the sight of her body again. Elizabeth clenched her fists at her sides, fighting for control of her breath.

He retrieved her wrap from the bedroom and, after drawing the flowing number in the same shimmering gold around her shoulders, Alexander stopped her from securing the button.

"Allow me, Elizabeth. Trust me to take care of you in every way." He fastened the button and rested his hands on her arms. "All night."

"I don't get a say in anything?" she asked. "You want me to be your slave? In public? I don't think so."

He barely stopped his jaw from dropping.

"I did some research."

Alexander didn't want a slave. No, that was his brother's predilection, but knowing Elizabeth was comfortable enough to research what he might want and wasn't bolting at the very mention, was promising.

"I will never be your Master, Elizabeth. The role has never interested me, and you...you are no slave. I am, however, your Dom, and perhaps one day, I will be more. Tonight, I ask you to put your trust in me. With the press, on the dance floor, and later...in the bedroom. You *always* have a say. You have a brilliant mind and a strong backbone, and I never want you to feel you cannot use them."

A hint of a smile curved her lips, and she hadn't dropped her gaze. Most subs he'd played with before were conditioned to never look their Dom in the eyes unless commanded to. He'd enjoyed the dynamic, on the surface, but the interactions had always left him wanting more. Now, he knew why. Elizabeth's strength and spirit made them equals, even when he commanded her.

Alexander offered her his arm. "You take my breath away."

"And you look good enough to eat," she said as they waited for the elevator and then immediately snapped her mouth shut, embarrassed.

Alexander laughed and pressed his lips to her temple. "Elizabeth, have you been drinking this afternoon?"

"I've had enough coffee to kill a horse," she replied with a nervous laugh. "I'm a little jittery. I didn't want any alcohol. The last thing I needed was to get drunk before we talked to the press. But, shit. Once we get there, I could really use a glass of wine."

He chuffed softly and pulled her closer. "I think I like you jittery. You stop thinking so much and let yourself feel. And speak your mind, apparently. We will absolutely have wine. But no getting drunk tonight, for either of us. Anything we do this evening will be done with your full awareness and consent. Not with impaired judgment."

She looked up at him, suddenly serious. "I want you. Whatever else is going on here, the chemistry between us is driving me mad. But I admit, I'm scared to death of what you want from me. And what will happen if I can't..."

Respect welled inside him. He knew he could be intimidating. Hell, he'd built an empire on his reputation for ruthless business practices and brutal negotiation tactics. "You stagger me, Elizabeth."

"For telling you I'm scared?" She frowned, confusion knitting her brows.

"Yes." He glared at the ancient elevator as the door slid open, hoping to scare the contraption into delivering them safely to the ground floor. As the car shuddered, he met her gaze. "What we have...goes far beyond simple chemistry, I think. Know this. Nothing will happen without your consent, and if you need to stop, use your safeword, and we will stop. Fear is natural. But I do not honestly think you could ever disappoint me as long as you are honest with me and with yourself."

The air in the elevator hung thick with tension until Elizabeth grinned. "Well, I'm hungry. And again, you do look rather tasty."

ELIZABETH STARED out the window as the glittering city streamed by, holiday lights in full splendor. Snow fell gently, dotting the sidewalks, coming to rest on the shoulders of men, women, and children bundled up in warm winter coats. A lightness infused her every movement today, unlike so many days before. Perhaps, they'd turned a corner now that they'd cleared the air about the lawsuit and Alexander's spectacularly poor manners on FaceTime.

At the Omni Parker House Hotel, thick, red carpet covered the stairs leading to the lobby with Christmas trees standing sentry on each side of the door. Sparkling white lights, red velvet ribbons, and golden stars added to the magic of the season.

Thomas opened the door, and Alexander alighted first, scanning the crowd. A smattering of reporters and photographers, plenty of security. Excellent.

As he helped Elizabeth to her feet, he marveled at her grace. A camera flash went off two feet away. Her fingers tightened on his, but she didn't otherwise react. Alexander gave her hand a gentle

squeeze, leaned over, and whispered in her ear. "Do not expect me
to ever stop touching you tonight, *chérie*. I simply cannot get
enough of you." Elizabeth blushed as he pressed a kiss to her neck.
"The press will jump on us when we get inside. Are you ready?"

"I guess."

Tucking Elizabeth's hand in the crook of his arm, he led her
up the steps of the hotel and into the opulent lobby. With his best
playboy smile firmly in place, he eased the cloak from her shoulders, then folded the wrap over his arm as he leaned in closer. "It
looks like someone detonated a Christmas bomb in here. There
may not be any spare lights left in the city."

Elizabeth laughed, tried to stifle it, and nearly ended up
snorting. She glared at him. "You're awful. You know that, right?"

Perhaps, but he'd coaxed a laugh out of her, and that was
worth it. A few feet into the room, a shrill voice called his name.
"Alexander Fairhaven! A moment for WGBH?"

Alexander turned smoothly with Elizabeth tucked close to his
body. "Of course. Miss...?"

"Paige Denick, Style Reporter."

The thin, waifish woman offered him a limp handshake. Her
burly videographer hefted a large camera on his shoulder. As a
red light winked on, the reporter smoothed her bright red hair
and cleared her throat.

"You've been almost a recluse these past few weeks, Mr.
Fairhaven," Paige teased. "Other than the short time you put in at
the Jimmy Fund benefit, you've been out of the public eye for
nearly two months."

"Can you blame me?" he asked, pausing to tip Elizabeth's face
up and plant a gentle kiss on her lips. "And please, call me
Alexander. This is Elizabeth Bennett, my reason for staying in as
of late."

"Of late? How long has this been going on, *Alexander*? Forgive
me, but you're not known for your long-term relationships. In

fact, I don't honestly recall you ever being seen with the same woman twice?" The reporter's tone was sweet, but her eyes hardened, and she pinned Elizabeth with an icy stare.

Elizabeth straightened her shoulders. The motion caused the citrine diamonds to wink in the bright lights of the hotel lobby. "Alexander and I have been seeing each other for several weeks now. And as for his past exploits, they are none of my concern, or yours, Miss Denick."

Alexander chuckled as pride bloomed in his chest. "Elizabeth is right, *Paige*. The past is most definitely the past. This lovely woman is my present, and I hope, my future."

Elizabeth pressed closer to him and gave a seductive laugh, but he could feel her discomfort. They were dancing towards dangerous territory—commitment. All before they'd even slept together.

"How did the two of you meet?" Paige asked them.

Elizabeth blushed and gave Paige a brief, rehearsed summary of their first meeting. "I'm afraid he had to work quite hard to get me to agree to a date, though. Given his reputation. However, I'm pleased I stopped listening to all of the gossip-mongering and gave him a chance. He's nothing like what the press makes him out to be."

"Elizabeth brings out a side of me I didn't know existed," Alexander replied.

"And what do you do, Miss Bennett?"

Elizabeth's fingers dug into his arm. Ben had prepared them for the question, but though she offered the practiced answer with apparent ease, Alexander felt her anxiety.

"Currently, I do a lot of volunteer work. I recently left a demanding position that left me unfulfilled, and I'm taking the next month or so to enjoy myself a bit and give back to the community that's nourished me for more than five years. But I have a business degree from Harvard, and I'm a licensed accountant, so after the first of the year, I'll be working freelance. Tax time approaches quickly."

"Now, Paige, you have grilled my lovely Elizabeth enough for one evening, and I fear we are expected upstairs," Alexander purred. "It was *an experience* meeting you."

The reporter narrowed her eyes at him as he steered Elizabeth towards the elevator. They were almost out of earshot when she spoke to her videographer. "I wonder how long he plans on keeping this one around."

Alexander stiffened and couldn't help the feral sound that rumbled in his chest. He turned back to the reporter, a quick glance at the camera ensuring the red light was dark. "As long as she'll have me," he said, unable to keep the venom from his voice. "And I'll thank you to treat her with more respect from now on or your network will lose a substantial investor and your boss will receive a personal call from me explaining why."

Paige sputtered out a hasty apology while Alexander wrapped a protective arm around Elizabeth's waist and pulled her against him.

"I suppose that's going to be a common reaction," Elizabeth murmured.

"Don't listen to her." Alexander jabbed the button for the twentieth floor. When the elevator doors closed, cocooning them protectively in the ornately paneled box, Alexander pressed Elizabeth against the back wall and crushed his lips to hers. He took possession with tongue and teeth, eliciting a low, throaty moan from the pliant woman in his arms.

She gazed up at him with half-lidded eyes after he pulled back. "What...was that...for?"

"You are mine, Elizabeth." Alexander cupped her neck. "I cultivated my playboy reputation. I let the press think I was aloof, impossible to tame or corral. It was easier that way. But I regret that now if it causes you even one second of grief."

The elevator doors opened, sparing Alexander from hearing Elizabeth's protestations. "Ready for a party, *chérie*?"

"No more reporters?" she asked.

"Oh, there will be more, I am certain, but they will be print or web only. No video cameras up here." He smiled and offered her his arm again. Not more than three steps out of the elevator, a flash went off in their faces. Elizabeth teetered for a moment, unsteady, but Alexander's arm held her up.

"Tami-Lynne Thorne, Mr. Fairhaven. I'm sorry for the flash. I write for the *Boston Globe*. A few minutes of your time?"

They repeated the dance again and again. The *Globe*, the *Post*, and even the local weekly gossip rag. Elizabeth was charming, holding her own but deferring to Alexander for questions surrounding the timing of their relationship and their holiday plans. "A couple must keep some secrets, wouldn't you agree?" he said to one particularly determined reporter.

Throughout the rounds, he never stopped touching her. A kiss to her neck here, playing with a lock of her hair there. It was well after eight when they extricated themselves from the requisite interviews, chit-chat, and introductions to his various business associates and found their seats at a silver cloth-covered table set with the finest crystal, flatware, and china. A perfect poinsettia graced the center. Nicholas and his slave, the not-so-brilliant Candy, were already seated, and Nicholas stood when they approached.

"Elizabeth, you look lovely," Nicholas said. He extended his hand and raised an eyebrow at Candy. She stood and toddled over on heels that were so high that she matched him for height. "Candy, this is my brother's girlfriend, Elizabeth Bennett. Shake her hand, dear."

Candy gave Elizabeth a wide smile. "Nice to meet ya," she said with a thick New York accent. Around her throat, Nicholas's diamond collar glittered. The thin silk of her low-cut gown barely hid tight nipples, and Alexander shook his head as Candy struggled to sit back down in a dress cut so high, it was practically obscene.

"Really, Nicholas? You could not have dressed her a bit more conservatively for the evening?" he whispered in his brother's ear once they were all seated once more.

"Hey, let me have my fun. Just because you've got a woman with some fashion sense and intelligence…"

Alexander took Nicholas's jacket from his chair and draped it over Candy's shoulders. "You must be chilled, Candy. Keep that on for dinner, will you?"

Nicholas grimaced as Candy looked to him for approval. "Do what he says, dear."

Wine arrived, poured by white-suited waiters. The conversation was sparkling, Elizabeth fitting in perfectly with the two Fairhaven board members and their wives, who joined them at the table. One of the wives, a small Asian woman named Sun who looked about ready to give birth, addressed Elizabeth. "So what do you do for a living?"

"I'm an accountant," Elizabeth replied.

"You count ants?" Candy asked.

Elizabeth swiveled her head towards Alexander, eyes wide, an expression of pure and total disbelief on her face. He shook his head sadly. Yes, his brother's current conquest was *exactly* that dumb. He turned to whisper in her ear. "You see what I had to deal with last Friday?"

"I take back every mean thought I had about you. And her," Elizabeth whispered back. She reached for his thigh under the table and gave it a squeeze. "No, Candy," Elizabeth told her. "I do taxes. I make sure companies pay their bills properly."

"Then why'd you say you counted ants?" She looked over at Nicholas. "I don't understand, sir."

Nicholas glared back at her. "I told you not to call me that in public," he growled, low enough only for Candy and Alexander to hear. "Let it go, Candy."

Alexander rested his hand over Elizabeth's. He was about to lean over and kiss her when her entire body stiffened, and she gripped his thigh so hard he wondered if he'd bruise. "Elizabeth?"

Her entire face paled as she stared past him. Through clenched teeth, she hissed out a single word. "Carter."

Alexander followed her gaze. An angry little man of sixty strode towards them. Graying hair, beady brown eyes, his hands balled into fists at his sides.

Quickly, Alexander pulled out his phone, tapped the screen, and engaged the voice recorder. Nicholas pushed to his feet and joined his brother, forming a protective Fairhaven wall around Elizabeth.

Carter glowered at the two men. "Excuse me, *gentlemen*. I need to talk to Miss Bennett."

"Not a chance. Didn't you get a copy of the protection order?" Alexander asked. "Elizabeth has nothing to say to you. You can address all of your vitriol to her lawyer." He flicked his gaze to Elizabeth. Stuttering breaths rasped as she trembled and stared at something—or perhaps nothing—across the room. Alexander angled his body so he could lay his hand on her shoulder.

"I could hardly be expected to know she'd be here tonight. But since she is, I need a few moments of her time," Carter said.

"I don't think so." Alexander gestured to one of the tuxedoed security guards around the room. They were unobtrusive, but their stance and their earpieces gave them away. "How much did you donate to the governor's pet causes last year, Carter? Five hundred thousand?"

"Seven-fifty," Carter spat.

"Oh, what a pity. Nicholas and I together donated more than two million. Not to mention the money we've pledged to his re-election campaign. And as it is *his* ball, I think I know who will be allowed to stay and who won't be." Alexander smiled, but he ached to punch Carter in his pinched jaw. Or throw it in the man's face that Fairhaven Exports would soon be suing them. But that was for the lawyers.

Carter leaned closer to Alexander and Nicholas as two security guards converged. "Listen to me. Fairhaven Exports is one of our clients. Miss Bennett is under a strict confidentiality clause. One she's apparently violated by associating with the two of you. We're going after her for everything she's got. You don't want to get caught in the middle."

Alexander held up his hand to stop the two security guards from interrupting. "That sounds suspiciously like a threat."

"You're goddamn right it is," Carter replied.

"Then may I introduce you to the governor's security detail?" Alexander nodded, and the two men took Carter by the arms.

"Sir, you'll need to come with us. Threats towards our guests are not permitted. Do you have a plus-one?" The taller of the two guards tapped his ear. "We have an incident. Escorting a guest from the premises for threatening the Fairhavens."

Nicholas blew out a breath once they'd hauled Carter away. "I'm really going to enjoy taking that piece of shite down a few notches."

"As am I. Elizabeth?" Alexander turned back to her and brushed his hands down her shoulders. "Are you all right?"

She looked up at him, her face paler than he'd ever seen. "I need some air," she managed.

He had her up and the cloak wrapped around her in a single breath. She practically sprinted for a set of glass doors leading out onto a balcony that wrapped around three sides of the room.

Heat lamps built into decorative columns kept them warm, despite below freezing temperatures outside. Elizabeth gripped Alexander's forearms and tried to force air into her lungs. "Can't breathe."

Alexander pressed her fingers to his neck. "Feel my heartbeat, Elizabeth. Focus on it. Listen to my voice and take slow, deep breaths." He kept up a steady stream of words, holding her with his eyes, his arm around her, and his voice. Several minutes passed before her breathing evened, and she sank against his chest.

"Sorry. Second attack this week. I thought I was past them."

"You have nothing to apologize for. Are you all right now?"

Her nod and small smile drew back the curtain of fear that had closed itself around him. "How did you know how to do that?"

"A Dom must be able to calm his sub quickly. I've never had a woman panic during play, but Nicholas has. We've both had training."

Elizabeth straightened and stared out over the city skyline. Her voice, when it came, held a tinge of sadness. "Carter's going to keep making trouble for you. Hayes is even worse. Pastack is the only halfway decent one, and he's so old that he barely comes into the office any longer. For all I know he's not even involved."

"Carter can make as much trouble as he wants." Alexander spared a glance inside the ballroom. His brother had his phone pressed to his ear, while Candy examined her nails. "Nicholas is likely talking to Ben right now. I recorded Carter's threat, and the two security guards heard it. There's nothing else to be done tonight but try to enjoy our evening."

"I'd really like that."

Nicholas met them at the door. "The security detail has Carter detained in the basement. The police are on their way. Violating the order of protection—at a party—won't get him more than a couple of hours in jail, but by the time they process him and he gets in touch with his lawyer, it'll be 2:00 a.m."

"Good. We'll be home by then, and I'm not letting Elizabeth out of my sight this weekend." Alexander brushed a kiss against her cheek. "We'll stop by your flat tomorrow and pick up some clothes for you. You'll stay with me for a few days. All right?"

Elizabeth grimaced as she nodded. "Okay. I can get my neighbor to watch River."

Nicholas rested a hand on her shoulder, earning a glare from Alexander. "Once we bring the Feds in on Monday, you'll be legally protected. No more lawsuit, nothing they can do to you. Alex will make sure you don't have to deal with those arseholes this weekend."

She shivered. "I know. I...I did my job. I always thought Carter was a misogynist, but he was never mean. Merely dismissive. This isn't like him."

"Which is why I'm keeping you close," Alexander said with a tender kiss to her knuckles. "Let's get back inside. I believe dinner is about to begin." Alexander kept his hand at the small of Elizabeth's back. He'd meant what he'd said. She would be safe. She was his, and he always protected his own.

---

DINNER WAS PASSABLE: tiny pillows of pastry filled with a salmon mousse, lobster, bitter greens, and whipped potatoes. Elizabeth relaxed after a glass of scotch and a few well-placed kisses to her neck and behind her ear. Soon, she was laughing, and the rosy glow returned to her cheeks.

Throughout the meal, they exchanged stories. She told him about her first week in Boston, getting lost, discovering Mike's Pastry in the North End, and subsequently gaining five pounds in a little over a month from an overdose of cannoli.

Alexander's stories centered around his time in the Royal Army, including the attack that had left him with a scar that bisected his chest and the tattoo he had on his right arm. "When I recovered from the grenade attack, my division brought me to the tattoo parlor before I reported in to my commander. All five of us were inked that day."

"Will you show it to me later?" she asked, trailing her hand over his bicep.

"Oh, most definitely."

After the crème brûlée dishes had been cleared away and coffee served, an adjoining room opened up, glittering with white lights, and a ten-piece band started to play.

"I'm not a great dancer," Elizabeth said wistfully. "Darren always said I had two left feet."

Alexander wrapped his arms around her. "Elizabeth," he said, kissing the tip of her nose. "I thought we'd already established that Darren is an idiot." He swept her towards the dance floor, holding her so securely that she couldn't possibly fall. "Smile, *chérie*," he whispered into her ear. "Tonight, I plan on showing you exactly who you are. I want that dress off of you, my silks binding you to my bed, and you begging for more as I taste you."

Elizabeth shivered. She followed his lead, her feet landing lightly only centimeters from his. They waltzed around the dance floor, their bodies pressed together, moving as one. "What are you thinking?" he asked.

"That I haven't locked myself in my own head since we sat down to dinner. That this party is stuffy and overdone, but being with you is refreshing. That I could talk to you all night, but I really want you naked." Flecks of gold shone in her eyes, and Alexander wondered just how far he'd already fallen, and how much further he could go.

"If it wouldn't be seen as a snub, I would carry you out of here right now," Alexander replied.

They danced off and on for an hour, and Elizabeth never faltered a single step. Her cheeks glowed. Alexander shed his jacket and longed to loosen his tie. When the tango began, she begged for a rest, and they moved off the dance floor.

A tall man with dark brown hair shorn close to his head hailed the two of them from next to one of the open bars. Alexander guided Elizabeth over to him. "Governor, may I introduce my companion? This is Elizabeth Bennett."

"It's a pleasure, Miss Bennett. Call me Marco." The governor took her offered hand and shook it firmly. "I've heard rumors that you've tamed one of the city's most eligible and cantankerous bachelors."

Elizabeth laughed, light and musical, the practiced tone she'd used on the press all night. "I don't think anyone tames him, Governor. Marco. If anything, I've brought out his cantankerous side even more. He doesn't seem to like me out of his sight."

"I can't say I blame him. However, I would like to steal him away for a brief moment. Business and all." The governor's smile faded.

"Of course. I need some fresh air anyway." Though her words were polite, Alexander noticed the tick in her jaw at being relegated to the sidelines. In that single moment, he knew. He'd fallen for her, and he might not ever let her go.

"Marco, Elizabeth has a head for business, and there's nothing I wish to hide from her. You can speak freely."

The governor raised a brow but then inclined his head as he gestured to a table far from the crowd.

"It's coming up on the end of the year. I've sent several requests to your office this week inquiring as to the timing of your donation to my re-election campaign, and none of them have been answered."

*Money? This was about money?* "I'm afraid I've been a bit distracted of late," Alexander said. "All of the companies under the Fairhaven umbrella are undergoing a full financial audit. It's something we do every few years, and it's fallen on me and my brother directly to oversee it. I'll get you a check next week."

"Alexander," Elizabeth said. The drape of her fingers tickled the fine hairs on the back of his hand. "Trust me on this. If the governor can wait, make your donation on January 1st. It'll be a lot easier tax-wise when you file next year, and you'll be able to contribute a bit more." She leaned closer and pressed her lips to his ear. "You're going to get a major settlement when this is through. The political donation in the next tax year will help offset your bottom line."

"You heard the woman, Marco. I'm sorry, but we'll make the bulk of our donation on January 1st. To ameliorate the delay, I'll add ten percent. Is that acceptable?"

"Oh, quite," the governor said. "I apologize for bringing down the evening with business, but a politician's job is never done. I love this state too much to give it up."

Alexander's world tilted on its axis. He knew how the man felt. He couldn't give Elizabeth up. He wouldn't. Not if she'd have him. He rose and shook the governor's hand. "It was a pleasure, Marco. We've had a lovely time, but, I'm afraid we must be going. Elizabeth and I have a…binding engagement to get to."

# CHAPTER FIFTEEN

*A*lexander tugged at his bowtie, loosening the knot and then winding the silk around his fingers. Elizabeth tracked his movements, remembering the silk and hemp rope he'd wound around her wrists the last time they'd played.

He'd been quiet, though he'd kept her tucked against him the entire ride. Did he think she'd run away? Or could he sense her nerves? As the limo hit a pothole, Elizabeth couldn't stifle her grunt of surprise. The noise seemed to snap Alexander out of his thoughts, and he brushed a curl away from her cheek.

"Are you all right?"

"I'm nervous." Desperate for a distraction, Elizabeth slid the thin strip of silk from his fingers and let the soft material trail over her palm.

A possessive sound rumbled in Alexander's chest. "Give me your hands."

His voice sent warmth pooling in her belly. No longer the concerned boyfriend, his stare, his tone, and even the set of his shoulders said they were now about to play.

The silk strip wound around her wrists, and his deft fingers secured the knot as she trembled. She hadn't paused a breath before obeying him, and as he guided her bound hands over his head, she stared up at him, waiting for his next command.

"You are mine tonight, Elizabeth. From now on, you will give me audible responses. What is your safeword?"

"Red."

"Very good. Do you willingly put yourself in my hands? He stroked her sides, lightly digging his fingers into her hips.

"Y-yes," she stammered. The thin scrap of silk under her dress was already wet. He lifted her into his lap, and the bulge of his erection pressed against her.

A predatory smile quirked his lips. "I want you out of that dress."

Elizabeth flushed. Not here. Not in the limo where she'd have to exit the car. "Alexander."

"You have a cloak." He reached around her, finding the tiny catch under her left arm. He flicked it open, slid down the zipper, and rolled the dress down to her waist. Her cloak fell open. "Shite. You look...exquisite."

Under her dress, Elizabeth wore a fitted golden corset. It pushed her breasts up to form soft pillows, tapered at her waist, and ended below her belly. Alexander's gaze roved hungrily over her body. He laid her down on the seat, guiding her hands to the grip bar on the far door. "Don't let go."

The dress shimmied down her hips, then landed on the seat across from her. Under the corset, gold silk barely covered her mound. Alexander ran his hands up her thighs. Velvet and heat and an itch she couldn't scratch. His fingers danced under the silk at her hips, and she quaked with desire.

"Alexander," she gasped.

"Yes, *chérie*? You want something?" He teased her inner thighs with tickling kisses. His hands on her spread knees kept her from writhing completely off the limo's seat.

"Touch me, please."

"Oh, but Elizabeth, you know that you are mine tonight. Mine to do with as I wish. Are you certain you want me to touch you?"

"Yes, please!" Two minutes and she'd already reached the point of begging. His teeth scraped up her inner thigh, and she cried out and shoved her hips towards his face.

"Hold still," he commanded. "You will not move, Elizabeth. Do you understand?"

"Uh-huh, God. Please."

Alexander grabbed the silk panties and yanked them aside. Two fingers plunged deep into her drenched channel, and Elizabeth screamed. Her hips bucked and caught Alexander in the chin. He withdrew his fingers and growled at her. "That is one, Elizabeth."

So far gone, she didn't respond to his words until he cupped her chin and urged her to meet his gaze. "Did you hear me?"

"N-no."

"That was one. One time you disobeyed me. Each time, I will count. If you reach ten, you will be punished. Do you understand me?"

Elizabeth struggled to sit up, but Alexander pressed his hands to her shoulders. "I told you not to move. Now answer me. Do you understand?"

"Um, yes."

"When we get home, I'll bind you to make things easier on you, but for now, I want you perfectly still. Do not come until I say."

"O-o-kay."

His teeth bit down on her inner thigh, and Elizabeth gasped as her clit throbbed. Alexander kissed and licked a burning trail towards her mound, growling softly when he tasted her arousal. "Spread your legs wider," he said as he lifted her left leg to rest on his shoulder.

A single finger slipped inside her, swirled around, then trailed down her inner thigh, followed closely by his lips.

"You are delicious. Summer rain. Almonds." Every hot breath sent goose bumps racing along her skin. Their combined scents and the rich leather of the limo coalesced into an intoxicating, heady fragrance she wanted to live in. Her thighs trembled as she struggled to hold back, and she couldn't catch her breath.

"Please," she mewled. "I can't."

"You can," he growled.

"No." The hoarse, desperate whisper took all of her focus. Her inner walls clenched and she couldn't help herself. When he slid two fingers inside of her and curled them up into her G-spot, she lost control. Her channel drew tightly together around him, and he bit her inner thigh, hard.

"Not yet!"

She was too far gone. As the orgasm overtook her, she screamed. Tears trailed down her cheeks, back towards her ears. He grabbed her bound hands and pulled her up against him with his arms banding around her.

She collapsed, boneless, into his embrace. "I'm sorry," she whispered. "I couldn't—"

He silenced her with a gentle shushing sound. "That is two, Elizabeth."

"I tried."

"I know. And this is new to you. But there are rules to our play —both for my enjoyment *and* your safety. Now relax. We're almost home." He tugged the knot in the silk, and her wrists were freed immediately. He held her in his lap, wrapped her in the cloak, and let her body shake against his.

The limo pulled to a stop, and Thomas rapped on the privacy screen. Alexander folded the discarded dress over his arm and cupped her cheek. "Can you walk?"

"Yes." She pulled the cloak tightly around her body. It covered more of her than the dress, but she was still embarrassed by what they'd done only a few feet from Alexander's driver. He must have heard her scream. But Thomas averted his eyes when Alexander alighted and helped Elizabeth out of the limo. A man in a dark blue suit opened the front door of the home so they could enter, but kept his eyes downcast as Elizabeth passed.

"Thank you, Samuel. That is all for the evening. Elizabeth and I will be upstairs until morning."

"Very well, sir. Good night."

Once Alexander had shut the bedroom door, he stared hungrily at Elizabeth. "Take off your cloak."

Elizabeth loosened the button and dropped the shimmering material onto a chair. In nothing but her heels, the golden corset, and soaked panties, she felt exposed but also...appreciated as Alexander smiled. "Beautiful. I am a lucky man, Elizabeth."

He swept her against him and claimed her mouth with a savage intensity. Grasping at anything to ground herself, she fisted his shirt, then, when that wasn't enough, ran her fingers through his hair. When he released her, she found herself pressed against the bed. She hadn't even noticed that he'd lifted her up to the platform.

"Look at me, *chérie*." His gaze smoldered, and she was powerless to look away. "What are we at now?"

"Um, two?"

"Very good," he said with a smile. "Sit down and relax for a moment. I need to choose the silks for you tonight."

"Alexander?" Elizabeth asked before he turned away.

"Yes?"

"Will you, I mean, can I ask a question?" With so much spare time while Alexander had been in meetings and Ben had been dealing with her court case, Elizabeth had read everything she could find on BDSM. Some Doms preferred their subs didn't speak without permission.

Alexander cupped her cheek. "Unless I tell you to be quiet, you can *always* ask questions. I want you to enjoy this, Elizabeth. Tell me everything you're feeling. Everything you're thinking. And ask any questions you want. I know this is very different than anything you have done before and I don't want you to regret tonight."

She blew out a breath, relieved. "Will you tell me what everything is used for?"

Alexander held out his hand, then led her to the cabinet. "Some of my toys you will need to experience to understand, but I will tell you what I can." He withdrew a silk blindfold and raised his brow.

"I know what that's used for."

Tilting his head, Alexander pondered the rest of the items all arranged on neat pegs and shelves. He selected two strips of long silk and hemp rope with metal eyelets at each end, along with two black leather cuffs. "Remember your safe word, Elizabeth," he said as he fastened the first cuff around her wrist.

Her heartbeat pounded in her ears. The padded leather didn't hurt, but Alexander tested the cuff by tugging on a metal ring attached to the side, and Elizabeth tried to stifle her shudder. As he secured her other wrist, sliding the diamond bracelet up so it wouldn't get caught, she sucked her lip beneath her teeth.

"These will be easier than the rope, *chérie*. Are you comfortable?" Alexander cupped her cheek and brushed a thumb over her lip. "If you need a moment, say yellow."

"I'm...okay," she managed. "Just...nervous."

Draping the long strips of silk over his shoulder, he returned to the cabinet. Two wide pieces of silk with leather buckles confused her. "Wh-what are those?"

"You are an active one, my sweet sub. Always wriggling. With what I've planned for you—for us—you could very easily hurt me if you move too quickly." Alexander dropped to one knee and fastened the silk around her right thigh. Thin strips of soft rubber on the inside of the wrap held it in place a few inches above her knee. "I'm going to bind you well tonight, Elizabeth. But I can release you in a few seconds if you need."

He finished his preparation with padded ankle cuffs, then stepped back to admire her. "Stunning."

When Alexander hefted the flogger he'd used on her the last time, she shivered.

"Would you like to know what this feels like on your bare skin?"

"Yes," she whispered.

He tossed the flogger on the bed, where it thudded softly. "There is only one more item in here that I want to use on you tonight, but I would like to keep it a secret for now. Will you trust me?"

"I—" Elizabeth met his gaze, finding a mix of compassion, concern, and lust churning in his eyes. "Yes."

"Then turn around and wait for my next command."

A strange sound, half rustling, half clinking, reached her ears, but she resisted the temptation to glance back over her shoulder.

Alexander pressed his lips to her neck, then kissed up towards her ear. "Remember, Elizabeth. *Red* stops everything. If you need me to slow down, back off a bit, say *yellow*. We won't abandon our play, but *yellow* will give you the time you need to decide if you need to safeword or whether we can continue. Do you understand?"

His velvet lips made it hard to think, but she forced herself to focus on his voice. "Yes. Red stops everything. Yellow slows things down."

"Brilliant. Now come with me."

# CHAPTER SIXTEEN

"*B*ack on the bed. Against the pillows, knees up, legs apart," Alexander said as he led her up to the platform.

Once he'd positioned himself between her knees, he ran his hands up her thighs. "Remove my shirt, Elizabeth. I want to feel your hands on me."

One button at a time, she parted the crisp material, until she could peel the shirt from his shoulders. A chiseled chest gave way to a six-pack that led to a *V* angling into his dress pants. A deep scar carved a trail across the right side of his chest with smaller imperfections spread out around it. Elizabeth ran her fingers over the long-healed wound, then leaned forward to kiss the length of the scar.

Next, she turned her attention to the tattoo on his arm—a lion perched on top of a crown. That, too, she kissed, savoring the taste of him. Up to his neck, then a quick nip to his ear, and Alexander groaned.

When she reached for the button on his pants, he captured her hands. "That's enough for now, Elizabeth," he said as he returned her hands to her sides. "Do not move."

Alexander sunk his fingers into her tresses, pulling one hair pin after another from her golden locks. Once her curls fell in gentle waves across her shoulders, he fastened the blindfold over her eyes. The loss of her sight made her heart race, but his presence, his heat reassured her. "Comfortable?"

"Yes," she breathed.

He cupped the back of her neck, then brushed a tender kiss to her lips. "I will never leave you alone while blindfolded or bound, but I won't always be touching you. All you have to do is say my name, and I'll answer."

Elizabeth drew in a sharp breath as he released her and tried to listen for him. "Okay."

Another gasp as he guided her hips forward. Settling deeper into the silky pillows, she tried not to panic when he pressed her left palm to his lips, then stretched her arm over her head. After two snaps, he tugged on whatever bound her to the headboard, and then she couldn't move her arm at all.

"Still green, *chérie*?"

Was she? After she tested the restraint again, she said, "Yes." But then he disappeared, and she tried to swivel her head, hoping to catch some glimpse of him, even though the blindfold obscured every bit of light in the room. "Al—"

As she'd started to call his name, he lifted her other wrist, then kissed her palm. "I told you I wouldn't leave you. Trust me, Elizabeth. I will never lie to you."

"I'm sorry," she whispered as he secured her other wrist and caressed her arm.

"Shhh. No apologies for this. You are doing very well." He brushed his lips against hers, and she strained to keep contact with him when he pulled away. Gentle fingers drew her panties down her legs. "I love your body, Elizabeth." The bare skin of her mound became his singular focus for a brief moment, and then he made a satisfied *mmm* sound. "So smooth. So sweet."

Her hips moved of their own accord, and Elizabeth tried to

dig her heels into the mattress for purchase. "Please," she whispered. "I can't hold still when you do that."

Tiny spasms made her thighs tremble as he kissed a trail down to her knee. "Are you asking me to bind your legs?"

"Yes," she cried as he danced those talented fingers over her folds.

"You are a joy, Elizabeth. But I won't restrain your legs yet. Wriggle to your heart's content."

Kisses traced a burning trail down one thigh and back up, and his hands held her hips steady as he slipped his tongue very briefly between her slick folds. She cried out and quaked uncontrollably, but he quickly withdrew and kissed down the other thigh.

His weight left the bed, and a drawer opened. "This is something I don't keep in my cabinet. It also contains no silk, but I think you'll enjoy it." He pressed a firm, cool piece of rubber to her channel. A vibrator? It slipped inside her and pressed against her G-spot. Another piece of it rested against her clit. Even the subtle pressure was almost too much. She gave a tiny moan and shuddered in her restraints. A click and the vibrator buzzed to life. Elizabeth yelped. "Oh God. I...I can't. Please."

Alexander crushed his lips down on hers and swept his tongue into her mouth. She moaned into his kiss, writhing, desperate to release the pressure gathering inside of her. As she thought she couldn't possibly hold on another second, the vibrator shut off and she whimpered.

His hands smoothed down her sides and slid behind her back. He deftly unhooked the dozen little catches of her corset and tossed the material away. Through the haze of her body's arousal, she was dimly aware that she was completely naked other than Alexander's silks.

He palmed her breasts and squeezed them gently. "Perfect."

She'd always thought her breasts were too small, but Alexander cherished them, stroking and pinching, kissing and licking, sucking and biting. Shocks of pain and pleasure zipped through her body. His mouth fastened around one nipple and the vibrator started up again. She flew towards the edge, so ready to let go with her orgasm, but then the vibrator stopped, leaving her panting. His lips gave a single parting kiss to her right nipple, and he moved back on the bed a few inches. Her chest heaved as she fought for breath.

"Please, Alexander. I can't . . ."

"You keep saying that, Elizabeth. I think you can. Now, I have one last little trick up my sleeve before I make you come. This is something I very much enjoy." He sucked on a nipple until the tender bud was firm. Then, a searing pain consumed her. Her hips bucked, her ass came off the bed, and she screamed as the sensation tore through her, down to her pussy.

"Yellow! Oh God, yellow."

Alexander slid his fingers into her channel and brushed his lips against her ear. "Breathe, *chérie*. The clamp is on the lightest setting. I have to attach the other one before we continue."

She shook her head violently. She needed the blindfold off. Her arms pulled involuntarily at the silks binding her. Metal *clinked* above her head. "No, don't. Yellow. Please. Yellow."

"Let me try one thing, Elizabeth. One thing and if you are still at yellow, I will remove the clamp, all right?"

Elizabeth could barely breathe. Her nipple throbbed, but her clit pulsed with the same cadence. How could this much pain push her this close to the edge of ecstasy? His hands on her skin moved in calming circles. "Uh-huh," she gasped.

The vibrator buzzed to life, and the combination of pain and pleasure overwhelmed her. She keened softly, pressing her hips into the mattress to try to release the intense pressure gathering inside her. Her toes curled against the sheets. "Oh God. I need to come."

"Not yet, Elizabeth," Alexander said sharply as the vibrator turned off.

"Please," she sobbed until her mouth was smothered by Alexander's firm lips and his fingers teased her free nipple until the pain exploded over the sensitive nerve endings from the second clamp. This time, though, his kiss and the pleasure from the vibrator combined to distract her. Bare skin and firm muscle pressed against her, over the clamps. A soft braid of silk lay between her breasts, and she wrapped her legs around Alexander's waist, desperate to feel...more. All of him.

Alexander chuckled as he toyed with the diamond hanging from her left ear. "Not against the clamps now?"

Shaking her head, she begged, "I need you. Please." The delicious ache in her arms and the helplessness of being unable to move or see thrilled her.

"Not yet." Alexander freed himself from her legs, then secured her ankle cuffs to the thick pieces of silk wrapped around her upper thighs. "You are the most beautiful woman I've ever seen, Elizabeth. I want to watch you come."

Every breath tortured her further, and she focused on one word. *Come. He's going to let me come soon. Hold on. Hold on. Hold on.*

"How should I do it, I wonder?" he asked. His fingers trailed down her inner thigh. She wasn't ticklish, but his light touch sent tremors and quakes all through her. The vibrator sprang to life again. Her channel clenched, and she pulled at the silk that bound her hands.

"Please, Alexander," she cried.

The silk between her breasts lifted, and he pulled on the clamps just enough. Whatever invisible force that connected her nipples to her pussy shattered her from the inside out. "Come now, Elizabeth," he commanded. With one more tug on the silk, she flew apart. His name exploded from her lips, and her body strained against the silk that held her securely.

She didn't even notice when the vibrator was removed. Alexander rubbed her arms, brushing her lips with gentle kisses, and crooning to her.

"Elizabeth, are you with me?"

"Y-yes," she whispered. "What... God. What was that?"

"You respond so well to bondage, *chérie*. So well. There is so much I want to introduce you to," he murmured. He kissed the tears from her cheeks. "Do you want more?"

Elizabeth's breath caught in her throat. "Y-yes. But I don't think I can."

"Will you let me try?" Alexander asked as he caressed her shoulder. When she nodded, then managed a vague sound of agreement, he spread her knees, his warm palms pressed to her inner thighs. Still riding the high of her orgasm, Elizabeth jerked when he slipped a finger inside of her.

Her mewl escaped as she spasmed again, and she almost said *yellow*, but then Alexander kissed her right knee. Back and forth he went, left leg, right leg, left leg again, kissing all the way up to the juncture of her thighs. Elizabeth moaned when he slid his hands underneath her to cup her ass, holding her firmly.

So secure, unable to move, the blackness of the blindfold all encompassing, Elizabeth had to imagine Alexander's body, his face, and his smile as he praised her for some response or another from her body.

"More," she breathed, and he rewarded her by swiping his tongue over her sensitive folds.

"My God, you taste exquisite," he said, his voice almost a growl. Teasing with tongue and teeth, nipping, laving her clit, exploring the round globes of her ass with deft fingers.

Returning to her slick folds, his breathing changed as he shifted the intensity of his ministrations. Two fingers twisted inside of her, swirling around her G-spot. Elizabeth's hips threatened to come off the mattress, but the firm pressure of his mouth on her kept her grounded.

"Mmmm. Alexander. Mm-hmmm, need..."

"Come, Elizabeth."

The silk between her breasts twitched again, tugging on her

nipples. She whimpered, her entire body imploding with sensation. Inhuman, guttural, desperate sounds filled her ears. She only recognized the sounds as hers when she ran out of air and had to suck in a gasping breath. Her channel clenched around his fingers, over and over again, and Alexander drank her in, the growls and grunts of desire vibrating against her.

Time stopped. Her arms hung limply in the restraints, her entire body spent, but he wasn't done. When he pulled away with a final kiss to her smooth mound, she let her head fall back against the pillows.

Alexander slid away from her, and the pressure of his body on the bed disappeared. Elizabeth wasn't thinking. She couldn't. But she knew he was close, releasing first her left arm, then her right, then her ankles. He massaged her tight muscles, alternating his firm, kneading strokes with kisses.

"I'm going to remove the clamps now. It will hurt a bit. Are you ready?" The concern in his voice surprised her until the pressure on her left nipple fell away, and blood rushed back into the sensitive flesh.

Elizabeth sobbed, incoherent and dazed. "No-no-noooo." Alexander blew on her nipple, then soothed the throbbing nub with his tongue. When he'd freed and tended to her other breast, he gathered her in his arms.

"Do you want more?"

"Can't," she whispered.

"Not yet, then. A few minutes to rest first. Then you can decide." He shifted, then pressed a bottle of water to her lips. "Drink a little."

She obeyed, resting her head against his chest. He smelled so good: sandalwood, vanilla, and cloves. Muscles flexed as he unfastened the silk wraps from her thighs. "Enough of those for tonight." As Elizabeth tried to offer him her wrists, he chuckled. "Oh, I'm not done with the cuffs yet. How do you feel?"

"Shaky. I want to see you." Holding her breath, Elizabeth

hoped Alexander would remove the blindfold, but he merely brushed her cheek with his knuckle.

"Not yet. This is part of the trust you give me, Elizabeth. I will push you tonight. I have pushed you. Trust me a bit longer, yes?"

Though she didn't think she could possibly take any more, he'd been right about everything else. Even the damn nipple clamps. "I trust you."

"Can you stand for me?" Alexander lifted her gently. Boneless, she only swayed once before she found her footing. "I want you to enjoy my flogger, Elizabeth, I want to see your lovely arse reddened and show you how intense an orgasm can be with a little pain added in. But I need your consent. This will hurt—a little. You can stop me at any time. Do I have your permission to keep going?"

A single finger traced down her cheek, and she melted, any reservations she had disappearing in the heat of Alexander's touch. "You can...keep going."

Alexander wrapped his arm around her body and guided her forward. Panic set in as she feared she might fall off the platform. Her stomach lurched, and she tried to pull away. Alexander slapped her ass sharply. "That is three, Elizabeth. You need to trust me. I will not let you fall."

She knew he wouldn't, but something about being blind heightened every fear. "I'm sorry."

He kissed her then, reassuring. "As this is your first time, I'll indulge you, but one day soon, you *will* endure a punishment from me." Sweeping her up into his arms, he carried her across the room.

From the few minutes she'd been in his bedroom without the blindfold, she thought she knew where they were when he set her down next to something smooth and cool. "Oh God," she whispered. "Alexander."

"One word and I stop, *chérie*." He spread her legs, and with gentle caresses lifted each foot up onto a platform and attached her ankle cuffs to the St. Andrew's Cross. Kisses trailed along her shoulders until he raised first one arm, then the other, and urged her to curl her hands around thin bars high on the arms of the cross. Once he'd secured her, a nibble to her ear sent tremors down her legs. "You are a vision."

The rustle of fabric as he unzipped his pants gave her a thrill. Suddenly, his entire naked body pressed to hers, his skin hot enough to brand her and his cock jutting urgently against her hip.

"I will be inside you soon, but not before I redden that arse of yours. Will you take a bit of pain for me?"

"Y-yes."

The soft falls of Alexander's flogger trailed over her arms. A bead of moisture rolled down her inner thigh, to her knee, and tickled her calf. Why was she so incredibly turned on? Resting her forehead against the wood, she let the tiny spasms from her body's pleasure scrape her nipples along the cross.

Alexander touched nearly every inch of exposed skin with the flogger. No pressure, no stinging pain, only soft suede.

Palming one of her ass cheeks, he rubbed, gently at first, then harder. When he'd tended to both cheeks, he nipped her shoulder.

"Relax, Elizabeth." She drew comfort from his smooth voice. "Count for me."

She'd barely processed his words when the flogger snapped across her ass. "One," she cried. A stinging burn spread over her left butt cheek. The second strike came only a second later. "T-two."

The next two strikes fell harder. The two after that, harder still. Her ass was on fire, but her pussy dripped with need. As Alexander struck lower, down to the crease between her ass and thighs, down halfway to her knees, then back up again, her voice faltered.

"I ache for you, Elizabeth. Your skin glows, and the sounds

you make, my God, you are perfect." At twenty strikes, the flogger hit the floor, and Alexander's lips pressed to her ear.

"I'm going to take you now, Elizabeth. If you'll let me."

"Please," she moaned.

Ankles, then wrists were released, and he caught her in his arms when she collapsed. Blind, aching for him, she ground her hips against his length, and he groaned.

As her ass hit the satin sheets, she winced at the pain. "I'll soothe that ache soon," he purred. "And in a moment, I hope you won't even notice it."

A drawer opened, foil crinkled, and he let out a pent-up breath as he nudged her channel. At her moan, he slid deeper, letting her get used to the size of him. Once he'd pushed all the way in, he pinned her wrists to the mattress. "I want to see you come again for me."

As his cock rasped against her clit, she sped to the edge of the precipice. "Alexander! God, help me!"

He wrapped an arm around her, his bulk pressing down on her torso. Never had she been so desperate. The pressure in her core exploded in a kaleidoscope of colors behind her blindfold, a roar of blood in her ears, and a hoarse, guttural yell from her throat. Alexander shouted her name, thrust twice more, and lost himself in her.

# CHAPTER SEVENTEEN

*A*lexander slipped into bed and pressed his naked body to hers. "You were exquisite tonight, Elizabeth. I...shite."

The most intense sex of her life, more chocolate-covered strawberries, and a hot shower combined to leave Elizabeth's mind hazy, but his oath broke through the fog. "What?" Wriggling in his arms, she met his gaze.

"I think I'm falling in love with you."

Her world ground to a halt. "You...can't be. N-not yet."

*Too soon.*

Nothing could have prepared her for Alexander Fairhaven. His sculpted body, his arrogant attitude, but most of all, his penchant for surprising her. How could he love her already?

Regret swam in his eyes as he cupped the back of her neck. His kiss drove all rational thought from her mind, and despite her exhaustion, arousal heated her core. As he drew away, however, his words echoed in her mind. Only his finger to her lips silenced her protest.

"I shouldn't have said anything. But...I've been down this road, Elizabeth. I'm no whelp. No one has ever made me as happy as you do."

"The past few weeks have been wonderful," Elizabeth murmured. "And I care—" The buzzing of her cell phone saved her from the eventual "but." Who the hell would be calling her at this hour? Alexander retrieved her purse, and Elizabeth frowned when she checked the screen.

"What's wrong, Mrs. McGillis?"

Alexander sat next to her, worry pinching his brows.

"I'm sorry to bother you, Lizzie, but that damn cat of yours bit me hard enough to draw blood. She's howling from the top of the cabinets. The young couple that lives next door already came over to complain about the noise. I've tried everything: shaking the food bowl, turning off the lights, dangling her feather toy in front of her..."

"That's not like her. Crap. I'll...um...I'll come home and take her to the boarders in the morning. I'm really sorry about the bite. Are you going to be okay?"

Once her elderly neighbor confirmed the injury wasn't serious, Elizabeth hung up and then dropped her head into her hands. "I can drop River at her vet in the morning, but I can't leave her alone tonight. She's never once swiped at me *or* Mrs. McGillis. I'm worried there's something wrong with her."

"I'll take you to get her."

Elizabeth gaped as he strode naked into his closet. "What are you doing? It's after one. I'll call a cab."

Alexander's voice echoed. "Do you think I'm letting you out of my sight this weekend? Hardly, *chérie*. Not after what happened with Carter this evening. We need clothes for you anyway. River can stay here tonight. All weekend if you'd like."

As he emerged, clad in jeans and a tight green sweater, Elizabeth tugged on her dress. Needles of pain stabbed at her toes when she stood on the towering heels. At least she'd be able to pack comfortable clothes—and shoes.

Alexander draped the wrap over her shoulders. "I hope River doesn't mind sharing the bed."

ALEXANDER AND ELIZABETH were halfway up the steps to her building's outer door when tires squealed, and a car lurched to the curb only a few feet from Alexander's Mercedes. He stepped in front of Elizabeth but quickly relaxed as his brother jumped out of the Audi.

Nicholas still wore his tuxedo from the ball, but he'd ditched his tie—and his date. "Goddamn son of a bitch! If I ever see him again, I'm going to shove a squash ball so far down—"

Alexander cringed and met his brother at the bottom of the steps while Elizabeth huddled against the door for warmth.

"How did you even know we were here, Nicholas?"

"I went to your house first. Samuel told me. Smythe—the Board's secretary for fuck's sake—broke his confidentiality agreement. He's *friends* with Carter. Foyle's working on the lawsuit against him right now, and Ben's reached out to the Feds on Elizabeth's behalf, but it's fucking two in the morning, and he can't get anyone to answer the bloody phone. We've lost any chance to blindside them with the lawsuit. And given how angry Carter was earlier, I'm starting to worry about both of you. Increase security." Nicholas glanced at the Mercedes, clearly surprised Alexander hadn't brought the limo, and shook his head. "Or get some, for that matter."

Elizabeth hurried down the steps and clutched Alexander's arm. An icy breeze flapped her dress, but she barely noticed. "If they know...they'll come after me."

Wrapping his arm around her, Alexander pressed a kiss to the top of her head. "Ben put enough in motion today to ensure you're protected. Even now. We'll get you to the federal prosecutor in the morning. Sooner if Ben can get him on the phone. This isn't good news, but it won't ruin you. I won't let it."

She wanted to believe him, but under his self-assured smile

and intense green eyes, worry lingered. "I have to get River. Then...can we get out of here?"

"Nicholas, we're going to get Elizabeth's cat. See if Ben can meet us back at my house in an hour? I'll call William to arrange extra security for the next few days." Alexander and his brother exchanged glances, and Elizabeth almost asked them what they weren't telling her, but Nicholas was already dialing.

As Alexander held the outer door open for her, Nicholas swore.

"Oh, bloody hell, no!" After a breath, his cheeks turned red. "That little wanker is going to wish he was never born. Alex?" Nicholas tipped his chin at his brother. "Ben and Foyle need you. We need to notify the Fairhaven Charities executive board as well, and we need to do it now. We can't reach your admin assistant."

Alexander almost growled. "Can't this wait twenty minutes?"

"No," Nicholas said. "Carter's got a judge in his back pocket. He's suing us—the whole Fairhaven umbrella as well as the three of us individually—for defamation of character. Foyle just got the notification from the very pissed-off clerk who was dragged out of bed to file the paperwork. Carter's gone to the *Beantown Babbler,* and they're running some sort of libelous screed on us tomorrow —all about our *vendetta* against them for firing Elizabeth. He's not going to get away with this."

Alexander shook his head and blew out a tense breath. "*Beantown Babbler* has hated us ever since you dumped their Style editor's sister. We have to stop this now."

Elizabeth laid her hand on Alexander's arm. "Deal with this. I'll be fine. It's a secure building. Come up when you're done, or I'll be down in ten minutes with River." She kissed his cheek. "I'm really sorry for all of this."

"You did nothing, Elizabeth. Nothing but steal my heart. I confess I do not want it back." Alexander trailed his hand down her back, over her ass, and squeezed. "Hurry. I want to be safely home before the story breaks."

She forced a smile. "River's going to need a litter box. I don't really want to bring hers in the car."

"Samuel can handle that. I'll text him."

"Okay. Be right back."

Elizabeth dashed through the building's foyer and jabbed the elevator button. Alexander and Nicholas paced, each barking into their phones. Hopefully, none of the neighbors would complain.

As she pushed through her apartment door, she called, "River? Come here, kitty!"

A thud of feline paws and a blur of orange streaked across the living room and dove under the sofa.

"Shit, sweetie, what's gotten into you?" Elizabeth got down on all fours to peer under the sofa. The cat crouched, her tail three sizes bigger than usual, and her teeth bared. Elizabeth reached out, and the cat growled at her.

"River!" She yanked her hand back. "Fine. But in a few minutes, you're going to have come out from under there."

Teetering on her heels, Elizabeth ran a hand through her messy hair as she glanced around the room. Her laptop drew her gaze. She should bring that, too. As she headed for her darkened bedroom, she made a short mental list of necessities. Her toe caught on a loose floorboard, but she righted herself quickly and glared down at her feet in the semi-darkness. She'd been lucky she hadn't tripped and broken her neck before Alexander had picked her up tonight.

*Another maintenance request the super can ignore.*

As she flicked on the bedside lamp, a rustle of fabric and a soft exhalation of air sent terror flooding her. Spinning around, she was about to scream when a gloved hand slapped over her mouth, and an arm banded tightly around her torso, pinning her arms to her sides.

"Well, now. You weren't supposed to be here tonight, Miss Bennett. But you've saved me a trip later in the week, I suppose."

Elizabeth thrashed and screamed behind the glove, but so little sound emerged she feared no one would hear her. Her assailant hauled her up so her feet dangled off the ground. She tried to kick at him with her sharp heels but found only air.

"Keep quiet. If you don't, I'll make your last few minutes very painful."

*Oh God. He's going to kill me.*

Alexander. He'd come for her eventually, but did she have that long?

Her captor dragged her towards her living room. Elizabeth bucked and tried to wedge her feet against the door frame, but the man holding her slammed Elizabeth into the wall. Her hip and shoulder throbbed, and she let herself go limp, hoping to save her strength.

As the man shoved her face first onto the couch, she flailed her arms, trying to scratch, punch, hit...anything to get him off of her. Too soon, her lungs burned, and she feared she'd pass out.

"Stop fighting me, Miss Bennett." He pressed his fingers underneath her arm between two of her ribs. Every nerve ending in her body caught fire. The pain overwhelmed all conscious thought, and her tears soaked into the upholstery.

"Hurts, doesn't it?"

She needed more oxygen and tried to whine into the cushions. The asshole wrapped a hand in her hair but didn't let her up. "I'm well-trained in advanced torture techniques. I can cause you more pain than you could possibly imagine and never leave a single mark. So you're going to behave. You're going to take the pills I give you without a fuss, and I'll let you die peacefully. Otherwise, I'll gag you, and we'll have several hours together before I force the pills down your throat. Understand?"

The pressure holding her head against the cushions let up slightly, and Elizabeth nodded.

*He doesn't know about Alexander.*

How long had it been? If she fought, if she could stand the pain until Alexander came to get her, maybe she'd have a chance. Or maybe Alexander would die too.

"Now we're going to get up, calmly and quietly retrieve a glass of water from the kitchen, and return to the couch. Once you swallow all twenty pills, you're going to lie down. I promise you'll feel no pain. It'll be like going to sleep."

Elizabeth's oxygen-starved mind couldn't fathom why he'd use pills. Why not just snap her neck, take the diamonds, and run? As her assailant's hand shifted from her hair to the back of her neck, she tried to raise her head and managed to take a single deep breath before he squeezed his fingers, sending a wave of dizziness washing over her.

"I can render you unconscious in about half a second, so don't try anything."

She managed to nod again, and he pulled her to her feet. "Please," she whispered. "Just let me go. I haven't seen your—"

His thin, raspy laugh sent a chill down her spine, and as they rounded the coffee table, he gave her neck another squeeze, focusing his grip on pressure points behind her ears. Nausea churned in her stomach, and her vision blurred. "Shut up."

Elizabeth stumbled on her too-high heels, but his hand on her neck kept her upright. "Don't do that again."

The living room window opposite her overlooked the street where Alexander and Nicholas were likely still on their phones. The door? Or the window? Her gaze flicked to her coffee table. A small metal bowl held her spare mailbox key and a tube of lip gloss. Would it make an adequate weapon? Something about the table seemed wrong, like a melody half a note out of tune.

The man's gloved fingers tightened, and he prodded her towards the kitchen. "I won't ask you again."

Elizabeth took a step, feigning another stumble. "M-my...shoes..."

As her would-be-murderer shifted, Elizabeth slammed one needle-like heel down on his instep, twisted out of his grip, and screamed.

She leapt for the door, but the man grabbed her hair and spun her around, throwing her into her coffee table. Her head slammed against the edge. Blood gushed into her eye. Wood splintered. The bowl clattered to the floor.

Floating in a sea of pain, she couldn't react quickly enough when her attacker lunged, grabbed her ankles, and yanked her back towards him.

"Help me!" she screamed with all she had left. Desperate fingers clutched for anything to hold onto—anything she could throw at him. The bowl. Heavy silver. One chance. She swung for her captor's head. The solid impact sang up her arm, and the man roared an oath.

"You'll pay for that, bitch."

Elizabeth tried to focus on him through the haze of dizziness. Brown eyes. Black mask over his face. Black clothes.

She scrambled back, swinging the bowl in front of her. "Help!" she screamed again, kicking wildly. Her heel caught her assailant in the arm, and he ripped the shoe off her foot. Closing his hand around her calf, he yanked hard.

In the silky dress, she slid easily, and her head slammed into the floor. And then he tackled her. His thumb drove between her ribs again, and she saw stars. Unending spikes of pain shot through her. She could barely whimper.

Unable to muster the strength to fight him, Elizabeth begged, "Please." The world went white, and then darkness tinged the edges. Darker.

Dizzy, disoriented, she noted only an inhuman roar as her front door came half off its hinges, the massive weight on top of her lifted, and something crashed to her right.

Breaking glass. Footsteps. The room spun. "Alexander," she called weakly. "Help."

"Elizabeth, can you hear me?" He knelt next to her. She watched his lips move, but his words sounded tinny, then faded away completely. With a groan, the darkness enveloped her.

# CHAPTER EIGHTEEN

othing mattered but Elizabeth. Not even chasing down her attacker and beating the man within an inch of his life. As Alexander knelt by her side, he tried to keep her conscious, but her eyes rolled back in her head, and the world slowed, his entire focus on her.

"Shite," Nicholas gasped into the phone as he reached the doorway. "She's hurt. Send an ambulance, too."

*Why didn't I go up with her?*

"Elizabeth, please. Open your eyes." Alexander took her hand, rubbing the inside of her wrist as he prayed she'd come back to him. A swollen knot on her forehead streamed blood into her hair, and dark bruises were already forming on her shoulder and her arm. As Nicholas called their personal physician, Elizabeth's eyes fluttered.

Nicholas knelt next to his brother and rested a hand on Alexander's shoulder. "Terrance only lives half a mile from here. He's on his way."

"Thank you," Alexander managed over the lump in his throat. He replayed the last few minutes in his mind, seeing the attacker on top of her, hearing her whimpers. The man had fled into the bedroom, jumping over a skewed floorboard.

Why was the floorboard pulled up?

"Nicholas, check her bedroom. There's a loose floorboard in there her attacker leapt over. He wouldn't have done that—"

"—if he hadn't known it was there. On it."

Caressing her pale cheek, Alexander shifted closer. "Come back now, Elizabeth. You're safe."

In the next room, Nicholas cursed. He strode back to the living room and dropped a stack of papers on the couch. "Alex?"

"What?" Alexander answered without taking his gaze from Elizabeth.

"These are our tax returns. Both the originals and the doctored ones that we received. Notes attached *appear* to confirm her involvement."

The growl that escaped Alexander's throat had Nicholas stepping back and throwing up his hands before he continued. "I don't believe this for a second. Someone at CPH will do just about anything to avoid going to jail. I'm calling Ben. He needs to get over here."

Alexander's entire world lay unconscious in front of him. River meowed from under the couch, then crept forward to peek up at him. "I'll take care of her," he told the cat.

Nicholas hovered a few feet away, talking in hushed tones. After ending the call, he huffed out a breath. "Ben's on his way too. Along with the Federal prosecutor's chief investigator. Both warned against Elizabeth saying anything to the police about the lawsuit."

"She has to wake up first," Alexander whispered. Shite, he needed to hold her, but without knowing how badly she was hurt, he couldn't take the risk. Cold air swirled around him from the shattered window. He could at least keep her warm. Covering her with a blanket from the couch, he leaned down and brushed a kiss over her cheek.

"Mmmm-hmm." Elizabeth's azure eyes fluttered open, unfocused and glassy. "Alexander?" With a whimper, she tried to raise her head.

"Don't move, *chérie*. You're safe, but I don't know how badly you're injured." Resting his hands on her shoulders, he tried to hold her still.

"He was going to..." She struggled with her words, and panic ate at him until he didn't think he could stand another second.

Finally, she relaxed. "Hurts."

"I know. You may have a concussion. Before the police get here, tell me what that bastard wanted."

"He was going...to kill me. Pills." She fumbled for Alexander's knee and gripped it weakly. "Computer." Tears gathered in her eyes. "Not right. Tried...couldn't get away." She grew more agitated with each slurred word. Stuttering breaths wheezed from her chest, and her eyes glazed over. "Help," she managed.

"Elizabeth, breathe." As he had done earlier that evening, he pressed her hand to his neck. "Feel my heartbeat. Look at me. In. Out. In. Out." She stared up at him with watery, bloodshot eyes, fighting for each inhalation. Nicholas shoved the broken coffee table out of the way and knelt on her other side, taking her hand and rubbing the inside of her wrist in a slow, rhythmic pattern.

A bit of color returned to her cheeks, and Alexander's relief shuddered through him. "Try again, *chérie*. What's this about your computer?"

She turned her gaze to Nicholas and then back to Alexander. She struggled with each word. "On the wrong side. River doesn't bite. He was here. Check the computer." Her eyes fluttered closed.

Alexander frowned and looked over at his brother. "If he planted information in her bedroom, he might have left some on her computer as well."

Nicholas nodded. "Setting her up to take the fall. Fuckers."

"Elizabeth, listen to me very carefully." Alexander waited

until she opened her eyes again before he continued. "We think someone at CPH is trying to frame you. When the police come, will you trust me to explain what's going on? The lawsuit?"

Her face twisted in pain for so long that he wondered if she'd heard him at all. "Okay," she said finally. "Can't focus anyway. Hurts."

Alexander blew out the breath he didn't even know he'd been holding. He bent down and kissed her lips gently as two sets of heavy footsteps approached the door.

"Police!" came a strong female voice.

"Come in," Alexander replied. Two uniformed officers entered, a man and a woman. The woman took in the scene and rested her hand on her gun.

Nicholas rose, his hands well away from his sides. "I'm the one who called 911," he said. "Nicholas Fairhaven. That's my brother, Alexander, and his girlfriend, Elizabeth. I have identification in my jacket pocket. Can I show you?"

After the officers had glanced at Nicholas's driver's license, the female officer approached. "Ma'am, can you speak to me? You know these men?"

"Know...yes. Don't make him leave," she said as she fumbled for Alexander's hand.

The fierce wave of possessiveness that washed over him at her words nearly had Alexander pulling her into his arms. Nicholas returned to Elizabeth's other side.

"I'm Officer Taylor. What happened here?" The officer crouched down so Elizabeth could see her better. Her partner, a tall, lanky boy of no more than twenty-five, moved through the flat, observing, until his boots crunched on the broken glass of Elizabeth's bedroom window.

Elizabeth's fingers tightened on Alexander's. With slow, unsteady words, she explained. "There was a man here when I came home. Grabbed me." She grimaced. "Told me not to scream. Held me down. Wanted to kill me."

"Where were the two gentlemen?" Officer Taylor asked.

"Downstairs. We were here to pick up a change of clothes for her," Alexander supplied. "I should have been with her, but my brother and I are dealing with a sensitive legal issue with our company. The federal prosecutor and our lawyer are on their way. Elizabeth is a witness to a crime, and I believe her attacker was here to ensure she could never testify."

The elevator dinged, and moments later, light footsteps approached. "Alex?"

Dr. Terrance Dalton was built like a linebacker and towered over the petite cop as he flashed his ID. Light blue eyes zeroed in on his patient, and he ran a hand over his wiry black hair. "Officer, the ambulance is downstairs, and the EMTs are gathering their gear."

The police officer shook her head. "It's a goddamm party here. Don't touch anything you don't have to." As she stepped out of the way, she muttered something under her breath that sounded suspiciously like "must be nice to be rich."

Alexander tried to rise, but Elizabeth clutched his arm, her fingers curling against the soft wool of his sweater. "Don't go."

He leaned down to whisper in her ear. "Terrance will take care of you, *chérie*. I need to give him room to work and answer the officer's questions. I won't be far."

For a moment, her gaze locked on him, fear and pain swimming in her eyes. But then she nodded, wincing from the effort. "Okay."

Terrance took Alexander's place at her side, but Alexander couldn't tear his gaze away from the woman he'd known he loved the moment he'd seen her bleeding.

"While Alexander told me he'd met someone, he never shared your name, my dear."

"Elizabeth. Bennett," she said weakly. "Who...are you?"

"Most patients call me Dr. Dalton," Terrance said as he shone a light in Elizabeth's eyes. "But you can call me Terry. Now, can you tell me the date today?"

"Mr. Fairhaven?" Office Taylor cleared her throat. "I really need you to answer a few more questions."

Two EMTs hurried into the room, and suddenly Elizabeth's small apartment felt practically stifling. Alexander glanced over at Nicholas, who stood guard over Elizabeth's computer. As the other officer approached, Nicholas straightened and crossed his arms over his chest. "No one touches the laptop," he growled. "Not until our lawyer gets here."

"Sir," the young man said, but Nicholas handed the officer his phone and told him to speak with the Federal prosecutor's office.

"What the hell is going on here?" Officer Taylor asked. "You don't get to tell us what we do and don't touch."

"No, but I do." Ben hovered in the doorway. "Or rather, Judge Edelman does." He brandished a piece of paper, and Officer Taylor rolled her eyes.

Returning his focus to Elizabeth, Alexander tried not to bark out orders as she tried to sit up again. Terrance soothed her, though, and she relaxed with a sigh.

"Can I at least get a description of the guy?" Officer Taylor said. "Anyone?"

"Six-foot-four, at least two-ten," Alexander answered, though he couldn't look away from Elizabeth. "Black turtleneck and pants, black shoes. He wore a full balaclava. I was too far away to see his eyes."

"Brown," Elizabeth called weakly. "They were brown."

"Well, that's something." The officer turned away and pulled her radio from her hip. As she reported in, Terrance moved away from Elizabeth, letting the EMTs load her onto a thin gurney.

"She's in shock and she's got a mild concussion," the doctor said as he rested his hand on Alexander's shoulder. "I want to run a CT scan to rule out anything more serious."

*More serious. Fuck me.*

Alexander wasn't sure he could speak until Elizabeth whimpered in pain. Then he shot his friend a panicked look. "She'll be all right?"

"Alex." Terrance's patient tone grated, as did the sight of the plastic stabilization collar around Elizabeth's neck and the various shades of blue and purple swelling on her face and shoulder. "Look at me."

The doctor's sharp, commanding tone snapped Alexander out of his fog.

"If you want to accompany her to the hospital, you're going to need to come now." Terrance halted the EMTs and rested a hand on Elizabeth's arm. "Doing okay, Elizabeth?"

"Uh-huh. I just want to sleep."

"I know, dear. Not yet, though. A few tests first, then I'll let Alex take you home."

Elizabeth sought Alexander's gaze. "He's not Alex. He's *Alexander*. Alex is a computer geek. Not a sexy British billionaire."

Alexander's heart skipped a beat as her personality shone through her pain and injuries. He'd take care of her—take care of everything.

River meowed loudly, and Alexander glanced towards the couch. The tabby peered up at him, and a sense of calm determination settled over him. "Where's your cat carrier, Elizabeth?"

"Closet," she said as she tried to reach for his hand. But the EMTs had strapped her down, and she could only move her fingers. "You'll get River?"

With a quick glance at Terrance to confirm the ambulance would wait, he nodded, then headed for Elizabeth's bedroom. Officer Taylor tried to stop him but relented quickly when she saw the look in his eyes. Once Alexander had River stowed safely in the carrier, he passed the cat off to Nicholas. "I'll call Samuel and send him and Thomas for my car and the cat. Keep me updated."

# CHAPTER NINETEEN

The harsh lights of the ambulance hurt Elizabeth's eyes, but the EMTs kept ordering her to stay awake and asking her questions. The vibrations of her vocal cords seemed to reverberate through her skull.

She couldn't focus on anything but the pain and Alexander's hand on her ankle. His hushed, clipped tones as he held a phone to his ear worried her, as did the occasional word she made out —*security, armed, lawsuit.*

The straps and blanket held her still, and she let her mind wander back to earlier in the evening when she'd been secure in Alexander's silks.

"She's smiling," Alexander said to Terrance. "Something's wrong."

The harsh tone of his voice snapped her back to the present, and she tried to reassure him. "Fine. Thinking...about you."

She was tired of talking. Tired of fighting to stay awake. Tired of reciting baseball stats, basic mathematical equations, and names of movies she'd seen. Most of all, she was tired of seeing the fear in Alexander's gaze. "I'm gonna be okay," she slurred.

"Yes, you'll be fine," he replied with a gentle smile. "Just stay awake for me. What was your favorite *Doctor Who* episode?"

"Big Bang." Elizabeth forced her eyes open again. "Or Eleventh Hour."

The ambulance ground to a halt, and Elizabeth breathed a sigh of relief. But then the EMTs decided to break a land speed record getting her into a private room. Medical history, more tests to verify her mental state, X-rays, and scans followed at a dizzying pace. Finally in her bed some time later, she was rewarded with a shot for the pain.

She floated, not quite awake, but not allowed to sleep either. And to that end, Alexander kept up a constant stream of innocuous conversation.

"You're so pretty," she told him when she ran out of things to say. "Pretty and rich. Why are you here? I'm not rich. I shouldn't be here."

Alexander hushed her and lifted her hand to his lips. God, she wanted to kiss him. But she was too tired to move.

"Will you kiss me? I like it when you kiss me."

He laughed and leaned close. "Where do you want me to kiss you?" Alexander skimmed a hand down the rough hospital gown. They'd taken her dress at some point. The diamonds too. She couldn't remember when.

"Elizabeth? Come back to me now. Tell me what you want. Anything at all." Strain bracketed his lips. He'd asked her a question. Oh. Right. Kissing.

"I want you to hold me. I want to go back to your big, comfy bed and go to sleep. It's too bright here. I hate hospitals. Take me out of here." A tear burned at the corner of her eye, and Alexander made a low, strangled sound as he tried to dash the moisture away.

"I can't. Not yet. But as soon as you're discharged, yes. I'm taking you home to my big bed, and we'll sleep."

Even through the fog of the pain meds, Elizabeth knew she'd

probably be dead if Alexander hadn't broken down her door. Fear churned in her stomach. "Don't want you to get hurt," she murmured, her eyes fluttering closed. "They're going to try to kill me again, aren't they?"

"Elizabeth, look at me."

She complied, recognizing the tone he'd used with her earlier in the bedroom.

"There are two former Navy SEALs outside this door. At home, a four-man detail is already waiting, including a member of the Greek Special Forces and a former SAS man. No one will harm you again." Alexander braced his hands on either side of her shoulders and held her gaze. "I promise."

"Too much. I can't repay you for this."

An odd smile curved his lips. "You don't have to. I protect what's mine."

He had to be nearly as exhausted as she was, but he still looked as handsome as ever.

"What time is it?" she asked. Four hours after the attack— that's when the doctors had said she could sleep. But Elizabeth's room didn't have a clock, not that she could keep track of time anyway as fuzzy as she felt.

Alexander looked up from his phone. "Five-fifteen, *chérie*. Less than ten minutes since the last time you asked me that question. Do you have somewhere to be?"

"I dunno. Too tired. I like looking at you." Elizabeth rubbed her head, but as soon as she brushed the bandage covering the stitches, she winced.

"You really do not do well on pain medicine, do you?" He chuckled, then skimmed a knuckle along her jaw.

Terrance knocked, saving her the effort of answering. "Good news, Elizabeth. All of your tests came back normal. We're going to discharge you as long as Alexander agrees to wake you every two hours until tomorrow night and you tell him if you feel dizzy or if your headache worsens."

"Yes. Of course." Alexander tapped his phone screen a few times, nodded, and then returned his gaze to Terrance. "You'll check on her tomorrow afternoon?"

"I'll be there at two." Terrance took Elizabeth's hand. "It was a pleasure to meet you, my dear. When I see you next, I expect you'll remember it better. Alex will take good care of you."

Elizabeth grimaced as a nurse raised the bed, then patted Elizabeth's hand. "Let's get you dressed, shall we?"

"Someone took my clothes," Elizabeth said.

Alexander leaned over her and kissed her tenderly. "That would be the police, *cherie*. There was blood on your shoes and the hem of the dress that did not appear to be yours. You did some damage to the bastard. They're testing it. If they can get a DNA match, it will help them catch the arsehole."

"When did they come?" she asked. Her eyes weren't focusing properly, and Alexander's face swam in front of her. A single tear rolled down her cheek.

"Shhh, Elizabeth. It's all been sorted. Do not fret." Alexander handed the nurse a green bundle of fabric. "I'd love to help with these, but I need to make sure our security is ready to go."

Elizabeth protested, "These aren't mine."

"They are now," Alexander said with a smile, then strode from the room.

The bundle—a pair of satiny pajamas and a warm robe—helped her feel somewhat human, though every movement made her dizzier. The nurse belted the robe snugly around Elizabeth's waist. "There we go. You're a lucky woman, you know. That man looks at you like you're the most important person in the world."

"He's going to take me home. I want to sleep in that big bed. Every night."

"Of course you do." The nurse patted her forearm and winked at her. "You'll sleep tonight. Now into the wheelchair with you."

"Don't you need my insurance card or something? I don't even know where my wallet is," Elizabeth said.

The kind nurse chuckled. "Of course not. Mr. Fairhaven took care of everything. You were probably too out of it when you came in, but you're in the Fairhaven wing of Mass General."

---

ALEXANDER TUCKED Elizabeth into bed as Samuel, his majordomo, hovered behind him. She'd fallen asleep as soon as they'd reached the limo, and hadn't stirred when he'd carried her up the stairs.

"Nicholas brought her laptop?" Alexander asked.

"Yes, sir. And the cat is currently hiding under the bed. Mr. Hetherington left a packet of paperwork for you. I secured that with the laptop in your office safe. Milos and Carl are the day-shift guards. Viktor and Sergei are on duty now—one in front and one at the rear of the house. Kaleb and Brandon will trade off with anyone who desires a break." Samuel glanced at Elizabeth, and his brows drew together. "Will she be all right?"

Alexander turned and rested his hand on Samuel's shoulder. Exhaustion swamped him, and though he'd never admit this to anyone, he'd come close to breaking down during Elizabeth's CT scan. "Yes, she will. Though only by pure luck. I have to find a way to keep her here—living here. It's the only way I can protect her."

As the two men stared at one another, Samuel nodded. "I'll inform Donatella that there's a new member of the household." River chose that moment to meow loudly, then butt her head against Alexander's ankle. "Two new members."

Samuel knew Alexander better than most, and understanding passed between them. After the bedroom door closed with a quiet *snick*, Alexander stripped, set an alarm, and reclined at the far edge of the mattress. In Elizabeth's current state, if he accidentally rolled over or tried to pull her close while he slept, he'd hurt her.

Two hours passed in the blink of an eye, and the blaring alarm drew a groan. "Elizabeth? You must wake up for me now." He stroked her arm, and she whimpered.

"No...sleep."

"In a moment. Where do the Red Sox play?" Terrance had advised him to ask her at least one question every time he woke her, but for the life of him, he couldn't think of anything more complicated than that.

"Fenway." Elizabeth blinked slowly, struggling to focus on the dimly lit bedroom. River mewled next to her. "Did I fall asleep in the car?"

Alexander chuckled. "Yes. You didn't even make it two minutes."

"Thank you for bringing River," she said weakly as her eyes fluttered closed. A barely audible sigh escaped her lips when Alexander leaned over and kissed the tip of her nose.

At ten, Elizabeth cursed him. At noon, she rolled onto her side away from him. But she answered his questions without fail. As her wit sharpened and her replies bit harder, Alexander felt comfortable leaving her to sleep alone. He showered, dressed, and snuck out of the room.

Samuel found him on his way out of the kitchen. "Sir, Miss Elizabeth's phone has been ringing constantly."

Alexander rubbed his gritty eyes. "Where is it?"

"In your study. I plugged it in to charge. I haven't answered it, but she's received three calls from a 'Kelsey' and five from someone named Toni."

"Antonia," Alexander corrected.

Samuel's brow twitched. "There's something else you should know."

The edge to Samuel's tone spoke to a serious problem, and Alexander followed his household manager into the study. "The *Babbler's* story came out."

Scanning his iPad, Alexander swore.

*Boston Billionaire's Night Turns Violent.*

The article bordered on libelous. Though the *Babbler* didn't come right out and accuse Alexander of beating Elizabeth, they quoted one of her neighbors. "*He broke down the door to get to her, and I heard screaming.*"

A blurry photo revealed Alexander hovering over Elizabeth's hospital bed, and an anonymous hospital source listed her injuries and implied that Alexander had been the cause.

"*He wouldn't let the police interview her. Brought in a private physician and everything.*"

Alexander seethed. Ben was going to have a rousing good time with this.

"Have you notified Philippa?" Alexander asked.

"Of course, sir. Despite your admin's many talents, she can't get the story retracted, but she wanted me to inform you that as soon as Miss Elizabeth is able, she'd like to set up an interview for the two of you. Otherwise, the *Babbler* is going to continue to harp on this, and more reputable sites could pick up the story as well."

"Bugger and blast it," he muttered. When he was upset, little colloquialisms from his mother bubbled up to the surface. "I'll speak to Elizabeth when she wakes up. You took care of what she needs for the next few days?"

"Yes. I filled the closet an hour ago."

A dry chuckle escaped Alexander's lips. "Lovely."

"You didn't lock the door, sir."

Before he could reply, Elizabeth's phone rang. Too tired to think straight, he jabbed the screen.

"Who is this?" a woman's voice, rough with a Boston accent, demanded. "Where's Lizzie?"

"Resting." Alexander peeked at the screen. "Antonia...? I'm afraid I don't know your last name."

"Grimaldi. Are you him? Fairhaven?" The accusation grated.

"I am."

Toni huffed. "If you hurt her, you're going to have to deal with my whole Italian family. And I mean that in every stereotypical sense of the word. *Capisci*?"

"Elizabeth is safer here than anywhere else. A man broke into her flat last night and attacked her. She has a mild concussion, but she'll make a full recovery. I can't speak to her willingness to accept visitors, as she's sleeping, but I'll tell her you called. If she feels strong enough to see you, you're welcome in my home."

"Make sure she calls us. If she doesn't, I'm bringing my family over. You don't want that. Get her to call. Soon."

"I will. Goodbye, Miss Grimaldi. I look forward to meeting you."

An hour later, after scheduling a meeting with the U.S. Attorney for late afternoon, having a tense conversation with Ben, and exchanging a dozen messages with Nicholas, Alexander returned to the bedroom.

The bed in the dimly lit suite was empty, save for the cat, who'd settled in the bunched-up blankets. "Elizabeth?"

Moving gingerly, she limped out of the bathroom. Worried she might shatter with each step, Alexander wrapped his arm around her waist and guided her back to the bed.

"I'm capable of walking on my own," she said, glaring at him through swollen eyelids as she shuffled next to him.

"Most of the time, yes. Right now? I'm not so sure." Alexander pulled back the blankets, much to River's ire.

"Back in bed with you, *chérie*."

"Alexander."

"Now," he commanded, raising his brow. This was his bedroom, and if he had to, he'd use that fact against her. "Please," he added when she bristled. "I'm worried about you."

As Alexander slid his hand up to cup her neck, she sighed and sagged against him. "No more pain meds. Ever," she said as she let him help her down, then arrange the pillows behind her.

"Elizabeth, we need to talk." He sat at her hip, her hands held firmly in his.

*I'm in love with you.*

"Oh God. Did I make a fool of myself last night? I don't react well to drugs. What did I say?"

"You and Nurse Betsy had a rather racy chat about what you'd like to do to Benedict Cumberbatch. Nurse Betsy is...adventurous. You simply wanted to have a proper snog."

The parts of her face not purple and blue flushed bright red as she looked away. "Kill me now."

"I found your drug-addled burble quite endearing." Alexander walked over to the dark blue draperies. "May I?"

She waved her hand in acceptance. He parted the drapes to reveal the dramatic view of the Charles River Esplanade, decorated for the holidays.

Elizabeth squinted in the bright winter's light. "What time is it?"

"A little after one. Donatella is making us lunch."

"I have to go home. You broke down my door. I won't have anything left. And my computer. He was on my computer." Elizabeth shoved the blankets down her legs, but Alexander's firm hand on her shoulder stopped her from getting up again.

"Your computer is in my safe, and your door and window will be repaired as soon as the police release the crime scene. Until we know who was sent to hurt you, you're staying here."

"I can't—"

Alexander's fingers trailed down her arm and, lifting her hand, he kissed her bruised knuckles. "Anything you need from your flat, we'll send for, or I'll go myself. Marjorie arranged for a few days' worth of clothing for you. Anything you don't like, we'll return. But we're having visitors today, and I assumed you wouldn't want to receive them in your robe."

"Oh. Thank you." Elizabeth lay back against the pillows. "Wait, visitors?"

"Nicholas is coming at three. Ben and the federal prosecutor are coming at four. We should also speak to the press."

"Why?"

Alexander pinched the bridge of his nose. "Someone snapped a photo of us—of me standing over your bed—at the hospital. The *Beantown Babbler* claims *I* beat you."

"Oh shit."

"Yes, that was my reaction as well. We will need to do a bit of damage control." Alexander held out her phone. "And your friends have been calling."

Elizabeth scrolled through a few of the messages, growing more agitated with each one. "Nine calls? Two dozen texts? Toni thinks you hurt me."

"I know." Alexander sighed. "But if we speak to the press, we should be able to head off those rumors without too much difficulty. Still, you should ring your friends to explain."

Her cheeks flushed. "I don't know if I can deal with them right now. They'll go all Mother Hen on me, and one overbearing control freak is enough for me today."

Alexander chuckled and leaned in so his lips were only inches from hers. "Very well, but I am not a 'control freak,' *chérie*. We're in the bedroom, and in here, I'm in control. Remember?"

She made a low, appreciative sound. "I remember."

His cock stirred. If she weren't injured, he'd take her right now, but instead, he just brushed a tender kiss to the corner of her mouth. "Would you like lunch in bed or do you feel well enough to go downstairs?"

"I want to get up."

Alexander helped her into her robe, but she refused his arm and limped out of the room ahead of him. Before they reached the stairs, however, Elizabeth turned, her eyes unfocused. "I'm... dizzy," she whispered as she wavered on her feet.

Wrapping his arms around her, Alexander let her lay her head on his shoulder. "You need more rest." He helped her to the upstairs sitting room and settled her on a love seat next to the window.

River padded in, her inquisitive green eyes investigating the space, and meowed. "You'll forgive me for all this turmoil once I ply you with tuna," Alexander said after he retrieved a blanket from a cedar chest in the corner. The cat met his stare. He wouldn't look away. He was the master in this house, not her. Eventually, the cat looked down at her paws and started to purr. "Good girl," he said, scratching her behind the ears.

Chef Donatella's quick entrance saved him from embarrassing himself with declarations of love or *control-freak* behavior like carrying Elizabeth right back to bed and making her stay there.

"Lunch will be ready in a few minutes, sir," Donatella said. "I thought you and Miss Elizabeth could use some coffee." She set a silver tray with a press pot of coffee and two china cups on the table in front of them.

"Elizabeth, this is Donatella. If you're ever hungry, she can fix you anything you want. I'll warn you now, though, she doesn't like it when I raid the pantry."

The chef smiled. "I only chide Mr. Fairhaven because he has an annoying habit of putting empty cracker boxes and chip bags back where he found them. Avoid that, and you and I will get along fine. Now if you'll excuse me, I'll be back in a few minutes with your meal."

Alexander poured Elizabeth a cup of coffee, then draped his arm around her shoulders, urging her against his body. He tipped the cup to her lips, and she made a feeble attempt to bat him away. "Elizabeth," he warned, "you are trembling too severely to hold a cup. Let me help you."

She looked up at him with so much uncertainty that his heart threatened to break, but took a sip of the coffee. When he set the cup down, she reached for his hand. "I'm scared."

"I protect those I care about; I told you that last night. There's a six-man security team guarding the house, and you're not going anywhere alone. Once the prosecutor gets here, we'll figure out our next steps."

Elizabeth shook her head, winced, and slumped back against him. "I know the next steps. I'll testify, but the case could last six months to a year. And they'll keep coming after me until it's over. There's only one solution." She tried and failed to stifle a sob. "Witness protection. Alone." Tears lined her eyes as she peered up at Alexander. "Why did I have to meet you now?"

Alexander ached to crush something—or someone. Namely, whoever sent a hitman after the woman he loved. But as she shuddered and tried not to cry, he smoothed a hand over her hair. "Witness protection might be the easiest option, but not one I'm prepared to live with. Do you *want* to leave?"

"No," she said with so much fervor that he smiled. Gently, with as much care as one would give an orchid, he tipped her head back and kissed her. Quick nips to the side of her mouth, a dart of his tongue, his teeth tugging on her lower lip. If she weren't so fragile, he'd have her underneath him in a heartbeat. But right now, he satisfied himself plundering that delicious mouth.

After a simple lunch of grilled cheese and tomato soup and more coffee, Elizabeth's hands had stopped shaking, and her color had improved.

"Will you rest for a bit before Nicholas gets here?" Alexander asked.

"Not yet. You said you had my computer?"

"I do. Wait here." As he jogged down the stairs to his study, he realized he still didn't know what had happened in the ten minutes Elizabeth had been trapped in her apartment with the hitman.

*You're too knackered to think straight,* he berated himself. Then again, as tired as he was, hearing the details of her injuries might have him doing something he'd regret—like going after Carter alone.

Alexander took his time ascending the stairs, debating how much to press Elizabeth for details. As he set the laptop in front of her, she smiled up at him. "Thanks."

He dropped down next to her, watching her search for recently modified files. Dozens filled the screen, at least half of them opened when Elizabeth had been firmly bound in his silks. Once she took several screenshots, she tried to open one of the files.

"FHE—Fairhaven Exports." A password prompt appeared. "That's not mine," she said. Four more files produced the same prompt. "These are all CPH clients. The guy…" Her voice broke, but she clenched her fists in her lap and continued. "He had pills. He was going to make my death look like a suicide."

Alexander saw red, then purple as he met Elizabeth's gaze. With a firm hand, he shut the lid on the laptop.

"Alexander, didn't you hear me?"

"I did." Gathering her close, he took a deep breath. "There is something I haven't told you yet about last night. There was a loose floorboard in your bedroom. Underneath it, Nicholas found a stack of papers. Copies of Fairhaven Exports' tax returns for the past three years. The doctored versions and the originals. All with Carter's signature on them. And notes with your name on them confirming the fraud."

Tears gathered in Elizabeth's eyes. "I didn't. Alexander, you have to believe me. I never worked on your returns. I didn't have anything to do with the fraud. Oh God. I wouldn't lie to you. I've never…"

Catching her around the waist as she tried to push to her feet, Alexander urged her into his lap, cradling her against him. "I know, Elizabeth. I know," he said as he rubbed her uninjured arm. "As does Nicholas. Someone breaks into your home, tries to kill you, and *then* we find evidence that links you to the fraud? I have no doubt that you are smart enough to pull this off if you so desired. If there was a dishonest bone in your body." He cupped the back of her neck. "Which is why I know you wouldn't be so daft as to leave an open floorboard easily seen in your bedroom. I retrieved your wrap before we left. The floorboard wasn't loose then. I never suspected you for a moment. Neither did my brother."

She wrapped her arms around him and buried her head against his sweater. "Thank God. I...you saved my life." Wriggling, she tried to burrow closer. "I didn't want this relationship. But you wouldn't leave me alone, and now I don't want to let you go."

"Then I'm a fortunate man."

# CHAPTER TWENTY

*T*errance knocked at the study's door. "How's my newest patient this afternoon?"

Elizabeth drew away from Alexander and tried to force a smile. "Exhausted and sore."

"That's to be expected. Still, upright, I see." The doctor gave her a slightly disapproving look, but then the corners of his mouth tugged up. "Perhaps you'll let me examine you back in bed?"

"You're as bad as Alexander," she grumbled, but the bed didn't seem like a bad idea—even the few minutes of standing had left her a little wobbly.

Alexander chuckled. "I believe the term she used, Terrance, was *control freak*." With an arm around her waist, Alexander guided her back to his bedroom, then tucked the blankets around her legs once she'd reclined against the pillows.

"Not inappropriate," the doctor replied as he opened his medical bag. "It seems her wit and powers of observation are perfectly intact."

"Much to my relief." Alexander moved away, then dropped

into a chair in the corner of the room. "Though I wish she'd have stayed in bed all day."

Watching the two men verbally spar gave her insight into the man she thought she just might be falling in love with. Alexander's focus never left her, and though he'd been firm, even controlling, at times this morning, he'd never been anything but caring.

Terrance shone a light into each of her eyes and asked her to track the movements of his finger up, down, left, and right. "Very good, Elizabeth. Now let's check those stitches. Any dizziness?"

"I—"

"She was unable to navigate the stairs," Alexander interrupted.

Elizabeth shot him a look that she hoped would imply her displeasure, and he inclined his head in apology. "I can speak for myself, Alexander, thank you. This might be your bedroom, but —" Flushing with embarrassment, she redirected the conversation. "My head hurts, and I'm shaky. Yes, I was dizzy earlier, but I hadn't eaten anything."

As Terrance pressed a series of butterfly bandages over her head wound, he tried to stifle his laugh, ending up with a wide smile. "Perfectly normal, my dear. And your stitches look excellent. If you're careful, you can shower and wash your hair."

"Thank God." Despite Alexander's scent infusing the sheets, the pillows, and even the whole room, she could still smell antiseptic, blood, and the foul stench of her attacker. "And, um... normal activities?"

"Let me check that shoulder."

As soon as she'd removed her night shirt and clutched the silky material to her breasts, Alexander's eyes darkened. He shifted in the chair, uncrossing his legs. Elizabeth's gaze flitted to the St. Andrew's Cross in the corner of the room, hidden behind a thick drape.

Terrance probed the bruises gently and checked her range of

motion. "Nothing too intense, Elizabeth. None of Alexander's... usual toys."

Her cheeks caught fire. "Um, you...know?" she asked as she stared from Terrance to Alexander.

Alexander stood and adjusted his painfully obvious erection as he grinned. "Terrance and I used to frequent a local BDSM club before my face became well known in Boston. We've tested floggers and crops on one another before."

"Wh-what?" The blood drained from her face so quickly she felt herself pale. "The two of you?"

"A responsible Dom always knows what his implements feel like," Terrance replied as he stepped back to rummage through his medical bag. "Otherwise, someone could get hurt." He glanced over at Alexander, then back at Elizabeth. "I'm sorry if I made you uncomfortable."

She waved her hand weakly. "I should have known. You have that same...command to your voice that he does."

Both men chuckled and Terrance handed Elizabeth a bottle of pills. "Alex told me you refused the Percocet. Vicodin shouldn't leave you as loopy, but it will ease the pain. At least half a pill every four to six hours for two days. All right?"

"I don't like drugs," she protested. "And I have to be lucid for—"

"*Chérie*," Alexander said firmly. "Every time you move, I can see the pain in your eyes. You'll try the Vicodin. At least once." His voice had changed—more like the authoritative tone he'd used when they'd played.

She sank back against the pillows, hating that he was right. Everything did hurt. "Fine. After we meet with the prosecutor, though. I can't have my mind all foggy for that."

Alexander inclined his head. "Very well."

Terrance leaned forward and dropped his voice to a whisper. "I've never seen anyone change that man's mind before, and I've known him for ten years. You, Elizabeth, are a very special woman." Straightening, he looked over at Alexander. "Walk me out? Elizabeth probably wants some rest."

Alone, she rolled onto her uninjured side and clutched Alexander's pillow to her chest. He'd changed in the past few weeks. Softened, perhaps. Because of her?

*I think I'm falling in love with you.*

His words—were they just last night?—warmed her, though the nervous churning in her stomach wouldn't go away. How in the world could she love him—or even stay with him—with someone trying to kill her?

With that thought in her head, she drifted off to sleep.

Milos, one of the bodyguards Alexander hadn't met yet, knocked on his office door. "Sir?"

The hulking Greek, with closely shorn black hair and the build of a boxer, stood at attention when Alexander looked up from his desk. He'd checked on Elizabeth, found her sleeping, and busied himself with returning the dozen calls that had come in since the *Babbler's* story had broken. "Yes?"

"There's a reporter from WGBH at the door. He would like to speak to you about an article on the *Beantown Babbler* and the report of Miss Elizabeth's hospitalization. I assume you'd like me to send him away, but..." Milos's brow quirked. "I'm not certain how strongly you'd like me to *word* that dismissal."

Alexander sat back in his chair, impressed. This man might make an excellent permanent addition to the staff. Assuming they ever found Elizabeth's attacker and could lower security at all. "Where's Samuel?"

"In the basement, sir. The cat...is apparently sneaky. And hiding in the storage room."

Chuckling, Alexander shook his head. "Inform him that I'm

not receiving visitors right now, and he can contact Philippa James at Fairhaven Charities for a statement."

"Yes, sir." Milos practically snapped his heels together as he turned. From what little Alexander remembered of the roster he'd approved sitting by Elizabeth's hospital bed, Milos had been a rather high-ranking soldier in the Greek Special Forces.

Despite his exhaustion, Alexander's mind raced over the reporter's presence. Rather bold to show up at the house unannounced. Perhaps...

Alexander leapt up and jogged to the front door, reaching Milos as the man had his hand on the knob. "Hold on a moment, Milos. I'd like to talk to the man."

The Greek's dark eyebrows shot up momentarily, but he merely nodded and stepped back enough to let Alexander take his place at the door. "Of course, sir. I'll wait right here, though."

A blond-haired young man with a round face and freckles stood on the short porch with a voice recorder in his hand. "Mr. Fairhaven? Mark Joont with WGBH. The *Beantown Babbler* ran two scathing articles this morning: one that implied you beat the woman who accompanied you to the Fire and Ice Ball and the other that accused you and your brother of defamation of character, unfair business practices, and sexual harassment. Care to comment?"

Well, *that* was interesting. The second story had only come out an hour ago. Alexander clasped his hands in front of him, and Mr. Joont's gaze slid to Alexander's knuckles, narrowed, and then returned to his face.

"Both Fairhaven Charities and Fairhaven Exports have full legal departments available to take inquiries seven days a week. The entire company undergoes sensitivity training every year, and we have a zero-tolerance policy for domestic violence and sexual harassment. Now, ask the next question. The one you really wanted to ask."

The reporter cleared his throat and straightened his shoulders. "What happened to Elizabeth Bennett last night?"

"She was injured. Try again." Dancing with the press was an art form, one he'd mastered once his brother had started gambling. Or...at least losing.

Mark shifted his voice recorder to his other hand and then thumbed through his notebook, pausing when he found the right page. "Miss Bennett was fired from Carter, Pastack, and Hayes a few weeks ago. Then last night, you had a run-in with Harry Carter at the Fire and Ice Ball. Several reports claim threats were made, by Carter, towards Miss Bennett, you, and your brother. Is there a connection between the run-in last night and Miss Bennett's hospitalization?"

*Impressive.*

Alexander let his hands drop to his sides, keeping his calm expression firmly in place. "That's better, Mr. Joont. Unfortunately, you'll need to address all of your questions to my lawyer, but stay close to your phone. An important call might come in sometime this afternoon. Good day."

Once Alexander had closed and locked the door, Milos met his gaze. "Sir, why did you speak to him—if you don't mind my asking?"

"Elizabeth and I will need to make a statement to the press later today because of the sodding photograph from the hospital. When trying to dispel an unfavorable news story, it helps to have a few reporters...on your side. Provided they're competent. Mr. Joont didn't push me on the sexual harassment claim. That's the sexy story—especially with the specter of domestic violence thrown in. He immediately switched his focus to Elizabeth, but did so in a way that told me he knew CPH was involved." Alexander spread his fingers, palms down, so Milos could see his knuckles. "Did you notice him glancing at my hands?"

Milos nodded.

"Mr. Joont will be one of the first reporters Philippa calls when she arranges the news conference. Now, I have to check on Elizabeth. My brother, someone from the U.S. Attorney's office, and Ben Hetherington will be here soon. When you've cleared them, have Samuel set them up in the living room with coffee."

"Yes, sir."

# CHAPTER TWENTY-ONE

*A*lexander slid a hip onto the bed and watched Elizabeth sleep. Her screams echoed in his ears, and every time he closed his eyes, he saw her as she'd been last night. Bloodied, half-incoherent, and terrified. Her brows pinched together in slumber, and when she mewled and twitched, he ran a hand over her back. "Shhh, Elizabeth. You're safe."

A little gasp punctuated her shudder, and her eyelids fluttered open. "Alexander."

The single word held such need he had to stifle his possessive growl as he gathered her against him, careful to avoid her injured arm. "I'm here, *chérie*. Just a nightmare."

Nothing could have prepared him for the overwhelming emotion of falling in love. After so many conquests in his youth, then so long without finding *anyone* who held his interest for more than a few hours, his overwhelming desire to *know* this woman, to hear her stories, to learn her quirks staggered him.

"Do you want to talk about it?" Alexander rubbed her back in gentle circles until she stopped trembling.

"I want this to all go away," she murmured against his neck. "Everything but you."

*Mine.*

The single word roared through his thoughts, and he couldn't help himself. "I love you, Elizabeth," he whispered.

Her arm tightened around his waist, but she didn't respond, and Alexander cursed himself for not being able to hold back. She wasn't ready for love yet—she'd all but confirmed it last night. Easing her back, Alexander searched her gaze. "Nicholas will be here soon. Then Ben and the prosecutor. I wish we could delay until tomorrow, but Ben wants to have everything filed by tonight. Would you like to get dressed? Or receive them here?"

Elizabeth chewed on her lip for a moment, uncertainty swimming in her eyes. "Help me shower?"

The mere thought of Elizabeth's naked body sent his cock straight to attention, but he focused on the purple swelling above her eye and got himself under control. "Of course."

Soon, steam swirled through the marble bath, and as Alexander helped Elizabeth off with her shirt, he grimaced at the mottled bruises that covered her left side.

"I'm okay," she said as she drew the backs of her fingers over his cheek. "Really. Nothing's broken. Bruises fade. This—" she gestured to the gash on her forehead, "—is going to scar. But I was lucky." A single tear spilled over as she glanced down at her feet. When Elizabeth met his gaze again, her dark blue eyes carried a deeper hue. "You saved my life, Alexander. He would have killed me. Thank you."

As she levered up on her toes to kiss him, Alexander realized he'd do anything, spend any amount of money, change anything about himself or his lifestyle to make sure Elizabeth was safe.

Before he made a proper idiot of himself and told her he loved her again, he stripped off his clothes and then stepped into the shower.

Angling the four shower heads to avoid Elizabeth's stitches, he watched her intently for any signs of distress. She sighed as the hot water cascaded over her breasts, and then let her hands trail down her sides.

*Shite.*

Her naked body drove him mad, and on the heels of nearly losing her, Alexander's need to claim almost overwhelmed him. With a breathy moan, Elizabeth reached for him, and he couldn't mistake the glint in her eyes.

"You're injured, Elizabeth. No."

"Terrance cleared me. Please." She angled her hips to press against his erection. "You'll be gentle."

"I can't," he managed, his voice rough and strained. "Not the way I feel right now. Seeing you like this..." Alexander tucked a blood-stained lock of hair behind her ear. "I couldn't be gentle."

"Try." Elizabeth retreated until her back pressed against the shower wall, then spilled some of his soap into her hands and started caressing her breasts in slow, maddening circles.

Unable to ignore his throbbing cock, he growled at her, "Stay here and keep playing with yourself."

She nodded, and he skidded on the wet floor as he ran into the bedroom to snatch a condom from the nightstand drawer.

When he returned, Elizabeth's head rested against the wall, her eyes closed, tiny sounds of pleasure escaping her parted lips.

*She's perfect.*

As he stepped back into the shower, he twisted one of the shower heads to send hot water sluicing over those perfect breasts. Elizabeth opened her eyes with a smile. "Tell me what to do."

My God. His woman wanted to play, as injured as she was. Fine. He'd give her what she wanted. Despite his words, he *was* gentle, circling her wrists with a firm grip and holding them at her sides. Nipping down her right shoulder, he kissed a trail to her breast, then took one pert nipple in his mouth. With an arch of her back, Elizabeth moaned, then started to tremble under his ministrations.

Angling her so the water wouldn't drown him, Alexander sank to his knees. Laving his tongue over her bare lower lips, he tasted her arousal, and when he found her clit, she whimpered, "Oh God. More."

Releasing her wrists, he tipped his head back, his reward seeing the flush to her breasts, her hard, dusky pink nipples, and the haze of desire in her eyes. "I am going to ravage your delicious pussy, Elizabeth. And while I do, I want you to go back to toying with those perfect breasts. Do you understand?"

With a shaky smile, she started to pinch and tug at her nipples. "Yes."

Her stomach quaked as she let her head rest against the river rock wall, and Alexander returned his attention to her slick folds. The scent of her arousal filled the enclosure as he started tracing patterns on the sensitive bundle of nerves that he loved so well.

As the trembling spread to her thighs, he shifted, nipping and biting a trail from her inner thigh to her hip and back again.

Elizabeth gasped and tugged harder on her nipples when he returned his attention to her clit. "Please," she begged. "I need to come."

"Not yet," he growled against her pussy. "Not until I say."

A keening moan escaped as he sucked at her nub, and Alexander braced his arm across her belly to steady her as he slid two fingers into her throbbing channel. With one twist of his fingers, he found her G-spot.

"Now," he ordered, then swirled his tongue around her clit. "Come now." A final nip to the throbbing flesh and she imploded, his name tearing from her lips as she screamed and shuddered. He took all of her, lapping at her folds, her release so sweet and heady on his tongue.

As she came down from the high of her release, she slid her fingers into his hair. "More," she whispered. "I want you inside me."

"That is exactly where I want to be," he managed as he got to his feet. "But I don't know if I can do that without hurting you."

Elizabeth kissed him and wrapped her fingers around his aching cock. "I think you can."

Once he'd rolled the condom over his length, he assessed her. Small lines of strain marred the corner of her lips. Elizabeth's left shoulder slumped lower than the right, but her eyes were clear, desire churning in the azure depths.

"Do exactly as I say," he ordered. Once she nodded, he bent slightly, then wrapped his arms around her thighs and lifted her against him. "Do not use your left arm to hold on, Elizabeth."

She'd been about to drape both arms around his neck but obeyed, and he pressed her back gently against the wall.

"If I hurt you—at all—you say *red*." Already, his cock demanded attention nestled so close to her channel, but he'd endure the worst case of blue balls ever to avoid causing her even one moment of pain.

"I will. Please. Inside me." Each word was punctuated with a stuttering breath, and Alexander wasted no more time.

Slowly, watching her face for any pain, he slid home, and they both groaned as she tightened around him. With each thrust, he raced closer to the edge, and as his balls tightened, he ground his hips into hers. Elizabeth moaned.

"Alexander!"

He dipped his head and sucked a nipple into his mouth. As he scraped his teeth over the tight bud, she lost control, and a second climax ripped through her. Alexander let go and flew over the edge with her.

---

ELIZABETH TRAILED her fingers over half a dozen sweaters, jeans, tanks, and t-shirts someone on Alexander's staff had purchased for her. "I'd be mad at you, but these are all things I'd buy.

Though, my versions would be way less expensive." Lifting the sleeve of a cashmere sweater, she frowned. "This sweater probably cost more than my monthly grocery bill."

"Marjorie had your sizes, and the police wouldn't let Thomas go through your closet." Alexander tugged on a pair of black jeans. "Tomorrow, Milos and Carl can escort us to your flat, and you can pick up anything else you need."

"I don't think I'd have wanted Thomas going through my underwear drawer," Elizabeth said as she pulled on a pair of black lace panties.

Everything fit perfectly, and once Elizabeth had laced up the white Keds, she surveyed herself in the mirror in the corner. Alexander's closet was bigger than her entire bedroom. Despite the bruises, including a tiny one under her arm that throbbed with every breath, she didn't *feel* awful, but she looked like death. Her cheeks had lost their usual color, dark circles braced her eyes, and the knot on her forehead had swollen to the size of a baby's fist.

Alexander was scrolling through his messages when she returned to the bedroom. "Shite. We need to make a statement to the press tonight. The *Babbler's* speculation that I was rough with you has gained a bit of traction."

"Oh God. Yes, of course. Should we do it now? Before the Feds get here?" She rolled her shoulders to release some of the tension, then had to stifle a wince.

"No. We'll put it off."

Alexander's sudden about-face had her meeting his gaze. He looked stricken, as if he'd just seen her bruises for the first time.

"I'm not risking your health."

"For fuck's sake." She straightened before marching over to him. "I realize I look like a punching bag, and maybe that's not the best image to present, but spending a few minutes telling the press they're full of shit isn't going to 'risk my health' in any way."

Taking a step back, Alexander's brows arched. "You challenge me, Elizabeth. Your independence. Your spirit. I don't know what I'd do if anything happened to you. I need you in my life."

"If you want me to stay in your life, you can't treat me like I'm made of glass. Even if I am right now." She rubbed her sore shoulder. "I love that you've taken care of me—hell, ever since we met in some ways. But I'm okay. I can do this. If I don't have to—" The memory of their earlier conversation brought a lump to her throat, and she sucked in a deep breath, trying to calm her pounding heart. Alexander linked their fingers, and she drew strength from his touch.

"If my life is still mine after the Feds leave, then I can do this. I have to do this for...us."

He ran his hands up and down her arms, careful to avoid her bruises. "Your life is always going to be yours. You're not going into witness protection. And despite my *control freak* tendencies, I never want you to feel as if you are not my partner. I'm sorry if I sometimes overstep. I'm not used to feeling like this."

Something warmed inside her. Love? She couldn't be sure. Affection, yes. Desire, definitely. Connection, without a doubt. But love?

"Just trust me," she said as she tipped her head to meet his gaze. "I'll try not to push myself too hard just to prove I'm not a total mess. But I can only make that promise if you trust me. Otherwise, I can't help getting a little defensive."

"Fair enough," Alexander said with a chuckle and then wrapped her in a gentle embrace. "Nicholas should be here in a few moments. Feel like trying the stairs again?"

"As long as you're with me," Elizabeth said, praying she was mostly done with the dizzy spells.

Alexander pressed a kiss to her lips. "There's nowhere else I'd be."

# CHAPTER TWENTY-TWO

*E*lizabeth fidgeted with the hem of the cashmere sweater. A fire crackled in the hearth a few feet away, and River stretched out on the warm bricks.

Humming a Christmas song, Donatella carried coffee service into the formal drawing room, then smiled at Elizabeth as she set the tray down. "You look better, miss."

"Please call me Elizabeth." All of these servants, the formality, even the perfection of this house made her uncomfortable. She didn't belong here. With Alexander at her side, she could ignore the doubts that filled her, but he was getting her laptop and some paperwork from his office, and despite the fire and the blanket he'd draped over her lap, she shivered.

As Donatella handed her a china cup, she nodded. "As you wish, Elizabeth. Can I bring you a snack? Chocolate chip cookies?"

Her stomach rumbled at the thought, and Donatella laughed. "I'll be right back."

She passed Alexander on her way out of the room, and he said something Elizabeth couldn't hear. Donatella nodded, smiling.

As Alexander sank onto the sofa next to Elizabeth, he stifled a yawn. "The press conference is scheduled for six-thirty. We'll make a short statement, take a few questions, and be done with it."

"I wish I had some makeup." Elizabeth brushed her swollen temple lightly. "I'd rather not look quite so...beaten up."

Alexander cupped her cheek. "You're beautiful, Elizabeth. Even with the bumps and the bruises. But I can send Samuel for anything you'd like. Or...perhaps you could call your friends. They want to see you. We could have dinner if you think you'd be up for it."

"I guess I should get that conversation over with. You realize they're not going to go easy on you, right?"

Alexander chuckled. "I'd expect nothing less."

Fueled by Donatella's chocolate chip cookies and more coffee, Elizabeth rang Kelsey, then almost cried with relief when the call went to voicemail. This wasn't a conversation she really wanted to have on the phone. *"Yes, I'm dating a billionaire. Yes, I'm staying at his house. Someone's trying to kill me. There are armed guards around the house. I'm scared I might have to go into witness protection. Oh, and by the way, can you bring me some concealer?"*

Rather than try to explain everything, she opted for a simple message. "Hey. I know you and Toni have been worried. I'm okay. I need a favor, though. Can the two of you come for dinner tonight? At Alexander's? And um, bring your makeup kit? I'll text you the address."

Once she'd sent the text, she tucked her phone into her pocket and gestured towards her laptop. "I want to look at those files again before the feds take this away from me."

The doorbell rang as she entered her password, but she barely noticed until the shouting started.

"Sir," a deep voice called. "Please—"

"Goddammit. I'm his bloody brother. If you think *I'm* the problem, then Alex has clearly made a big mistake hiring you."

Alexander rolled his eyes as Nicholas burst into the room, followed by a burly, olive-skinned man the size of a small mountain. "You couldn't have shown them a photo?" Nicholas asked.

"I've been a bit preoccupied. Or did you forget that we didn't get home until after six this morning?" Despite the harsh edge to Alexander's tone, he poured his brother a cup of coffee. "It's all right, Milos. My brother isn't normally this...testy."

"Yes, Mr. Fairhaven." Milos turned on his heel and strode out of the room.

"Apologies," Nicholas said as he tugged at the neck of his white Oxford shirt, then turned his focus to Elizabeth. "How are you feeling?"

*Nervous. Terrified. Exhausted.*

Elizabeth forced a smile. "I've been better."

"Shite, Alex. Aren't you taking care of her?"

Alexander clenched his fists on his thighs. "Nicholas..."

Elizabeth covered Alexander's hand with hers. "He's taking care of me. Maybe a little too well."

"Oh?" Nicholas accepted the coffee with a raised brow. "Care to explain?"

She blushed. "He's just a little overprotective."

"I believe the term she used was control freak," Alexander muttered.

Nicholas nearly choked on his coffee. "She's good for you, Alex."

At this, Alexander relaxed. "Philippa set the press conference for six-thirty. We'll address my supposed domestic violence. The second article that accused us of being tossers in every way, we'll ignore for now. Let the lawyers handle it. Will you stay?"

Nicholas nodded. "Of course. A united front. Foyle called half an hour ago. He and the U.S. Attorney are on their way. Our accounting department finished their research. We overpaid by a grand total of forty-two-point-one million over three years."

"Shite." Alexander pinched the bridge of his nose. "With that size of a payout, no wonder they tried to eliminate Elizabeth."

"She'll be safe after we speak with the U.S. Attorney. Ben already filed the lawsuit listing her as the primary witness. The partners will be served tomorrow, once Elizabeth signs her affidavit."

The china cup rattled in her saucer. "They can still try to pin it all on me," she said quietly. "That's what they were trying to do last night. Plant evidence that I was responsible, make my death look like a suicide, and they stay out of jail. Sure, they have to pay the money back, but they'd be free. I bet they've invested it all, made millions more. There's probably an account somewhere with my name on it containing a shit-ton of money that can be traced back to CPH clients." Elizabeth started scrolling through her files, searching for anything out of place. "I wish I'd paid more attention to my boyfriend in college. He wrote a couple of password cracking apps."

"How did you know?" Alexander asked, a strained edge to his voice. "About your computer. You weren't making much sense last night. You worried me." He brushed his knuckles along her jaw, such a tender and intimate gesture that she shifted closer to him.

"I didn't mean to," she said with a shy smile. "My mouse was on the right side of my laptop, and the laptop was closed. When I left with you for the party, the lid was open, and I use the mouse with my left hand."

"But you're right-handed," Alexander said, his brow furrowed.

Elizabeth chuckled. "That I am, Mr. Observant. But a lot of full-time accountants mouse left-handed. At work, I had an external number pad on the right side of my keyboard. The guy must have moved my mouse when he was putting the files on my laptop, and then he shut the lid when he was done."

While Nicholas and Alexander discussed the suit Fairhaven Exports would file on Monday, Elizabeth tried to break into a couple of the protected files. Her eyes felt gritty, but she *knew* there had to be something there.

"Gotcha," she muttered as the screen filled with dozens of spreadsheets, documents, and screenshots. One particularly large document drew her attention. As she paged through the images, she started to feel sick. "Well, this alone damns me."

Alexander peered at her screen, grimaced, and then turned the laptop towards Nicholas so he could see the email message.

*I've completed the Fairhaven files. Eight percent, as we agreed. I expect the bonus in my account by morning. —Elizabeth*

"Well, shite."

"She didn't send that email, Nicholas," Alexander said sharply.

Nicholas sighed and leaned back, draping his arm over the top of the couch. "I *know* that, Alex. If I thought she had anything to do with this, I wouldn't be here. I'd have sent my lawyer instead. Bloody hell, you can be over-protective."

"I protect those I love. You should know that by now."

Elizabeth's heartbeat thudded in her ears. Then skipped a beat. If Donatella hadn't entered at that precise moment carrying a fresh carafe of coffee and more mugs, Elizabeth would have gaped. While he'd told her earlier that he loved her, saying it in front of someone else?

"Dinner will be at seven, Mr. Fairhaven. How many will there be?"

"Nicholas? Do you want to stay?" Alexander asked.

His brother waved his hand. "No. Candy will be waiting for me by then. If I don't feed her, she gets whiny."

Alexander glanced at Elizabeth. "Your friends will come?"

Checking her phone, she nodded. "Yes." The six text messages she'd received confirmed they'd show up *and* that they planned to interrogate Alexander without mercy.

"We'll be four, then."

Donatella nodded at Alexander. "And the extra staff? They will be staying?"

"For now. I know this is extra work for you and I'm sorry for that. Have Samuel book you and your daughter a week somewhere in January, anywhere you want to go."

Donatella beamed. "Thank you, sir. Teresa has always wanted to go to Cancun."

The chef left as Milos led Ben, Paul Foyle, and a woman and another man Elizabeth didn't know into the room. Alexander stood, then helped Elizabeth to her feet.

Ben smiled and offered her his hand. "You worried us, my dear. I'm glad you're all right."

Foyle nodded curtly in greeting, took a seat next to Nicholas, and withdrew his laptop. "I'm only here to observe and take notes," he said. "You're a material witness to our case against CPH, and I don't want to be blindsided in court."

The woman scanned the room, her limpid blue eyes lingering first on Nicholas, then Alexander. She smiled warmly and extended her hand. "Carola Roy, U.S. Attorney for the State of Massachusetts. I'll be handling the case against Carter, Pastack, and Hayes. It's a pleasure, Alexander, Elizabeth."

Carola's smile dropped as soon as Alexander extricated his hand from hers. Elizabeth eyed the magenta power suit, the white shirt that opened to reveal a slice of lace, and decided she didn't much care for the woman.

"My chief investigator, Tyler Gilvers," Carola said as she gestured to her companion.

Tyler, tall and ruggedly handsome with only a hint of gray in his brown hair, shook Elizabeth's hand first. "Good to meet you, Miss Bennett. Please accept my apologies. I had to go through your apartment with a fine-toothed comb this morning. I did my best not to leave it a mess."

Elizabeth's cheeks burned. "Lovely. Since you've likely seen my underwear, medical records, and recent reading material, I think you can call me Elizabeth."

"It's my job, Elizabeth. I don't judge. Regardless of what I find. You have nothing to be ashamed of." Tyler took a seat next to Carola. His dark hazel eyes flicked to her laptop. "Ben told me last night that you'd taken this with you. May I?"

"I'd prefer to show you what I've found if that's all right?" Elizabeth said. She turned the machine so Carola and Tyler could see the screen and summarized her findings.

Ben took detailed notes and handed her a flash drive to copy all of the altered files when she'd finished. Carola ordered Tyler to take the laptop into evidence.

Elizabeth's thoughts started to wander as Alexander and Nicholas asked Carola about the timing of the Fairhaven lawsuits.

She was tired. Exhausted even, and she still had to deal with the press this evening. And her friends. Even after five years in Boston, she'd only grown close to a few people. She needed Toni and Kelsey, needed to feel normal for even an hour, but if they took an instant dislike to Alexander, Elizabeth didn't know how she'd get through dinner.

Alexander's voice permeated her thoughts. What was he saying? She squeezed her eyes shut for a moment, trying to focus.

"What is the likelihood they'll come after her again?"

Carola cleared her throat. "It's hard to say. Though, after tomorrow it won't do them any good."

"Tomorrow?" Elizabeth asked as she forced her eyes open.

The attorney spared her a brief glance before turning her smile back to Alexander. "Two things are happening tomorrow. First, we're raiding CPH's offices at 8:00 a.m. Second, we'll take Elizabeth's deposition tomorrow at our offices. Say, at eleven?" Without waiting for a response, Carola continued. "Tonight, we'll put her into protective custody. She'll be there until the case is settled, and after that, if we still think there's any sort of threat, the witness protection program is certainly an option."

Elizabeth's stomach flipped as Alexander, Ben, and Nicholas all started speaking at once. Her fingers tightened on Alexander's thigh. Unable to look at him, her throat too tight for her to say anything, she prayed the death grip on his leg conveyed her fear.

"Enough!" Alexander roared. When silence descended, he pinned Carola with an icy stare. "Elizabeth isn't going into protective custody."

Carola leaned forward, the lace gaping to reveal the tops of her breasts. "It's the safest place for her, Alex."

A muscle in Alexander's leg tightened under Elizabeth's touch as the anger rolled through him. "Ms. Roy, my name is Alexander. But I'd prefer you address me as Mr. Fairhaven. That gentleman who frisked you on your way in was a major in the Special Projects division of the SAS. They're very much like your SEAL team. His partner? A member of the First Raider Brigade from Greece. Off-shift, downstairs, I have a former Secret Service agent and three former SEALs. Elizabeth is safer here than anywhere. What would you do for her? Stick her in a small hotel room with a single police officer as a babysitter? Only let her leave for court dates? Ben tells me that the case will likely not be tried until the first of the year. I will not let her spend Christmas alone, nor will I stand for being forcefully parted from her."

Carola sputtered. "There w-would be two of th-them."

Alexander glared back. "I have six, and I can get a dozen more with a single phone call. You don't have the resources I do."

"Elizabeth—Miss Bennett—this is irresponsible," Carola pleaded. "CPH defrauded their customers out of close to four hundred million over the past five years."

Elizabeth's headache throbbed with each beat of her heart. "Oh, so *now* you're willing to acknowledge that I'm sitting right here? I'm not blind, Ms. Roy. Nor am I stupid or irresponsible. What I *am* is exhausted and tired of you looking at Alexander like he's your prize for having to be here on a Saturday. I need a minute. Excuse me."

Elizabeth pushed up, proud that she didn't sway on her feet. Alexander stalked after her as she hurried from the room.

"You should have seen her face," Alexander said as he slid an arm around her waist. He sobered when she turned to him, tears lining her eyes. "What's wrong?"

"I just need a minute. A bathroom. You have one down here, don't you?" Elizabeth tried desperately not to let her tears spill, but as Alexander tucked her against him and brought her into a small home gym, she lost the battle.

At a half-bath in the corner of the room, Alexander rested his hands on her shoulders and held her gaze. "If you ever ask me to let you go, I will. But until that day, you never have to face anything alone. We'll get through this together."

Elizabeth nodded, fighting against the nausea that threatened. "If I hadn't left, I would have said something I regretted," she managed. "Go back in there. I won't be long. I just need to splash some water on my face."

For a long moment, Elizabeth didn't know if Alexander would let her go, but eventually, he nodded. "I probably should make sure she hasn't captured Nicholas in those talons of hers."

Elizabeth almost laughed, and once she'd run a washcloth under cold water and pressed it to the back of her neck, she steadied.

Just outside the parlor, raised voices met her ears.

"This is foolish, Mr. Fairhaven. The police haven't found any sign of the man who attacked her. He's still out there somewhere," Carola snapped.

Alexander swore. China rattled. "So find him."

"We're working on it," Tyler assured him. "There was enough blood on the heel of Elizabeth's shoe and her dress to run DNA. Unfortunately, it wasn't a match for anyone in the system. Whoever he is, he hasn't been arrested before. And without a detailed description, we're going to have a hard time searching for him."

"Which is why we need her to agree to protective custody. I don't care how many former SEAL team members you have," Carola said. "I won't be responsible for her safety if she doesn't agree to come with us this evening."

"No." Elizabeth stepped through the doorway into the parlor, and everyone turned towards her. "Once I give my deposition, nothing they do matters, right? They could kill me, and it won't damage your case against them?"

No one in the room said a word for several tense breaths until Carola broke the silence. "We've got them dead to rights. We want you to testify so CPH can't sue you. Once you give your statement, under oath, the only legal challenge they could possibly have goes away."

"They're not stupid," Elizabeth said. She limped back to Alexander and sank down on to the leather sofa. His arm curled around her, soothing her in ways she'd come to depend on. "I don't think they'll come after me again. If anything happens to me now, they'd be the prime suspects. And they've taken too much already. They took my job. They broke into my home. I don't even know that I'm going to be able to sleep there again without thinking about the asshole who tried to kill me. I won't lose anything else to those bastards."

*Especially not Alexander.*

Alexander's shoulders melted away from his ears, and he blew out a relieved breath. Elizabeth straightened as best she could. "I'll come in for the deposition tomorrow, and I'll testify whenever you need me to, but other than that, I'm done. You have my computer, and you can request copies of my bank records, tax returns, and any other personal data you need to prove that I had nothing to do with the tax fraud. I don't have anything to hide. I'd like to see the papers you found under my floorboards. You said there were notes on them?"

Tyler withdrew a stack of papers sealed in plastic and passed them to her. On the top sheet, a Post-it contained a hastily scrawled note. "We've tested it for fingerprints, but it's clean."

*Per our agreement. This is the last remaining copy of the original return. —E. Bennett*

"That's not my handwriting," Elizabeth said. "Ask anyone in the office. I don't use blue pens. Ever. I don't own any. Red and black only. And at CPH, I went by Lizzie. If I were going to put my name to something it'd be L. Bennett."

Tyler pulled out a legal pad and a blue pen. "Will you submit a handwriting sample?"

"Of course." Elizabeth copied the text verbatim. There were subtle differences in the curve of her l's, the serif on her t's and the slant of her n's. Tyler sealed the sample in another clear plastic bag and signed his name across the flap. "Is there anything else?"

"I have a list of questions," Carola said, withdrawing two printed sheets of paper from her black leather briefcase. "I'd like to go over them now."

For the next two hours, the prosecutor peppered Elizabeth with questions. By the time they were done, darkness had fallen beyond the large picture windows. Goodbyes were exchanged, and Carola, Tyler, and Foyle left together. Ben and Nicholas remained behind for the press conference.

Alexander turned to Elizabeth and tucked a lock of hair behind her ear. "Your friends will be here shortly. How are you holding up?"

"I feel a little better. Knowing—deciding—that I'm not going to have to give up any more of my life helped." Her stomach growled. The scents of rosemary, chicken, and butter wafted through the house. "And I really want to get the next hour over with."

"The press conference or dealing with your friends?" Alexander asked.

"Both."

# CHAPTER TWENTY-THREE

"*E*lizabeth?" Alexander rubbed his hand up and down her arm, and she forced her eyes open. "Your friends have arrived."

He smiled down at her, tucked against his side and wrapped in a soft cream-colored blanket. She'd tried to stay awake when he, Nicholas, and Ben had started talking about the upcoming lawsuit Fairhaven was preparing to bring against CPH, but between the fire in the hearth, her injuries, and Alexander's comforting warmth, she'd lost the battle.

"Miss Elizabeth is in the parlor," Samuel said as he led her two best friends into the room.

"Oh my God," Toni said as she rushed in and pulled Elizabeth into a tight hug.

"Ow!" Pain shot through her shoulder, and Toni jerked back, horrified.

"What did I do?" Toni ran a hand through her short brown curls and looked from Elizabeth to Alexander. Kelsey hovered just behind her, eyes wide.

Sensing Alexander seething beside her, Elizabeth forced out a breath. "I'm pretty banged up," she said. "You didn't do anything wrong. Just...let me do the hugging, okay?"

After Toni nodded, Elizabeth twined her fingers through Alexander's under the blanket. "Um, this is Alexander, his brother Nicholas, and Ben, Alexander's lawyer."

"*Our* lawyer," Alexander corrected. As Nicholas and Ben stood to shake hands with the women, he turned to Elizabeth, searching her gaze for a long moment to confirm she wasn't in severe pain. At her nod, Alexander rose. "A pleasure," he said as Kelsey shook his hand.

Toni jammed her hands on her slim hips and glared up at him. "I don't care how much money you have. She looks like she's been run over by a train. What. Happened?"

"Toni!" Elizabeth tried to get up, but her muscles screamed in protest, and she sank back down quickly.

Alexander motioned for Nicholas and Ben to give them all some privacy, and they headed for Alexander's office behind the stairs.

"Miss Grimaldi, you don't know anything about me, but I care very deeply for Elizabeth, and if I could have stopped her attacker sooner, I would have."

The two faced off for several tense breaths. After a brief glance at Elizabeth, Toni relented. "Okay. I believe you."

Alexander held out his hand, and Toni paused for only a beat before returning the gesture. "I'm sure you would like some time alone. I'll leave you until five minutes before we're expected outside." He leaned down and kissed Elizabeth. Staking his claim, his tongue danced with hers, and he pulled away only after nipping at her lower lip.

"Where will you be?" Elizabeth asked. Suddenly, she realized how little she knew of the home's layout, and nerves—both over the press conference and her friends' interrogation—had her voice trembling.

"In my office with Nicholas and Ben. Down the hall and to the right of the stairs."

With one last lingering brush of his thumb over her lips, he left them alone.

"Makeup. Now," Elizabeth insisted. She gently pushed her hair back, and both Toni and Kelsey gasped. "I'm *not* going to talk to a bunch of reporters with cameras looking this bad."

Kelsey set her makeup kit on the coffee table and started rummaging inside. "Spill it, Lizzie. All of it."

Elizabeth sighed.

"Last night, my neighbor called as we were about to go to sleep. River was acting weird." The cat heard her name and offered a little *mrrp* from her spot next to the fireplace.

"He moved you in here?" Toni shook her head. "I take it back. That's just...not cool. You're locked away behind men with guns?" She dropped her voice. "I can call my uncle."

Elizabeth tried not to roll her eyes. "You will do no such thing. I'm staying here because it's the safest place for me. Now stop jumping to conclusions and listen."

As Kelsey started applying foundation, Elizabeth shared what she remembered from the previous night. By the time she'd finished, Kelsey had progressed to powder and blush.

"He really said he was falling in love with you?" Toni asked.

Her cheeks flushing, Elizabeth smiled. "He did."

"So, what's it like? Living in this big house and having the staff call you 'Miss Elizabeth'?" Kelsey asked as she carefully arranged Elizabeth's hair over her stitches, then added a couple of pumps of hair spray to hold the locks in place.

"This isn't...anything I was prepared for." Elizabeth fiddled with the hem of her sweater again, the expensive wool softer than any of her clothes at home. "He buys container ships for a living. I don't even shop at the Container Store because it's too expensive. What if we're just...too different?"

"People have overcome more. Hell, my father didn't even

speak English when my mother met him. They've been together forty years," Toni replied.

Alexander cleared his throat from the doorway, and Elizabeth gasped. One look at his face and she knew he'd heard her confessing her fears.

Elizabeth rose, still unsteady, and he met her halfway across the room. "I thought we were past this," he said quietly. "I love you. Isn't that enough?"

"I want it to be."

He slid his arm around her waist, and she melted against him, but when he spoke, his tone still carried an edge. "We're expected outside. Ladies, Samuel will show you into the media room where you can watch on television."

"Lizzie?" Toni reached out and took her hand. "Are you okay?"

Elizabeth tore her gaze away from Alexander. Her friends pressed together, a united front ready to protect her or fight for her if she asked them to. "Go with Samuel," she said. "Alexander and I will be a few minutes, and then we'll have dinner."

Alexander's majordomo appeared behind him with a leather coat in his hands. "Miss Elizabeth, it's freezing outside."

"Thank you," she managed as Alexander took the coat from Samuel. Once they were alone, she stepped back, the hurt and confusion in the emerald depths of his eyes too much to bear. "You can't tell me you haven't thought the same thing."

"I haven't. Not once."

"Alex," Nicholas appeared in the doorway. "Whatever this is, we don't have time for it now."

"Shut it, Nicholas. This does not concern you. The press will wait." Alexander helped her into the coat, then wrapped his arms around her from behind. His warm breath tickled her ear. "I didn't intend to fall in love with you, Elizabeth. Honestly, I wasn't sure I was capable of the emotion. But now...I can't imagine my life without you. Don't give up on us because of differences that mean nothing."

Elizabeth slumped in his hold. "The press is going to jump all over me. Maybe not tonight, but soon. I'm unemployed. They'll dig up all the crap with my parents. My bank account, credit rating. All of it. Aren't you worried about that? About what they'll say about you for dating me?"

"No." The single word carried his every emotion, and he turned her around with his hands on her waist. "I care about *you*, Elizabeth. I can handle the press, and if they come after you, they'll regret it."

"Are we quite done with the carrying on?" Nicholas asked. "The longer we make them wait, the more rabid they're going to be."

Elizabeth searched for any hint of deception in Alexander's eyes, any sign he might be putting on a front so she wouldn't worry. But she only found determination, love, and a hint of pain at her lack of trust in him. "I won't give up on us," she whispered, and his smile warmed her down to her toes.

"You look lovely," he said as Samuel opened the door for them.

Bright lights blinded her, and she raised a hand to shield her eyes as they stepped out onto the porch. Camera flashes went off in her face. Philippa, a tall brunette in her forties, stood in a heavy coat at a small podium that had been erected on the porch.

"Ladies and gentlemen, Mr. Fairhaven and Ms. Bennett will make a brief statement and take a few questions. Please do not interrupt." Philippa stepped aside, allowing Alexander and Elizabeth to approach the microphone.

*Oh God. You can do this.*

Elizabeth gripped the thin wood sides of the podium with white knuckled fingers.

"Last night, a man broke into my apartment and tried to kill me." A titter went through the crowd, and another few flashes had her raising a hand to her eyes briefly. "I went up ahead of Alexander while he handled some business. The assailant was already inside. He threw me into a table. I sustained a mild concussion. Alexander heard me scream and probably saved my life. He stayed by my side all night in the hospital because I needed him there. The notion that he could have done this to me —as the *Beantown Babbler* reported—is ridiculous and patently false. I won't dignify their claims with any further discussion."

Philippa joined them at the podium. "You've heard from Ms. Bennett in her own words. She and Mr. Fairhaven will take a few questions. Mr. Joont, I see your hand."

"Mr. Fairhaven, Ms. Bennett. Mark Joont, WGBH. Can you confirm that this has something to do with the lawsuit you've filed against Carter, Pastack, and Hayes?"

Ben cleared his throat from behind them and raised his voice to be heard. "I'm representing Ms. Bennett. This isn't a question we're prepared to comment on at this time. However, I will confirm that she is a material witness in the tax fraud case and that Harry Carter threatened both of them last night at the governor's ball. You can draw your own conclusions."

"Was the concussion the only injury when you were attacked?" another reporter called out.

"The only serious one," Elizabeth replied.

Philippa pointed to a woman with flaming red hair and lips to match. "Hilary Wasser, BBC, do you have a question?"

"Is Fairhaven Charities bringing its own lawsuit? What about you and your brother?"

Alexander leaned closer to the microphone. "Fairhaven Charities employs independent accountants. As for Nicholas and me personally, we have no current plans to sue CPH. I will not speculate on whether our lawyers will bring suits against the *Babbler* for their false and hurtful claims."

"What is the status of your relationship?" a woman called out from the crowd.

Alexander started to reply, but Elizabeth squeezed his hand. "Let me." She sought out the blond woman who'd asked the question. "Alexander is probably used to all this attention, but I'm not. No one reports on my relationships. At least not until now. How would you feel if a stranger on the T came up to you and asked you how your sex life was? Whether you'd made plans for Christmas? Or whether you were in love?"

"I'm not news," the reporter replied.

"Clearly." Next to her, Alexander stifled a chuckle. "I'm not going to comment on the intimate details of our relationship other than to say that Alexander has been nothing but kind and caring this weekend. There's nowhere else in the world I'd rather be right now. Well, except inside, warm, and away from all of you fine people."

Half of the reporters laughed, and the others glared at her. She couldn't tell if she'd just made a terrible mistake or a brilliant show of bravery.

"That's all for tonight, ladies and gentlemen. It's close to freezing, and Elizabeth needs rest. I'll thank you for a bit of privacy in the next few days. Any other questions you have can be directed to our attorney, Fairhaven Exports' legal department, or my press secretary." Alexander led Elizabeth back inside, Nicholas, Ben, and a chorus of camera shutters following them.

# CHAPTER TWENTY-FOUR

*E*lizabeth sank into the luxurious leather seat of the limo with a groan. Even the slightest movement aggravated her headache, and she'd broken down and taken one of the Vicodin before she'd let Alexander help her out of Ben's office.

Four hours of deposition hadn't left her with any reserves, and she closed her bloodshot and gritty eyes as Alexander slid onto the seat next to her.

CPH's lawyer, Oliver Forrester, had a kind face. Until the questioning started. Gold digger, two-bit hussy—who even used that term anymore?—and fraud were the milder terms he'd called her, and though she'd held her own, she'd barely managed to keep the panic at bay.

"Are you all right?" Alexander's deep voice drew her out of her thoughts. "You look knackered. We can skip going to your apartment and head straight for Maine."

"I don't want to go back there." She wasn't proud of the tremble in her voice, or the nausea that churned in her stomach.

"We don't have to. I'll call Marjorie, and you can order whatever you need for the next few days. She'll have everything sent over within the hour." Alexander framed her face with his hands, and she met his gaze. The cognac flecks in his irises seemed richer and brighter today.

"No, I need to do this. It won't get any easier the longer I wait. I'm glad you're coming with me."

"I don't plan on being anywhere else but by your side for some time." His lips brushed hers. He tasted of coffee, rich and strong and dark as night. Elizabeth could believe everything was going to be okay whenever he kissed her.

Milos and Carl—two of Alexander's security detail—flanked them as they stepped out of the elevator. Elizabeth had expected the worst, but her newly repaired front door gleamed with fresh paint, and as he pressed the key into her hand, she took a deep breath.

Orange soap, disinfectant, and a hint of fresh wood stain were the only scents she could discern as she stepped over the threshold. Her broken coffee table was gone, along with the bloodstains. The silver bowl rested on her counter, full of River's cat toys.

"You did this," she said, turning to Alexander.

"Well, not me, personally, but yes. As I was the one to damage your door, I thought I should have it fixed. Were you terribly attached to that coffee table?"

She snorted "No. It was from Goodwill."

Milos cleared the apartment and nodded to Alexander as he took his place next to Carl at the front door.

In her bedroom, the floorboard was back in place and the window sparkling and new.

*Keep quiet. If you don't, I'll make your last few minutes very painful.*

Her open closet door drew the memory of her attacker's voice. He'd been hiding there, she knew now, and her shoes were in disarray. As her heart rate spiked, she pressed her hand to her chest and forced a deep breath before dropping to her knees and trying to bring some order back into her personal space.

"Elizabeth?"

A couple of her blouses had fallen off the hangers, and as she clutched them to her chest, a whiff of her assailant's sweat and greasy hair floated up. Tossing the clothes into the hamper in the corner, she pushed to her feet.

"You're upset." Alexander reached for her arm, but she side-stepped him, slipped out of the room, and closed herself in the bathroom. No. She couldn't let herself give in to the panic.

Drumming her fingers gently against her eyebrows helped bring her heart rate down.

*I'm never going to be able to sleep here again.*

The light knock startled her, and she yelped. "I *said* I need a couple of minutes. Go buy another container ship or something."

The bathroom door swung open. "There aren't any more ships for sale today," Alexander said. "And you're trying not to cry. You can't very well expect me to leave you alone in that state. Come sit with me and tell me what's wrong." He guided her back to the bed and sat with his arm around her shoulders. Even his warmth couldn't quite calm her here.

*I'm warning you.*

She shook her head, trying to wipe the memory of her attacker's threats away. "Don't let go," she whispered to Alexander.

"I couldn't let you go if I tried." He pressed her palm to his heart and waited patiently for her to speak, tracing patterns on the back of her hand.

"I don't know if I can stay here again," Elizabeth said. "He was in here when I came in. In the bedroom. He dragged me back out to the living room and held me down. I couldn't breathe." She turned her head into Alexander's neck and inhaled his scent. "This place wasn't much, but it was mine. I always felt safe here."

Alexander threaded his fingers through her hair and held her securely against his body. His lips brushed her ear. "This isn't a decision you have to make now, Elizabeth. You're not staying anywhere alone until the man who hurt you is arrested."

"He's a professional. A...hitman." The one word she hadn't let herself say before sent her panic over the edge. As she hyperventilated, Alexander guided her head towards her knees, then rested his hand on the back of her neck.

Elizabeth jerked away. "Don't. Don't touch me there."

Alexander held up his hands. "What is it? What did I do?"

"There's a spot...he said there was a spot he could use to render me unconscious if I fought him. I don't want to keep feeling his hands on me."

Anger twisted Alexander's mouth into a snarl, and he went to her window, shoving his hands into his pockets and staring out over the alley behind the building.

After several tense minutes, Elizabeth managed to calm enough to speak. "Come back."

"Not if I'm going to frighten you." Emotion thickened his tone, and he refused to turn around.

The entire room smelled wrong. Felt wrong. Elizabeth went to Alexander, took his hand, and returned it to her neck. Locking her eyes on his, she tried to focus on his scent, the warmth of his touch, and the steady beat of his heart under her palm.

"I don't want to be so scared."

"Fear is...a part of life, Elizabeth." Alexander's voice cracked, and he slid his other arm around her. "I close my eyes and I hear you screaming. I see him hurting you. I'd be happy if you never came back here again. But whenever you want or need to be here, I'll be with you."

As Alexander pulled her close, she laid her head against his shoulder. Home, safety, love. She'd never associated scents with those thoughts before. Alexander's soap, his aftershave, and the very essence of him would now forever be branded with those words.

Once her heart rate returned to normal, Elizabeth extricated herself from his embrace, then returned to her closet. Packing a duffel bag with jeans, her favorite sweater, a couple of flannel shirts, and underwear, she tried not to let her mind wander.

"Snow attire?" Alexander asked.

She dug in the back of her closet for her snow pants and boots. "We're not sledding, are we? I hate sledding."

"No," he chuckled. "But there's a storm headed for the coast that should hit tomorrow afternoon. We might end up walking to dinner tomorrow, or skiing if the roads are too slick. It's a small town. We could be stranded for a few days."

A reluctant smile tugged at her lips. "You'd like that, wouldn't you?"

"It wouldn't upset me."

———

AN HOUR LATER, Alexander pulled out onto the highway. Behind his Mercedes, Milos and Carl followed in a black SUV. BBC streamed from the radio.

"We've about ninety minutes," he said, "if you want to take a nap."

"Where are we going? All you ever told me was 'Maine.'" Elizabeth stifled a yawn, then reclined the seat slightly to take some pressure off of her shoulder.

"York Beach. I go there when I need to escape the city. During the winter, half the town shuts down. There are a few people who know me there, but they're discreet. We won't be bothered."

The way he spoke of the town made her think this wasn't an ordinary destination. "Have you ever brought anyone there?"

They turned onto Interstate 95. Snow danced outside the windows, tiny flakes that had no direction or destination. Alexander flicked on the wipers. "No. You're the only one. I'm not even certain Nicholas knows about it."

"Oh."

"You're very special, Elizabeth. You have to know this by now.

I want to share everything with you. Including parts of me I never share with anyone else."

They drove for almost two hours. The snow piled up along the interstate. By the time they entered Maine, Alexander's knuckles had paled as he clutched the steering wheel in a vise grip and he hunched forward in the driver's seat. Through the white curtain outside her window, Elizabeth caught glimpses of the sea. Five years in Boston and she'd never made it to Maine, despite Kelsey and Toni pestering her to join them every summer.

Alexander pulled off the main road and turned up a small hill. But even the snow tires couldn't keep up with the ice and snow gathering on the winding road. They skidded, righted, and skidded some more. When they pulled into the driveway of a small, single-story home, Alexander stopped the car and blew out a breath. "Bloody hell. That was the worst sodding drive I've had in years."

The black SUV pulled in to the driveway next door. Milos stood by their car while Carl checked the perimeter.

"No footprints around the house, sir, and the alarm hasn't been activated. Do you want us to check inside?" Carl asked when he returned.

"No. We'll be fine. The caretaker stocked the fridges here and at the cottage next door this morning. I have the panic button." He held up a small pager. "Go relax. If we need you, you'll know."

"Yes, sir," Milos said, and the two headed for a small bungalow on the adjoining property.

Alexander hefted their luggage and his laptop, despite Elizabeth's protests. "You can get the keys, *chérie*," he said with a grin.

From the gleam in his eye, she had a pretty good idea where those keys were. As she slipped her hand into the tight pocket of his jeans, his cock stirred against her fingers. Though the keys rested high in the pocket, she dug deep and scraped her short nails along his hip.

"Careful now," he said. "Or I'll strip you naked and make you sit quietly on the couch while I build a fire to warm up the house."

"You wouldn't!" Elizabeth gasped, withdrawing the keys and unlocking the door as quickly as she could.

"I would. You've been lucky not to earn a punishment from me yet, Elizabeth, but that time is coming." Despite his ominous words, he smiled at her.

She shivered, but not from the cold.

Alexander flipped light switches as he led Elizabeth through the house. In the living room, a light blue sofa sat in front of a brick fireplace with a flat-screen TV mounted above.

Floor-to-ceiling windows looked out over the snow-covered backyard. Inky blackness beyond the fence confused her for a moment.

"Wait. Is that the ocean?"

"It is." Alexander dropped the bags and then wrapped his arms around her waist from behind. Angling her to the left, he pressed a kiss to her ear. "Watch."

Brilliant red and white lights winked on and off. "That's Nubble Light. It's been standing since 1879. The little nub of land it sits on—that's how it got its name—is really only accessible by this motorized tram—more of a bucket, really."

Alexander sighed, and his voice took on a wistful tone. "I discovered this place after a particularly....bad time in my life. I needed to be somewhere else, and I came up here for a fortnight. The very first time I saw the lighthouse, I couldn't look away. I sat in the parking lot for an hour watching the waves and the sunset, and the rest of my problems faded away. I bought this place the very next week.

"This is the only place I can go and be completely myself." He nuzzled the back of her neck and feathered kisses along her earlobe.

"So you haven't been completely yourself with me until now?" she asked.

Alexander bit her ear, and she yelped. "You bring out the real me, Elizabeth. I've not needed this place since I met you. The only reason we're here now is that I want to share it with you."

"Oh." She twisted and looked up into his dark green eyes. "Thank you for that."

He kissed her tenderly and sucked her lower lip between his teeth before releasing her. "Relax while I build a fire and fix us some dinner."

"I can cook."

"You can have a rest."

Elizabeth scowled. "You're the one who drove more than two hours in a raging snowstorm to get us here. You've slept less than I have the past two days. Let me cook something for us. Please."

"Elizabeth, you're still injured, and you need rest." He brushed a finger along the edge of the bruise on her temple.

"I'm not planning on running a marathon. I'm going to cook dinner. You can unpack our bags if it makes you feel better. Even do the dishes." She jabbed his shoulder softly as she skirted him, but he caught her around the waist and pulled her against him.

"Someone is feeling feisty," he said roughly.

"You're the one who told me not to give up who I was—my strength—in the rest of our relationship. If you want a future with me, you can't expect me to do what you say all the time." She tried to wriggle out of his grasp, but he held her tightly.

Alexander's eyes softened. "I didn't mean to imply that I expect you to...obey me...outside of the bedroom. I worry about you. I cannot look at you right now without seeing you unconscious and bloodied on the floor of your flat or seeing that tosser's hands on you, causing you pain. I'm going to be a bit overprotective for a while."

"We're going to have to figure out how to make this work," she said. "Some sort of balance. You're . . . intense."

He laughed. "I am. That is part of the reason we're here. Time alone. Time to learn about each other. Find that balance. I'm used to getting what I want. But the one thing I've never found...is love. Not until now. I'm out of my element."

Alexander released her with one last kiss. "I've fallen for you, Elizabeth Bennett. There's not much I wouldn't do to ensure you one day feel the same about me."

Elizabeth watched him slip out the glass doors to the backyard, presumably to get wood for the fire. "I'm pretty sure I'm already there."

The SubZero refrigerator had been stocked for an army. Once she'd selected two steaks, potatoes, and kale, she *tsked* as she pulled a bottle of Champagne from the bottom shelf.

"What did you say?" Alexander asked, dropping a pile of logs in a metal bin next to the hearth.

"Champagne should never be stored in the refrigerator for more than a few hours, you know." Elizabeth waved the bottle at him, then set it on the counter.

"I *do* know. Apparently, my caretaker does not." Alexander stacked logs and arranged kindling while Elizabeth chopped potatoes. Mischief glinted in his eyes. "We could drink it."

"Not tonight. Steaks." She pointed to the package of meat. "There's a bottle of Bordeaux in the wine rack that's appropriate for what I'm making."

"Where did you learn about wine?" he asked, striking the match and lighting the kindling.

"Parents. Any daughter of theirs had to be able to host a dinner party appropriately." She seasoned the steaks as the potatoes started to sizzle in the pan. "We traveled to Paris, London, and Rome every year. Family holiday. Every trip included cooking classes for my mother and me. Dad and Darren got to spend the time drinking or gambling."

*You're late. Dinner was supposed to be ready when I got home.*

In her memories, Darren chided her, and she braced her hand against the counter forcing deep breaths.

Alexander cut her off with a kiss that left her breathless. "I see the fear in your eyes, Elizabeth. Why?"

"Memories." Elizabeth's cheeks flushed with embarrassment, and she pulled away to start heating up the cast iron pan for the steaks. "Darren...screwed me up. In a lot of ways. I stopped doing all these things I enjoyed because he expected me to do them. I loved to cook until he insisted that I have dinner ready every night before he came home. He never raised a hand to me or even yelled, but..."

Alexander tenderly stroked her cheek with the back of his hand. "He mistreated you. Even if he never laid a hand on you. And one of these days, I plan on laying him out flat and telling him so."

"The part of me that's an adult says you should be the bigger man and let it go." She shot him a quick smile. "The part of me that thinks he's a vile, petty, childish prick wants to watch."

Alexander bellowed out a laugh. "Then the next time you go to Seattle, I'll go with you. Now, can I help you at all with this?"

"No. Go unpack. You have ten minutes before I could use an extra set of hands. This is a simple meal with steaks this expensive."

"Simpler, perhaps. But not simple. I fall more in love with you every moment." Alexander left her with a quick kiss and a promise to not only unpack but to build a fire in the bedroom for later.

Elizabeth watched him walk away, and any doubts she'd had melted away. She'd fallen in love with him, too.

# CHAPTER TWENTY-FIVE

*O*ver dinner, they shared stories of their youth.

Alexander's exploits on the rugby field, Elizabeth's brief stint in the drama club, and stories of their parents—Alexander's parents anyway. Elizabeth couldn't bring herself to speak much about the people who disowned her.

When they moved to the couch, Elizabeth curled against him as he stared into the flames. "And conquests?" she asked with a smile as she wrapped her arms around his waist. "Rumors are, you've had a long line of them."

Alexander's body language changed, his back stiffening. "Not as long as the tabloids claim, but...I haven't been a monk, by any means."

She drew back to cup his cheek. "Alexander, I don't care. I've only had four serious relationships, plus a couple of hookups in college. My boyfriend freshman year at Harvard taught me how to crack passwords and rewire a light switch. Howard used to sing in the shower, and he tried to encourage me to switch my major to pre-law—against my parents' wishes. Once they found out... well..." Memories threatened, ones she didn't want to delve into tonight. "I could never stand up to them."

"Until you did. Until you had something you knew you had to fight for." Alexander ducked his head so he could give her a quick kiss. "Your strength amazes me, Elizabeth. Truly. That's what drew me to you in the first place. And every day since, your spark, the fire inside of you...I can't get enough of you. In or out of the bedroom."

She blushed and fiddled with the blanket he'd drawn over her legs. "I've never experienced anything like being your...being in your silks."

"Yet still, even saying the word sub makes you uncomfortable. Why? Because you're such a strong woman?"

She shrugged. "I...yes. I've been alone—no family, few friends—for five years. Kelsey keeps telling me it doesn't have to be me against the whole world, but that's how it feels sometimes."

Alexander pulled her closer with a nod. "Ten years ago—right before I bought this place, I was in a relationship. It was... serious." Sadness laced his tone, and Elizabeth tried to shift so she could meet his gaze, but he stared into the flames as if he barely saw her. "Serena and I were a good match, on paper. Mother was pleased. We met at boarding school when we were both seventeen, dated for a bit, and then when I took over Fairhaven Charities, I asked her to move to Boston to see if we had something tenable. She agreed, and we dated exclusively for two years. She loved me. I cared for her deeply, but I don't think I ever fell in love with her. She very much wanted to get married. I was new to being a practicing Dom at that time. Serena was amenable to play, but though she was submissive, she lacked anything approaching a backbone, in or out of the bedroom." He closed his eyes for a deep breath, and when he opened them again, there was pain there.

Elizabeth nestled closer. "You don't have to—"

"I do. For both of us." His gaze trailed over the room, settling on their empty wine glasses. "I'd purchased a new crop. Serena was desperate for a commitment and willing to do almost anything to please me. Even the one thing she knew she should never do."

"What was that?"

"She refused to safeword. I hit her too hard. Lost in the moment. Young. Inexperienced. I didn't know that I was truly hurting her. I bruised her. Badly. The second I saw the blood welling purple under her skin, I stopped, but the damage that injury caused to our relationship never healed. I stayed with her for six months after that, largely out of guilt. But we never played again. Eventually, she confessed to me why she hadn't told me when it started to hurt beyond the light pain I intended. She feared I would leave her."

"She wasn't strong enough to stand up to you when she needed to."

"I think that's why I never fell in love with her. Strong women make the best submissives, Elizabeth. I can trust you because you'll always tell me if I push too far. We're tremendous together. With you, I feel as if I'm completely myself."

Elizabeth straddled him, draped her arms around his neck, and captured his lips. As she tasted him, the wine they'd shared, a hint of wood smoke from the fire, and his arousal, she knew what she wanted.

"Alexander, will you tie me up?"

---

"SAUNA? YOU HAVE A SAUNA HERE?" Elizabeth asked as Alexander cracked eggs into a bowl the next morning.

"In the backyard. I take it you'd like a session?" He chuckled as he glanced over at her, perched on a stool at the counter, dressed in nothing but a robe. Their play the night before had been incredible, but nightmares had plagued her, and Alexander hated feeling so helpless to take away her pain.

"Hell yes." She rolled her head on her shoulders and tried to stifle the tightness around her mouth and eyes. "And a massage. My shoulders need attention. Among other parts of my body."

"A massage—" He snapped his mouth shut and tried not to grin. Once he lost the battle, he threw a towel at her. "You're sending me up."

She loosened the belt on her robe, exposing the gentle swell of her breasts. "Maybe."

"Elizabeth."

Her breath caught in her throat. She knew his tone. "Yes?"

"Strip and follow me."

The robe hit the floor a few seconds after he'd turned around. Her bare feet made soft slapping noises on the hardwood floors, punctuated by her erratic breathing. Under his own robe, his cock throbbed.

Inside the bedroom, he whirled and caught her naked body in his arms. As she gasped, he thrust a finger inside of her bare folds to find her already slick for him. "Please," she whispered.

"Oh, you'll be begging before long, *chérie*. Now get on the bed and spread your legs for me. Audible answers now. Do you understand?"

"Yes."

Elizabeth reclined against the pillows and spread her long legs to expose her glistening sex. The scent of her maddened him. How the hell was he supposed to control himself long enough to give her the release she deserved? Alexander grabbed the blindfold from the bedside table and knelt between her legs. He positioned the silk carefully over her eyes, then dipped his head and brushed a soft kiss across her lips.

"Give me your left wrist."

She obediently held her hand out in the direction of his voice, and he fastened the cuff securely. The right one followed without a word, and then he used a clamp to lock the two cuffs together. He lifted her bound hands over her head and watched her face for signs of pain.

"Can you stand this? Is it too much on your shoulder?"

"I'm okay."

"If you hurt at all, say *yellow*. But otherwise, don't move unless I give you permission. Do you understand?"

"Yes."

He hooked the clamp to a part of the wrought-iron headboard, cursing himself for not equipping the room with places to secure his restraints. Though he'd never planned on bringing anyone here.

Once her ankles were cuffed and secured to the bedposts, he kissed the inside of her left knee. The clamp holding her wrists rattled against the headboard, and she keened, trying to shift her hips, remembering his command, and then trying again. Never kissing the same spot twice, Alexander trailed his lips erratically over her body. Her right knee, the top of her left foot, her navel, the curve of her jaw, her right ear.

"Still all right, *chérie*?"

"Uh-huh." Her voice was roughened with need, and he purred his satisfaction as he rose to his knees, relishing in the sight of her spread out like a banquet before him. The left nipple clamp slid on with a gentle pop, and Elizabeth cried out and bucked her hips.

"One. If we get to five, I'll punish you."

"Five?" she squeaked. "God."

"Yes, five. You know my rules now. You no longer need ten. Breathe for me, Elizabeth." The second clamp elicited another yelp. She tried to hold still, but her entire body jerked.

"Two."

"Hurts. And...I need...uh..."

He tugged the silk between the clamps as he laved his tongue over her clit. "You taste like honey." Every gasp and quake was a gift. Sliding two fingers deep inside her, he found the bundle of nerve endings he knew she loved. With a moan, she pulled against the ankle restraints and nearly caught him in the chin with her hips. "Three. I am going to enjoy punishing you."

"I can't...please let me come. It'll be easier then," she whimpered.

"Not yet." He toyed with her clit, enjoying her helpless mewls. Her thighs quivered.

"Can't..."

He bit her inner thigh hard, sucking the creamy flesh between his teeth while simultaneously yanking on the chain between her breasts. The pain should have stopped her orgasm cold, but instead, she screamed out his name, shuddering and undulating on the mattress as her release consumed her.

Alexander lapped up the essence that flooded from her channel, licking, sucking, and biting long after her quaking had ceased. Each time his tongue touched her, it set off another mini-spasm.

"I couldn't," she sobbed. Tears soaked her cheeks, and her head bowed so her chin almost rested on her chest.

"Shhh," he said as he released her ankles, then her wrists. "You'll learn how to control your body, Elizabeth. I'm not angry. But in a few minutes, I *will* punish you."

"I was at three." She tried to raise her head, but too spent, she gave up and fell back against the pillows.

"Four for coming without permission and five because you thrash about quite a lot when you come. Now hush. We're not done. Not by a long shot." He grinned and slid up to cover her body with his. A contented sigh escaped her lips as he rubbed her arms in tender circles.

"While I have you in such a lovely position, I have a question. Have you ever had a man's cock in your mouth?"

She sucked in a breath. "Once. It didn't go well."

"You gagged?" He kissed her chin and fondled her left breast. Her pale cheeks flushed bright red. "Yes."

"Would you be amenable to trying with me? Before you

answer, this isn't a command. Nor something I will ever insist on, and this is not your punishment. You can refuse." Alexander reveled in the blush that spread across her bare breasts, the gasp as one last tremor from her release ran through her, and the way she slid her thigh between his legs to press against his erection.

"I want to try."

His eyebrows shot up. With her limited sexual history and the reluctance to her tone when she'd admitted she'd gagged, he hadn't expected her to agree. "My cock?"

"Yes."

He kissed her neck, and she angled her head to afford him better access. "Thank you. You honor me, Elizabeth. Now I am going to redden that gorgeous arse of yours."

Pulling a long length of silk and hemp rope from the drawer, Alexander bound her legs together at mid-thigh, then locked the ankle cuffs to one another. "So you don't thrash about and hurt me," he said as he scooped her up and set her on her feet. She swayed in his grasp, panic tightening her lips. "I won't let you go, Elizabeth. Trust me."

With a shuddering breath, she nodded. Sitting, he draped her over his thighs and tried to stifle his laugh as her hair tickled his bare feet. Her arse beckoned him, and he massaged the creamy expanse of flesh. His sub liked a bit of pain. With how she'd responded to his flogger, he suspected she'd enjoy her punishment, and in this position, without her arms bound, he wouldn't aggravate any of her still-healing injuries. Every new thing he discovered about Elizabeth made him love her even more.

"Are you comfortable? Nothing hurts?"

"Nothing hurts," she said.

"Count for me, Elizabeth. Ten strikes."

*Thwap.* The crack of his hand against her bare arse made her yelp, but she didn't move beyond a quick flinch. "One," she whispered.

He swung again. "T-two."

Arousal coated his legs, and by his fifth strike, she'd started to quiver. At seven, she tried to grind her hips against his thighs, but he reached down and tugged on the silk between her breasts. "Three more, *chérie*."

He finished off the last strikes quickly, then flipped her around so she sat up against him. Her arse had to be on fire, but she collapsed into his chest. Was she even still with him? "Elizabeth?"

"Uh-huh?"

"I needed to hear your voice. You're a treasure. A lovely, wriggling treasure." Alexander tossed a pillow on the floor, then helped her to her knees. As her arse hit her heels, she hissed. "Damn."

"The pain is part of your submission and your punishment, Elizabeth. Will you take it for me? You can always use your safeword."

She tipped her face up, despite the blindfold, and her cheeks flushed. "It's...not um...bad."

Alexander chuckled. "You like the feeling?" When she didn't immediately reply, he cupped her cheek. "Answer me, Elizabeth."

"Y-yes. I...liked you punishing me."

With deft fingers, he released the clamp on her wrist cuffs. "Can you put your arms behind your back without straining your shoulder?"

A tiny wince tightened her lips as she moved, but she relaxed as soon as she clasped her hands together. "Yes."

He considered for a moment, uncertain she was being completely honest with him. "I'm not going to lock your wrists together. Not today. Keep your fingers laced like that if you can, and take this." Pressing a bell into her hands, he felt her confusion. "You won't be able to safeword with your lips around my cock. If you need to say *yellow* or *red*, drop the bell, and I'll withdraw. Okay?"

"Drop the bell. I understand," she said, her voice cracking on the last word.

Alexander brushed her hair away from her face, then kissed her. "Lick your lips."

When her tongue darted out, he stood so his cock was only a breath away. Sensing the warmth and the scent of him, she inhaled deeply.

"Breathe through your nose and part your lips. Press your tongue down, relax, and let me control the depth and the movement. All you have to do is listen and not bite me. Are you ready?"

---

ELIZABETH'S HEART POUNDED. Her ass throbbed. She wanted to shift her hips or lift her butt off of her heels, but she couldn't think with Alexander's arousal perfuming the air: salty, rich, sweet. The smooth head of his cock pressed against her moistened lips. "Taste me, Elizabeth."

Swirling her tongue around the thick flesh, she almost smiled. He tasted exactly like he smelled, and she wanted more. His voice was firm but gentle as he commanded her. As she rounded her lips into an *o,* he pushed in, just enough to force her tongue down. Prickling pain along her scalp traveled down to her ass, then back to her clit as he wrapped his fingers around her mussed locks.

"A bit deeper now. Breathe for me."

Elizabeth tensed as he approached the back of her throat. "Press your tongue against me, *chérie.* As far forward as you can. You won't choke."

Amazingly, she didn't. When her lower lip brushed against the smooth skin of his balls, she almost gasped. He'd filled her completely, but she could still breathe. Elizabeth lost track of time as Alexander coached her through licking, sucking, and tasting him. "Blast it, Elizabeth, you are brilliant," he groaned when she pressed her tongue against the thick vein on the underside of his cock.

Darkness enveloped her, but Alexander's ragged voice, his hands in her hair, the scent, and the taste of him rounded out her senses. Her own arousal dripped onto her heels. Unable to move beyond her lips and her tongue, blind, half-senseless with need, she couldn't think of another place in the world she'd rather be.

"Elizabeth, I can't deny myself much longer. If you don't want to take my seed, drop the bell now."

She did want this. Alexander loved her, and more than that, she trusted him. She could do this. Hoping he'd enjoy the sensation, she hummed, letting the sound travel to the back of her throat as he thrust deeper.

"Oh shite, Elizabeth. I love your mouth." His words dissolved into hoarse grunts, and he thrust twice more before he jerked against her lips and his seed shot to the back of her throat. She panicked for a moment until she heard his voice. "Swallow, Elizabeth. Now."

Even without full command of her senses, she could obey him. When his cock stilled, and he withdrew, she wanted to collapse on the floor, but he still had a hold of her hair and dropped down next to her instead to pull her into his arms.

Resting in his embrace, she relished the pounding of his heart under her ear. She'd done this to him, turned him boneless and sated him. She ached to see him, but she felt secure and too spent to move. Until he removed the clamp from her left nipple. She whimpered quietly, shuddering, while he sucked the abused flesh into his mouth and soothed the throbbing ache. The right followed. Tears streamed down her face, but she didn't care. The pain was intense, but held in his arms, she was more at peace than she'd ever been.

She didn't even notice when her thighs were released and he eased the bell from her hands. Or when he laid her on the bed and unbound her ankles. With a possessive growl, he guided her knees up and her feet flat against the mattress.

"I want your hands on me, Elizabeth," he murmured. "And I want to look into your eyes when you come." The blindfold fell away, and she blinked against the brightness of the daylight streaming in from floor-to-ceiling windows. A wall of pure white separated them from the deep blue of the sea. "Kiss me."

She draped her arms around his neck, moaning as his tongue swept against hers and danced over her teeth. When he toyed with the swollen nub between her legs, she fought not to thrust her hips against his hand. Her ass couldn't handle another punishment. Not today. Tomorrow, however... She stifled a laugh under his insistent lips.

"What's so funny, my lovely sub?" he asked with a smirk. His fingers dipped inside her, and she mewled softly when he found her G-spot and pressed against the sensitive nerves.

She shook her head. "I don't want to say. Yet."

"Secrets?" He nipped at her thighs. "No secrets between us. Not now. Tell me."

Exasperated, she let out a sigh. "My ass hurts. And...I..."

"You like the feeling?" He cupped one sore butt cheek as he toyed with her clit.

"Oh God. Yes. Please..."

Alexander laughed and rose up on his knees. "My favorite word out of your lovely mouth." Once he'd sheathed himself, he wrapped her hands around his hips. "You are everything I wanted but never knew I needed, Elizabeth."

The tears she'd held back tumbled down her cheeks. With every thrust, he swiped his capable fingers over her folds. Her toes curled against the sheets. This man loved her. He'd saved her life and shown her a part of herself she'd never known existed, but now couldn't live without.

"You're mine, Elizabeth. And I want you to come. Now. Come with me."

The climax that had been building for what felt like hours rushed towards her, starting deep in her belly, reaching for her toes, her fingers, even the top of her head. Alexander's eyes darkened with his groans of pleasure, and when he gave a final thrust and shouted her name, she let go.

When she next managed a coherent thought, she found herself in his arms, covered by blankets. He pressed a bottle of water to her lips. They didn't speak until his phone buzzed on the bedside table. He growled his displeasure, but she twisted out of his arms to grab it for him.

"Yes?" He listened for a minute and shook his head. "We'll be walking to lunch in an hour." He hung up and tossed the phone back onto the bed. "I'm glad their timing wasn't any worse."

She chuckled and wrapped her arms around his waist. "I wouldn't have noticed. I don't remember a thing after I came."

"You're good for my ego, *chérie*. A Dom enjoys hearing that from his sub."

His sub. Those two little words thrilled her down to her toes. Never in her life would she have imagined that being anyone's anything could make her so happy. Snuggling closer to him, she closed her eyes. Her mind wandered, bringing her to the top of a tall cliff, staring down at the sea. Her bare toes curled over the edge, sending rocks skittering towards the water. She smiled and let herself fall.

# CHAPTER TWENTY-SIX

*E*lizabeth huddled in the front seat while Alexander locked the door, then carefully made his way to the car. He'd had to dig the Mercedes out of its snowy cocoon this morning. They'd barely left the house for three days, and Elizabeth sighed as he sank into the driver's seat.

"What's wrong, Elizabeth?" Reaching over to twist a lock of hair around his finger, Alexander scanned her face, concern bringing out the whiskey-colored flecks in his green eyes.

She tried—and probably failed—to keep a bit of the melancholy from her voice. "How do you go back to reality after time here?"

He chuckled, then leaned closer so he could capture her lips in a tender kiss. When he pulled back, he'd sobered. "I'm not going to like leaving you to go to the office tomorrow. Promise me that you'll stay in the house?"

"For how long?" As he threw the car into reverse, Elizabeth twisted the hem of her old Harvard sweatshirt. The poor fabric had lost its elasticity years ago with all of her fidgeting. Anxiety sucked, and she hated feeling like she couldn't settle. "At some point, I have to live my life, Alexander."

As he turned onto the beachfront road and Elizabeth gaped at the deep blue ocean that spread out before her, all the way to the horizon. "Oh my God. It's so beautiful."

"Next time, I'll bring you out to the lighthouse," he said, a hint of longing in his voice. "I called, but they haven't dug out from the storm yet."

Several minutes passed before he answered her question, and Elizabeth spent every one of them chewing on her lip. She couldn't just hide away in that big house for the rest of her life. She had to find a job, make an effort to be a better friend, see Toni and Kelsey more often, get back to running, volunteering at the food bank...all the things she'd put off or just ignored

Alexander glanced over at her, then at a stoplight, took her hand, but kept his eyes forward. His shoulders held tension, and she squeezed his fingers. "I'm struggling, Elizabeth. There's nothing I want more than to keep you safe and protected," he said quietly. "Right now, that means inside the house. But I know that's not fair to you. Milos and Carl will be staying on. Ben's going to drop by this afternoon to update us on the case against CPH."

"And the...hitman?" Her voice cracked on the last word.

When he spared her another glance, she read the answer in his eyes. "Still out there."

Elizabeth released his hand as the light turned green, then turned her gaze to the sea. "I won't let him, them, anyone...take more of my life from me."

"I know, *chérie*. I'm going to send Milos for a defensive driving course, and I ordered a town car. William—my head of security—is working his magic to get the doors and windows reinforced."

Did he really think she was just going to let someone drive her everywhere? "I need to run, Alexander. To go hang out with Toni and Kelsey, go to the movies, out to dinner. With *and* without you."

He sighed, and his knuckles whitened on the steering wheel.

"I want you to do all of those things. But not at the expense of your safety. Please, Elizabeth. Trust me a little longer."

Though she wasn't sure he'd ever be okay with her going out alone again, she nodded. "Okay."

Relief changed his whole body language, but longing still lingered in his voice. "When we get home, there's something I need to show you."

"Care to elaborate? Or do I get to spend the whole ride worried?"

When he looked over at her, the glint in his eyes calmed her nerves. "Do not worry, Elizabeth. This...I hope...you'll like."

---

ELIZABETH SLEPT all the way back to Boston. Alexander woke her with a brush of his fingers against her cheek. "We're home, *chérie.*"

A yawn split her lips, and she hid behind a hand over her mouth. "Can't stay awake in the car to save my life unless I'm driving." She reached for the door handle, but Alexander stopped her.

"Wait for Milos."

"It's the middle of the day in front of your house. Do you really think there's a danger?" Elizabeth looked up and down the street. "There's no one around."

Alexander only had a moment to scowl at her before Milos appeared at her door and Thomas showed up to take Alexander's place behind the wheel.

Once he'd ushered her inside, he passed Samuel their luggage and accepted a small stack of correspondence with a Post-It note on top. His frown only lasted a moment, but Elizabeth's stomach somersaulted. "I have a few calls to make. Work related—nothing to worry about."

"Where should I, um, go?" This wasn't her house. Would

Samuel or Donatella be upset if she hung out in the kitchen or parked herself in the upstairs study? Would they even care?

"Anywhere you want."

River padded up to the both of them *mrrping* the whole way. She wound around their legs until Elizabeth picked her up and nuzzled her orange-striped fur. "Hello, sweetie." The cat purred and butted her head against Elizabeth's chin. "Miss me?"

"She slept on your bed," Samuel said from the parlor. "On Miss Elizabeth's pillow."

"She's gained weight, too." Elizabeth raised a brow at Samuel. "All tuna all the time now?"

Alexander's majordomo stared down at his shoes, but the corners of his lips turned upwards. "Perhaps."

After a quick kiss, Alexander strode to his office, and Elizabeth stood in the entry hall, River in her arms, unsure what to do.

"Would you like to see the library, Miss Elizabeth?" Samuel asked.

"There's a library?" At her surprised tone, River meowed and then wriggled out of her arms. "Sure," she said, though really, she just wanted somewhere she could feel comfortable again.

Samuel held her gaze for a long moment, understanding in his brown eyes. "I'll give you the nickel tour."

---

CURLED on the love seat in the upstairs study with a small plate of Donatella's chocolate chip cookies and a pot of tea, Elizabeth called Kelsey.

"How's the head?"

Elizabeth brushed her fingers over the still healing wound. "Better. The swelling's gone. Though my bruises are all a disgusting shade of yellow now."

"And Maine?" Kelsey's tone turned teasing.

"I didn't want to come back. Next summer, you won't have to

twist my arm to join you. Assuming I have a job. Or any way to support myself."

Her friend's sigh carried over the line. "Do you really think you're going to have to worry about that? Lizzie, you're dating the richest guy in Boston. No, scratch that. The richest guy in Boston is *in love* with you."

Elizabeth wished she could explain how Kelsey's assertion both thrilled her and terrified her at the same time. Instead, she stared out the window at the snow-covered streets and tried not to panic.

"Earth to Lizzie. Come in, please."

With a soft shake of her head, Elizabeth returned her attention to her friend. "Sorry. I just...this is all so much. When we came ho—back here, Samuel carried our bags upstairs, Donatella had a plate of cookies waiting, and I'm sitting in a room where the furniture probably costs as much as a small car."

"So?" Kelsey huffed. "Look, when David was alive, we sort of lived the dream, you know? Townhouse in the South End, trips overseas every year, vacations in Maine or Vermont. We weren't rich, but we didn't worry a lot about money. He was a damn good real estate agent."

"I remember." Kelsey wasn't usually this talkative about her late husband.

Sadness tinged Kelsey's words as she continued. "Now, I live in a tiny apartment that overlooks an alley. I'm happy—more or less. Happier than I've been since I l-lost him. And you know what else I am?"

"No."

"The same person I was when we had money. And the same person I was when he and I got married and had to live in his parents' basement for two years because we couldn't afford anything else." Kelsey sniffled once, but her voice didn't crack again. "Living in that big, fancy house with the fancy staff and the fancy address and the fancy furniture? It doesn't change who you are."

"But...how do I make sure I don't end up like I did before?" Elizabeth's voice dropped to a whisper. "With Darren."

"By keeping us in your life. Toni and I picked up the pieces when you left him, hon. We know the signs. Hell, we knew them back then, too, but you never opened up to us. And since we were both across the country, there wasn't a whole lot we could do." After a long, slow exhale, Kelsey lowered her voice. "You didn't walk us out the other night. Alexander did."

"Oh God. What did he say?" Her cheeks flamed, and she dropped her head into her hands, momentarily forgetting about the stitches.

"He gave us his mobile number. Told us to call him anytime, yell at him, berate him, do anything we needed to do if we ever suspected he wasn't taking care of you or respecting you. He said he knew a little about Darren, and that he might need help not making an ass—or arse—out of himself from time-to-time because he comes on pretty strong. Then told us we were always welcome and invited us for Christmas. Toni sort of gaped the whole ride back to Brookline. Kind of impressive, really. She's *never* speechless."

Hope warmed deep inside. "You're not worried I'm going to... change? Being with him?"

Kelsey chuckled. "Your parties are going to be a lot cooler now. Honestly, I could probably stare at Samuel all day and die a happy woman. But no, Lizzie. You're not going to change. You've got us. More importantly, you know who you are now."

---

ALEXANDER SLUMPED BACK in his chair. Three hours of phone calls, emails, and video conferences. Samuel had brought him coffee—twice—and now, his hands shook from all the caffeine. As he was about to get up, Nicholas rang him.

"About bloody time," Alexander snapped. "Foyle's been trying to reach you all day. Where have you been?"

"Trying to wade through the end of year reports. Foyle knows where my office is. He could have knocked. Penny's out sick, and I didn't request a temp. Figured it'd be better to keep my head down and finalize all of this shite." Nicholas sounded tired, but more than that, a deep sadness lingered in his voice.

Alexander rubbed the back of his neck and tried to put himself in his brother's shoes. "Can I help?"

"You're still in Maine, yeah?"

"Elizabeth and I came home this afternoon." Another quick scan of his email gave him the only update he truly cared about. "Fuck me. The U.S. Attorney found the bank account opened in Elizabeth's name. Six million and change."

Nicholas whistled. "But nothing on the hitman?"

"No. I don't know what I'm going to do, Nicholas. She wants to find a job, get back to her life." Though the two brothers hadn't always been close, and Alexander made a point not to discuss financial matters with Nicholas, at his lowest, he still turned to his older brother. Even though most of the time Alexander felt like the responsible one.

"Let her." Nicholas called Alexander's name to stop the tirade of curses and protests. "She's not a bird in a gilded cage. From what I've seen of her, she's got a backbone—and a hell of a brain. Get her a driver, a bodyguard, hell, find a safe apartment building, buy the damn thing, and outfit it with the best security system you can find for her. Or just ask Elizabeth to move in with you. But you can't keep her cosseted behind closed doors just because someone once wanted her dead. If the tosser who tried to kill her was a hired professional, which seems bloody likely, he probably knows by now that he's not getting paid, and he'll leave her alone. If not, that's what the security's for."

Grimacing, Alexander pushed to his feet. He needed a hot shower, a meal, and Elizabeth in his arms. "You're right. She's too bright a jewel to keep hidden away from the world. I should go talk to her. You'll be at the board meeting tomorrow?"

"Yeah. If I don't drown in these reports first." With a dry laugh, Nicholas hung up.

# CHAPTER TWENTY-SEVEN

*A*lexander found Elizabeth in the bedroom, sitting cross-legged on the bed with River next to her. She'd found the remote control for the television, and the strains of "White Christmas" filled the room as Bing Crosby and Rosemary Clooney serenaded one another. She absently stroked the cat's fur, and tears shone on her cheeks.

"What's wrong, *chérie*?"

She startled, a tiny yelp escaping her lips. "I love this movie."

He wandered closer as the two lovers on screen embraced. "I haven't seen it in years."

With a sniffle, Elizabeth swiped at her cheeks, then patted the bed next to her. As the final strains of the song played, she twined her fingers with his. "I missed the first hour. But it's on every day until Christmas. Maybe...we could watch it together?"

"Nothing would make me happier. Except one thing." Alexander brought their joined hands to his lips and kissed her knuckles. "Come with me?"

Elizabeth let him help her off the bed, but rather than lead her out of the room, he took a sharp turn into the darkened closet. "Please tell me you didn't buy me more—" Her hand flew to her mouth as he flicked on the light. While they'd been gone, Alexander had asked Samuel to rearrange the space to accommodate Elizabeth's belongings.

She ran her fingers over the empty shelves and hangers. The few clothes Marjorie had sent over—the ones she didn't bring to Maine—hung lonely, and Alexander held his breath. What if she said no?

"Elizabeth? Will you move in with me?" Alexander wrapped his arms around her waist and nuzzled her neck. "I hate the idea of you sleeping anywhere but in a bed we share. Every night."

Her eyes shimmered with unshed tears, and her lower lip tucked under her teeth. The azure depths of her gaze reflected so much. Fear, relief, uncertainty, and...perhaps love?

"What if you find out I snore?"

"You do. These soft little sighs that are among my new favorite sounds, for that means you're safe and sleeping next to me."

Some of the doubt receded, leaving a hint of excitement in her eyes. "What if I'm a slob?"

"Then Samuel will bring in the housekeeper more often. I've seen your flat. I'm not concerned." Alexander would find a counterpoint for every one of her arguments. His negotiation skills had been honed in the boardroom for more than a decade.

She pursed her lips, and uncertainty took over.

"Elizabeth, I need you in my life. I need to come home to a house we share. To know you'll always come home to me. You're the one I want to see every morning, the one I want to share coffee with, shower with, spend holidays and vacations with."

As she took a shuddering breath, he laid his heart bare. "I want to start the new year living with the woman I love."

"Samuel was on the phone earlier. Talking about an appointment on Saturday." She arched her brows.

"Movers. If you agree, anything you want from your flat can be packed up, and we'll find a spot for it."

"You have a whole home already filled," she protested. "None of my stuff will fit here."

"Any of your things—even that abysmally out-of-date furniture, will find a home here." Alexander didn't know why she'd possibly want to keep any of her furniture, but he'd find a spot for every single piece if she wanted.

"I can't give up my couch."

"The upstairs study then."

Elizabeth started to laugh, bracing a hand on one of the closet shelves as she tried to catch her breath. "That old thing...is a piece of crap." A half-sob, half-snort escaped, and she leaned her whole body against the door jamb. "Half of the springs are broken, and it's always smelled vaguely of fried rice."

"You're sending me up. And enjoying it." Snagging her around the waist, he hoisted her over his shoulder. Elizabeth shrieked with laughter and pounded on his back.

"Let me down, you cretin!"

"Oh, you'll go down all right." Alexander slid her off his shoulder and onto the bed, then caged her with his body.

"I had you going," she said as she met his gaze, joy and lust dancing in her eyes.

"You did. And you're going to pay for that. But you never answered my question. Will you move in with me?" He couldn't get enough of this woman, and as her chest heaved and she grinned up at him, he tried to decide just how many times she'd come before he let her off their bed.

Love softened her gaze, and she reached up and draped her arms around his neck.

"Yes."

---

THE NEXT DAY, after Terrance had stopped by to check on her, Elizabeth invited Kelsey and Toni over for lunch. Alexander had to work, and he'd encouraged her to do whatever she needed to in order to reclaim some normalcy—as long as she stayed at home until Milos completed his defensive driving course and the new town car arrived.

Though she'd wanted to protest—and venture out for a run—the idea of going anywhere the hitman could get to her didn't sit well. So, she'd agreed.

Donatella cooked chicken picatta, and after lunch, they sat around the hearth—on the floor, to Samuel's surprise— with mugs of hot cocoa.

"So, what's it like living in this mansion," Toni asked as Kelsey groaned, patting her belly as Elizabeth offered her the last sugar cookie.

"Um...odd. I guess it'll feel more like home once I get my stuff. Not that I'm going to bring much with me. Clothes, my accounting books, my Gram's teapot." She leaned against the leather sofa, absently rubbing her sore shoulder.

"What's wrong?" Kelsey asked as she gave in and snatched the lonely cookie off the plate. "I can't come over here too often unless I start walking from the South End."

Elizabeth scanned her friends' faces. "I haven't told him that... I love him."

Toni and Kelsey responded in unison, "What are you waiting for?"

"The right time?" Elizabeth sighed. "We had all these intense discussions up in Maine, and I kept wanting to tell him, but... something would happen. and I'd chicken out. Now it's like this *thing* I can't say."

Toni nudged her thigh. "You need a big glass of wine and a nice meal and—"

"Oh my God. You're right," Elizabeth said. "Can you get me a table at Guiseppe's for tonight? Before it gets all crowded?"

Toni shook her head, the mirth fading from her eyes. "We're closed tonight, hon. Thursday. Family meal and cleaning."

"Oh. Well...shit. I guess tomorrow then?"

Toni frowned, then grabbed her phone from the coffee table. After her fingers danced over the screen for a moment, she held up her hand until the phone buzzed a reply.

"Come at seven. Pops just agreed to meet me at the restaurant early. The rest of the staff doesn't show up until eight, and Pops and I will whip up some *linguine alle vongole* for the two of you."

"Really?"

"Hon, I love you. Friday nights are insane from open to close, and you look like you're going to burst if you don't tell him soon. Plus, this way, no one needs to worry about you out in a crowd with that asshole who hurt you still out there."

Elizabeth pulled Toni into a tight embrace, and Kelsey piled on. "We need to do this more often," Kelsey said with a laugh.

"Next Monday? The twenty-third?" Elizabeth asked. As the date registered, she pulled away. "Oh shit. It's Christmas next week. What the hell am I supposed to do? He's got more money than God, and I need to get him something."

Toni's laughter echoed off the stones of the hearth. "Oh sweetie, I think a visit to Kelsey at the Waxing Spa and some stilettos would do him just fine."

---

ONCE HER FRIENDS HAD LEFT, Elizabeth wandered through the house, looking for Samuel. She found him in a small room off the library, which appeared to be his office.

"Yes, Miss Elizabeth?"

"Um, I need some things from my apartment, and if I tell Alexander, he's going to insist on going with me."

"I can retrieve what you need. Do you have a list?"

"Some of them are...personal." The idea of Samuel going through her underwear didn't sit well.

He smiled at her like her favorite uncle, understanding and a little indulgence ghosting over his features. "Miss Elizabeth, you live here now. I will be folding your laundry. And though I work for both of you, if I facilitate you going anywhere on your own right now, he will have my head." Samuel clasped his hands on top of his desk, his dark brow arched slightly, as if he expected her to argue.

*And I suppose you probably know all about what happens in Alexander's—our—bedroom.* She rubbed the back of her neck and forced a deep breath. "Do you have a pen and paper?"

"Of course, miss."

"Elizabeth."

"Apologies, Miss Elizabeth, but that's not going to happen." Samuel chuckled, opened a drawer, and withdrew a notepad and pen so she could jot down her meager list.

*My pillow*

*The photograph of me, Toni, and Kelsey at Fenway Park from my dresser*

*My Gram's flowered teapot*

*The wooden box on my nightstand*

When she was finished, she stared down at her feet as Samuel gave her list a quick glance, folded the paper, and tucked it into his pocket. "I'll be back in a little over an hour," he said, a hint of amusement in his voice.

"I need one more thing that's not at my apartment."

"Yes?"

"A gift box big enough for the wooden memory box. And a bow or ribbon. Silk."

Samuel smiled. "I understand, miss." As he passed her, he paused, lowering his voice. "This isn't my place, but I'm going to say it anyway. You're a good match for him."

———

At six-thirty, Elizabeth tucked the wrapped box into her purse along with a little handwritten note. She'd agonized for an hour over it, finally settling on three simple lines:

*I kept every one of the ribbons and cards. Even when I thought your gifts were made of nothing but strings. I love you.*

Alexander walked out of the closet buttoning his cuffs. Tight jeans showcased slim hips and strong thighs, and his royal blue shirt brought out the cognac-colored flecks in his eyes. "More secrets?" he said as she fastened the clasp of her bag.

"Not exactly. But you'll just have to wait to find out."

When they slid into the limo, Alexander tucked an arm around her shoulders and kept her close. "Ben called today. My deposition is scheduled for next Monday down at his office."

"Oh! I told Toni we could have a girls' night next week. Monday actually. Do you want me to reschedule it?"

"Of course not. But unless you plan on having them over to the house, you'll take Milos and Carl with you. They know how to be unobtrusive."

"Our girls' nights usually involve a movie and a bottle or two of wine at someone's apartment."

"Then they'll wait outside. Or, use the media room."

"Control freak," she said, but secretly she was relieved. "You really don't want me to be...err...home after your deposition?"

"Elizabeth, I'm not looking forward to hours upon hours of questions. I have no doubt I'll be in a piss-poor mood. This way, by the time you're done with your friends, I'll have recovered." Alexander winked at her. "And I'll be able to show you how much I missed you."

"Oh. Well, okay then."

"Milos is scheduled for his driving course over the weekend. The town car arrives tomorrow. You should resume your life— with some alterations, that is. You'll have security when you leave the house. You'll need to go shopping with Marjorie for some enhancements to your wardrobe for parties and any business events you choose to accompany me to, and you'll need to forgive me occasionally for being—as you are so fond of saying—a *control freak*."

She laughed. "Maybe this won't be so bad. Though it'll be better once I get some clients and can pay for my own clothing. I don't want to keep taking your charity."

"It's not charity, *chérie*. I love you. You're not asking me to buy you a bridge. You're not asking me to buy you anything. I'm the one who's offering. And the first thing you need is a better coat."

"Why? Yours works fine," she teased. She wriggled deeper into Alexander's leather jacket, inhaling his scene. She could live in this coat and be perfectly happy.

"It does look lovely on you."

Guiseppe's was lit up with candles and dim, romantic lights when they arrived. After Milos circled the building and then walked through the kitchen and the dining room, they were allowed to leave the limo.

Toni greeted them at the door and showed them to the only set table in the entire restaurant, complete with a bottle of Chianti breathing in the center.

"Are we the only customers?" Alexander asked.

"We're technically closed tonight," Toni admitted. "But Pop was cooking anyway for our cleaning party, and Lizzie called in a favor. Trust me. This is *not* a problem." She winked at Elizabeth.

Elizabeth blushed and hung her purse on the back of the chair. She didn't know why she was so nervous. Alexander loved her. She loved him. Still, her hands shook and her heart pounded.

"Miss Grimaldi knows something I do not," Alexander said, holding her chair.

"She's one of my best friends. I think you can call her Toni. And she's trying to make trouble."

Elizabeth accepted the glass of wine he poured her and lifted it to return his toast. "To the rain," he said.

"The rain? Why?"

"Because if it weren't for the rain, I never would have met you, and that would have been a tragedy. I can't imagine my life without you, Elizabeth."

*There's so much I want to say to you.*

She took a significant gulp of her wine. "I hope you're hungry. Papa Grimaldi is the best. Nonno Guiseppe started this place. Papa's father. Toni manages it now, but Papa still cooks every night."

"I'm hungry for a lot of things," he said with a sly grin. "But dinner is definitely one of them."

Toni rushed out with a plate of sliced meats, a small basket of bread, and a bowl of herbed olive oil for dipping. "Your dinners will be up in about fifteen minutes. And Pop said you couldn't leave until he got to meet your man. After dinner, though."

Elizabeth rolled her eyes. "Probably wants to interrogate you," she told Alexander.

Toni chuckled. "I'd say that's likely. I'll go check on your clams." She winked at Elizabeth as she rushed off.

Elizabeth's stomach churned, and she fumbled for the clasp on her purse.

"Elizabeth, are you all right?" Alexander reached across the table and touched her arm.

*Get yourself together.*

"I...just need the ladies room. Give me just a minute?" What she really needed was fresh air, but since no one was going to let her take a walk around the block alone—least of all her own fears—she'd settle for splashing some cold water on her face.

Alexander rose and offered Elizabeth his hand to help her up. "Don't be long."

Latin American guitar tones filled the narrow hallway on the way to the bathrooms. Elizabeth rounded the corner, and a rough hand yanked on her wrist, spinning her around until something hard jabbed into her ribs.

"Don't make a sound, or I kill all of them."

# CHAPTER TWENTY-EIGHT

*T*he voice haunting her dreams belonged to a tall man with close-shorn black hair, dark brown eyes, and a scar across his cheek. He grinned, taking joy from her tears.

"We're headed out the back door, and you're going to keep quiet and do as I say."

She wheezed, her panic trapping the air in her lungs until she feared she'd pass out. Her stomach lurched, and an icy ball of pure terror surrounded her heart.

"You...can kill...me," she forced out, "...won't make...a difference. Lawsuit...was filed."

"Doesn't matter. He wants you to pay. So you'll pay. Now move." Her attacker forced her towards the exit, and she tried to pull her arm away, but the gun barrel jabbed harder into her ribs.

Elizabeth stumbled, throwing her hands up as she crashed into the wall. Rough fingers grabbed her neck, and her world started to shimmer.

"I've really had enough of you, bitch," he spat in her ear.

"Noooo," she moaned weakly as her vision darkened. A dull roar filled her ears. The burnt orange walls of the hallway blurred. Falling, she tried to call out, to scream, but her arms, legs, and voice wouldn't obey her commands.

Flopping helplessly as her attacker hefted her onto his shoulder, she fought to kick, claw at him, do *anything* but just hang there and let him carry her to her death. He clutched her legs tightly as he escaped into the alley.

The biting cold, her position, and her overwhelming panic conspired against her. "Help," she tried to cry, but barely a whisper reached her ears. They headed away from the busy street, down another even narrower alley. If she didn't escape, she'd die, and Alexander...

A sob tripped from her lips, and she forced herself to draw a deeper breath. Balling her hands, she slammed her fists into her captor's back, over and over again. He shook her, and then pressed his thumb against her inner thigh.

Pain shot up her legs, through her back, and wrapped around her skull. Still, she kept fighting. One of her blows must have hit a sensitive spot because the hitman stumbled enough to throw her off balance.

Elizabeth twisted her body as she tumbled to the snow-covered ground. The bone-jarring impact took her breath away. As her body struggled for air, she watched, helpless, as her would-be-kidnapper grabbed her under the arms. "Fucking bitch," he growled as he hauled her up. "You're going to pay for that."

"Get the hell away from her!" Carl's voice echoed down the alley. Barreling towards the man at full speed, he tackled the hitman, and as Elizabeth collapsed to her hands and knees, she sucked in a feeble breath.

"Help!"

Carl landed a punch to the man's gut and drew back for another blow.

*Crack!*

The sound reverberated against the tall buildings, and a

burnt, sweet stench filled Elizabeth's nose. Carl fell to his side, a small, dark hole in the center of his forehead.

"No!" Elizabeth scrambled back and tried to get up, but the assassin sprang for her and had his hand around her arm before she could find her footing.

He glanced down the alley towards a black van idling with its rear door open. "We've got to move!" he shouted to a shadowy figure inside the vehicle. With his meaty hand around Elizabeth's injured arm, he dragged her closer to the van.

Fifty feet.

"Please," she cried as she clawed at his fingers. The pain made it almost impossible to speak, but if he got her into that van, she was dead.

Forty.

Struggling to get her feet underneath her, she pulled as hard as she could against his hold.

Thirty.

"Elizabeth!"

Alexander raced towards them at break neck speed, a look of pure hatred in his eyes. "Let her go!" His voice held so much emotion. Terror. Panic. Love.

Twenty.

The assassin whirled around, raising his arm. Elizabeth swung at him, but he shoved her to the ground.

"Gun!"

The loud crack preceded Alexander's soft exhalation by a heartbeat.

*It's not like it is in the movies.*

The dim thought echoed as she watched Alexander's eyelids flutter, the dark lashes dramatic against his rapidly paling cheeks. He sank to his knees, almost in slow motion, pressing his hand to his side. Blood drenched his shirt just below where she thought his heart should be.

Hauling her up again, her attacker tried to pull her the last few feet, but she couldn't take her eyes off Alexander. "Let...me... go!" With more strength than she thought she possessed, she tore her arm from his grip. Shocked by the sudden move, he didn't react quickly enough, and Elizabeth drew back and drove the heel of her hand into his nose. Blood spurted from his nostrils, and he snarled at her.

"I've had enough of you." He raised the gun, but she flew at him with an anguished scream. Another shot echoed, her outer thigh burned, but she barely registered the sensation as pain. Grabbing his shoulders, she rammed her knee into his groin. He staggered again but didn't go down.

The gun slid upwards to point at her head.

"Elizabeth."

Alexander's gasping call seemed to startle both of them, and her assailant's eyes flicked away from her for a fraction of a second. Another shot rang out, and Elizabeth's world crashed down around her as she screamed in pain.

# CHAPTER TWENTY-NINE

*S*trong arms dragged Elizabeth away from the scent of blood and gunpowder. The hitman lay on the ground, panting, with his hands pressed to his abdomen. Blood gushed from between his fingers. A black-booted foot kicked the gun away.

"I've got you. Come on now. He needs you."

*Thomas.*

Milos shouldered past them, and Elizabeth focused on the gun in her bodyguard's hand, the wisp of smoke emanating from the barrel. Thomas pulled Elizabeth's arm around his shoulders and together, they rushed to Alexander's side.

On his back, legs bent awkwardly underneath him, Alexander's breath stuttered as he forced shallow, gasping inhalations. Elizabeth dropped to her knees next to him. "No. Look at me. You are *not* allowed to die on me!"

Thomas yelled into a phone. "We're in the North End. Just off Hanover Street. He's been shot in the chest. Struggling to breathe. Left side." The driver rounded Alexander and pressed his hands to the wound, the phone tucked between his shoulder and ear.

Eyelids fluttering, Alexander groaned.

"Open," Elizabeth ordered him. "Now."

He struggled to obey, and when he focused on her, a smile, almost serene, graced his lips. "Love. You." A gasp punctuated each word, and blood trickled from the corner of his mouth as he coughed.

Elizabeth tried not to sob as she cupped his cheeks. "Shhh, it's okay. You're going to be okay."

"Can't. Breathe." He fought for each word, each tiny movement of his chest. Thomas relayed his words to the 911 operator.

"The EMTs are only four blocks away. Hold on, sir."

Milos shouted at someone down the alley as sirens wailed. Bringing Alexander's hand to her lips, she fought not to retch at the scent of his blood. "Stay with me, you arrogant control freak. You're not getting out of us living together that easily."

His smile faded as he shuddered and his eyes rolled back in his head.

"Look at me, dammit. I have something to say to you, and I'm not going to tell you what it is if you die on me." Her tears spilled over her cheeks, landing on their joined hands. Alexander coughed again, his mouth opening and closing, but no words escaped. The short, stuttering breaths slowed.

Brakes squealed, and boots thudded towards them. Elizabeth was pulled out of the way, and as Alexander's hand slipped from hers, he tried to raise his head. "Eliz—"

"I'm right here," she called from behind the EMTs. "I won't leave you."

His lids fluttered closed, and Elizabeth's sanity faded away. She couldn't think—couldn't believe this was actually happening.

The EMTs worked quickly, loading him onto a gurney and pressing an oxygen mask to his nose and mouth. "We need to take him now," one of them said to her. She ran after them, but the tired EMT blocked her way. "We're going to Mass General. He's critical. We need the room to work."

As the door slammed in her face, shivers wracked her body.

Her hands went numb, then her lips. She couldn't breathe, her throat constricting painfully.

"Miss Elizabeth, come with me."

The familiar voice sounded hollow in her ears. Elizabeth couldn't move, couldn't do anything but stare at the ambulance pulling away with her heart trapped inside.

"Elizabeth!" Thomas snapped out her name as the buildings and cars spun around her. Hands forced her down to the ground and guided her head between her knees. "Breathe. In and out. Slow now. You have to calm down so I can take you to him."

Thomas rubbed her back. "Get her coat," he said to someone behind her. Moments later, with Alexander's leather jacket wrapped around her shoulders and his comforting spicy scent calming her, Elizabeth took her first easy breath. The second staved off the dizziness. The third strengthened her enough to raise her head and look into the driver's earnest hazel eyes.

"Better?" he asked.

She nodded.

"I'm going to take you to the hospital now. You've got some injuries yourself, and Mr. Fairhaven would want you looked after. And he'll want you close when they're done patching him up." Even though Thomas kept his words encouraging, she read the fear in the driver's eyes.

Three uniformed police officers approached, and Toni ran over and wrapped her arms around Elizabeth.

"Gawd, Lizzie, I'm so sorry. We usually keep that door locked, but I took the trash out earlier, and I guess I didn't—"

Elizabeth shook in Toni's arms. "My fault," she whispered. "He was after me. I need to go. I can't...I have to be there. The hospital. Pray. Please pray."

Toni released her. "Of course. Go. I'll be there as soon as the cops let us lock up the restaurant."

Milos appeared at Elizabeth's elbow. "Miss Elizabeth, I have to stay here with the police. I killed the man who hurt you. Viktor will meet you at the hospital. You met him at the house before you left. Do you remember him?"

She nodded, not trusting herself to speak.

"Don't go anywhere alone. Do you understand?"

"I won't let her. Don't worry," Thomas replied. "Come on."

"Wait!" One of the uniformed officers blocked their way. "We need to ask her some questions."

"Miss Elizabeth needs to go to the hospital, which is where I'm taking her," Thomas replied sharply. "Unless you think the bullet wound to her thigh should go untreated?"

"What?" Elizabeth asked.

"It's a graze, miss. But between that and your wrist, you need to be seen," Thomas replied. He gestured to the ripped material of her jeans. The deep gash oozed blood, but the pain barely registered. "You can talk to her at the hospital."

Thomas ushered her two blocks down to the limo. By the time he held the front door open, her wrist had started to protest and her thigh burned. "You'll ride up front so I can keep an eye on you." He waited for her to get in, and then shut the door firmly. When he slid behind the wheel, he turned, his face as serious as she'd ever seen it. "Buckle up. I used to be a stunt driver."

---

SIX HOURS LATER, Elizabeth sported a wrist brace and a thick bandage on her thigh. Samuel had brought her a change of clothes, and she'd changed into black wool pants and a rose-colored cashmere sweater she was certain hadn't been in the closet when they'd left the house.

Next to her, Alexander lay in the narrow bed, a heart rate monitor beeping regularly. *Too pale*, she thought as she stared at his bare chest, and the tube still inserted between two of his ribs. The bullet had pierced his lung and had taken a path dangerously close to his heart, but the doctors assured her that he'd make a full recovery—despite his blood pressure dropping dangerously low on the operating table.

Elizabeth sat next to the hospital bed and stroked her fingers lightly over the back of Alexander's right hand. She traced each of the veins along his skin, memorizing the feel of him, remembering the strength of his grip, the firm heat of his lips, and his commanding voice.

For two hours, she'd fought with the nurses. She wasn't family, and they'd refused to tell her anything or let her into the ICU. But then Nicholas had strode into the ward and told them that if they didn't put Elizabeth on the family list, he was going to call the hospital administrator and pull all Fairhaven funding for the rest of his natural life.

Now, he slipped back into the room. "The police won't bother you again until tomorrow," Nicholas said quietly. "The U.S. Attorney has Hayes and Pastack in custody, and Carter is spilling his guts."

"Thank you," she whispered and leaned into his hand on her shoulder.

Nicholas sighed. "He's a stubborn son of a bitch, Elizabeth. If you haven't learned that about him by now…"

"I know. I'll feel better when he wakes up." She tried to keep the wobble from her voice but failed miserably.

"You should get some rest. I know you want to stay, but you've been through a lot these past few days too. I'll keep watch over him. Thomas can take you home for a few hours."

"I'm not leaving him," she protested, and Nicholas drew his hand away so he could take a seat next to her. When she met his gaze, she found his pale blue eyes bloodshot and full of concern.

"It's two in the morning. He's stable. There's nothing else you can do right now."

"She stays." The whisper from the bed startled them both.

Elizabeth gasped. Alexander's eyelids twitched, and his lips parted as he groaned softly.

"Alexander, look at me," she begged, leaning closer and bringing his hand to her lips.

A muscle in his jaw flexed. He tried to take a deeper breath, but pain ghosted across his face, followed by a weak smile when his eyelids fluttered open and he focused on her.

"Hey there," she said, unable to stop her tears.

"Stay." The single word was all he managed before his eyes closed again.

"I'm not going anywhere. They'll have to drag me out with a team of rabid dogs."

"Dogs aren't...allowed."

"Well, then a team of rabid Candy Stripers. Do they even still have Candy Stripers anymore?" she asked Nicholas, who was chuckling quietly in the other chair.

Alexander's body flinched, and Elizabeth's heart skipped a beat until he spoke again.

"Don't joke. Hurts."

Despite her very poor joke—barely even a joke—he'd tried to laugh. He always laughed at her feeble attempts at humor. If he had the presence of mind to do so now, he'd be okay.

Elizabeth stroked his arm. "You're a fool, you know."

He opened his eyes again and managed to raise a brow. "Excuse me?"

"Running after me. After a man with a gun. You could have gotten yourself killed, and then what would I do? I love you, dammit." She hadn't meant to say the words. Not here when he could barely keep his eyes open, but she couldn't take them back now. Nor did she want to.

He tugged on her hand with tears in his eyes. "Come here."

"I'll hurt you." She eyed the amount of space left alongside his body.

"Don't care." He grimaced as he tried to urge her closer. "Need you against me. Come. Here. Now."

Elizabeth shook her head. "Not with a tube in your chest. But..." Dragging the chair closer, she lowered the side rail of the bed, then rested her cheek against his shoulder. "This will have to do for now."

"Don't expect me to ever give you up," he whispered. "Especially not to a man with a gun. I will always come for you."

"Well then don't get shot next time, all right?"

"Bloody inconvenient. I had plans for tonight that involved you. Naked."

"At least I got to keep my plans," Elizabeth murmured. She raised her head and looked into his eyes. "I love you. I wanted to tell you over dinner. I had it all planned out. I even had a little gift for you."

He smiled as he fell asleep again, and she laid her head against his upper arm. Under the antiseptic and the blood, a hint of his scent remained. Sandalwood, cloves, pure male strength. Alexander had come back to her, and now that she'd admitted her love for him, she let herself drift off, content knowing they'd survived together.

# EPILOGUE

*T*he soothing patter of rain lulled him halfway to sleep. No, not rain. The shower. Alexander forced his eyes open. The dim light of the bedside lamp cast a warm glow over the Egyptian cotton sheets and down comforter.

Alexander couldn't remember much about leaving the hospital. Terrance had arranged for a private ambulance to return him home, and he knew Elizabeth had been at his side, but beyond that, the day was a painful blur. All except for the twenty-two steps he'd had to climb with Roger—the nurse—to get to his bed. He remembered every one of those steps. The pain had nearly convinced him to go back to the hospital. But the thought of Elizabeth in the king-sized bed with him at night kept him from complaining. For two days, she'd slept in the thin reclining chair in his hospital room. Once he'd gotten his chest tube out, she'd perched on the edge of the narrow hospital bed for another night. The bags under her eyes had worsened by the hour.

As the last drops of water fell, he closed his eyes. The next thing he knew, the scent of vanilla, gardenia, and white ginger surrounded him in the darkness. Reaching for her, he winced at the lightning bolt of pain ripping through him. Any lascivious thoughts he'd entertained disappeared in an instant.

"Alexander? Do you need another pain pill?" Elizabeth rubbed her eyes and sat up, turning the lamp back on. Black silk draped over her breasts. Her golden hair tumbled loose around her shoulders, and Alexander winced again, but not from the pain. Red rimmed her puffy eyes, and she sniffled softly.

"No. I wanted to touch you." The sheets hid the lower half of her body, but he knew every inch of her. The curve of her hips, the long legs, the slender waist. She'd nibble a little on her lower lip if she were worried, and as the plump flesh disappeared under her teeth, he reached up—slowly—and ran his thumb along her jaw. "What's wrong?"

"Nothing. I'm fine."

"You're not. Turn the light off and come here. We haven't been truly alone at all these past few days. I need you."

She scoffed. "No sex. No silks. Not for at least another week. Doctor's orders, remember?"

"We'll see about that, but sex wasn't what I intended. Not tonight. I need to hold you. I need you to talk to me. And I need —" he traced the line of her eyebrow, "—you to tell me why you've been crying."

With a sigh, Elizabeth flicked off the light and snuggled against his chest. "I wasn't crying. I had a panic attack." As he stiffened, she rushed to continue. "Not a bad one. In the shower." Draping her arm over his body, carefully avoiding the bandages wrapped tightly around his torso, she pressed closer.

"You have nothing to panic about now, *chérie*. We're home. I'm going to be fine. You're safe now. Pastack and Hayes are in jail. The arse who tried to kill you and ran me through is dead."

After Milos had killed the assassin, he'd found Pastack wheezing in the back of the van. The oldest CPH partner had apparently masterminded the whole thing, spending his cut of the embezzlement funds on experimental cancer treatments overseas. Hayes had chosen the clients and falsified the tax forms. Carter, for all of his vitriol towards Elizabeth, had been innocent of everything other than being a thoroughly unpleasant wanker.

"Then why are there still men around the house?"

"Milos is a permanent addition to the staff. Viktor will be with us for another month or two until we're done with all of the court dates. We had this conversation."

"I think you had that conversation with the Percocet. Or maybe only with Milos. Because it certainly wasn't with me," she replied.

"Shite. I'm sorry about that. I can't say I remember much about the past few days."

Elizabeth wrapped her arms around his waist, and she brushed her lips to his jaw. "You should be." Despite her ire, she kissed him so long and so thoroughly that he was close to forgetting his own name.

"Now lie down, *chérie*, and spread your legs for me. The doctor said *I* could not orgasm for several more days. He said nothing about you. Care to see what I can do to you with only my fingers?"

---

ELIZABETH AND ALEXANDER BARELY SURVIVED. Now that Christmas is almost here, they're looking forward to some time at home.

If only Nicholas, Alexander's brother, wasn't in deep with the Italian mob.

Will Nick's gambling problems spell the end for Alexander and Elizabeth's happiness?

Find out now and **one-click CHRISTMAS SILKS now!**

---

IF YOU LOVED In His Silks, you'll love **BREAKING HIS CODE**, my sensual, geeky, and thrilling military romance.

**She's a wounded warrior. He's a former SEAL and a hell of an online gamer. Can their love survive the transition to the real world?**

After almost dying in an Afghanistan war zone, Cam found it easier to live in the virtual world than face reality. Until her flirtatious gaming buddy wants to meet face-to-face.

Even though West turns out to be a hunky former SEAL who doesn't seem to mind her cane, her instincts still scream "RUN."

As she resolves to give love a shot, her career-making programming project comes under attack by a hacker. Does she have enough ammunition to fight on both battlefields?

West is haunted by the mission that took the lives of his team. So when he befriends a gamer and former Army ordnance specialist with scars of her own, their connection soothes something in his battered soul.

After the sharp-shooting beauty surpasses his wildest dreams, he's determined to break down the armored panels she's built around her heart. When his own worst fears return, he worries he won't be able to face the coming challenges alone.

With new enemies and old phantoms from their past closing in, can Cam and West find the courage to lower their defenses and heal their wounded hearts with love?

*Breaking His Code* is the first book in Away From the Keyboard series of explosive military romantic suspense novels. If you like diehard female veterans, sexy cyber romance, and emotional journeys of healing, then you'll love this heartfelt tale of love after war.

One-click **BREAKING HIS CODE** now!

YOU CAN ALSO JOIN my **Facebook group** for exclusive giveaways, sneak peeks of future books, and the chance to see your name in a future novel!

**P.S. Reviews are like candy for authors.**

Did you know that reviews are like chocolate (or cookies or cake) for authors?

They're also the most powerful tool I have to sell more books. I can't take out full page ads in the newspaper or put ads on the side of buses.

Not yet, anyway.

But I have something more powerful and effective than ads.

**A loyal (and smart) bunch of readers.**

Honest reviews of my books help bring them to the attention of other readers.

If you've enjoyed this book, I'd be eternally grateful if you could spend just five minutes leaving a review (it can be as short as you like) on the book's Amazon page.

# ABOUT THE AUTHOR

Patricia D. Eddy writes romance for the beautifully broken. Fueled by coffee, wine, and Doctor Who episodes on repeat, she brings damaged heroes and heroines together to find their happy ever afters in many different worlds. From military to paranormal to BDSM, her characters are unstoppable forces colliding with such heat, sparks always fly.

Patricia makes her home in Seattle with her husband and very spoiled cats, and when she's not writing, she loves working on home improvement projects, especially if they involve power tools.

Her award-winning *Away From Keyboard* series will always be her first love, because that's where she realized the characters in her head were telling their own stories—and she was just writing them down.

*You can reach Patricia all over the web...*
patriciadeddy.com
patricia@patriciadeddy.com

# ALSO BY PATRICIA D. EDDY

## Away From Keyboard

Dive into a steamy mix of geekery and military prowess with the men and women of Hidden Agenda and Second Sight.

## Gone Rogue (an Away From Keyboard spinoff series)

## Dark PNR

These novellas will take you into the darker side of the paranormal with vampires, witches, angels, demons, and more.

Forever Kept

Immortal Hunter

Wicked Omens

Storm of Sin

## By the Fates

Check out the COMPLETE By the Fates series if you love dark and steamy tales of witches, devils, and an epic battle between good and evil.

By the Fates, Freed

Destined: A By the Fates Story

By the Fates, Fought

By the Fates, Fulfilled

## In Blood

If you love hot Italian vampires and and a human who can hold her own against beings far stronger, then the In Blood series is for you.

Secrets in Blood

Revelations in Blood

## Holidays and Heroes

Beauty isn't only skin deep and not all scars heal. Come swoon over sexy vets and the men and women who love them.

Mistletoe and Mochas

Love and Libations

---

## Restrained

Do you like to be tied up? Or read about characters who do? Enjoy a fresh COMPLETE BDSM series that will leave you begging for more.

In His Silks

Christmas Silks

All Tied Up For New Year's

In His Collar

Made in United States
Orlando, FL
16 March 2023

31106836R00165